The Lost Cantrell

by

Shamiso M. Lezard

The Lost Cantrell

Cover Art by *Lisa Dawn MacDonald*

The Wild Rose Press, Inc.
PO Box 708
Adams Basin, NY 14410-0708
Visit us at www.thewildrosepress.com

Publishing History
First Edition, 2022
Trade Paperback ISBN 978-1-5092-4365-5
Digital ISBN 978-1-5092-4366-2

Published in the United States of America

"Should I be worried?" I eventually asked him.

Zeke glanced in my direction. "No, you shouldn't be worried, Ella," he said.

"But you're worried," I pointed out.

"I don't like it when routines change, that's all."

I looked over at Chris, who was seated near the back of the plane with his eyes closed, dozing peacefully. "Chris doesn't seem worried," I said lightly. "That's a good sign, right?"

"Chris doesn't know the details of this trip. And even if he did, it wouldn't be his job to worry."

I searched Zeke's face, keeping my eyes intently on his. "Be honest. Can this trip end badly for me?"

The tension in his jaw tightened. "No. I said that I'd protect you, and that's exactly what I'll do. With my life."

"But there's a chance that something bad might happen, right?"

"There's always a chance that something bad might happen. Right?"

He had a point. I turned my face forward, leaning back as I closed my eyes in the hopes that I would get some decent sleep before we landed at our final destination.

Dedication

God first, as always. For it is only by His grace.

To my parents, Edgar and Molly Mlilo, who always encouraged a reading culture in me and framed my high school writing awards as a reminder of my potential. I couldn't have asked for a better, more loving home to grow up in.

And, of course, to my husband, Sebastion, who will always ask, "Have you done any writing today?" to keep me going. You are the perfect support system and an ever constant ray of sunshine to me. I love you.

To The Wild Rose Press, thank you for believing in my work.

And to all of you, my readers, I appreciate your support more than you know.

Thank you…

Chapter 1

I have always considered myself a fairly confident person. Fairly. It's not that I think overly highly of myself or anything. Not at all, actually. I just don't care what people think of me. I don't mind not being perfect. That's a certain type of confidence, right?

I'm not cocky, but I'm definitely not timid either. My confidence is balanced. Yeah, that's the word that best describes me in a nutshell. Balanced. I've always had just enough confidence to get by in this cruel, cold, judgmental world...and, clearly, enough dramatics, too.

That's why, looking back on the events that led to my present circumstances, I have no idea why I was practically shaking as I stared up at the tall, grand building that was The Lost Cantrell, a top five-star hotel in Midtown, Manhattan. I was there to leave my resume for a Kitchen Staff position that had been advertised for its restaurant, L'Annette. I had been perfectly fine in the taxi that I had taken from my apartment in Reign Hill, but as soon as I had stepped out of it at the hotel drop-off area, I was like a fish out of water.

It always fascinated me how quickly things changed in a second. Emotions, relationships, situations...they all changed so quickly. Confidence could turn into plain nerves and anxiety, just like that.

I inhaled deeply and released the breath slowly as I made my way closer to the hotel entrance doors. I could already smell the "rich people" air from my spot on the sidewalk. I fiddled with the sleek, low ponytail that I had tied my meticulously flat-ironed, long, black hair into, smoothing over non-existent stray strands. A side effect of having usually very, *very* unpredictable curly hair. Dropping my hand, I studied my approaching reflection in the glass door of the hotel, over-analyzing my dark-green turtleneck, tight black pencil skirt, and long black coat outfit combo. There was a security guard standing to the side of the doors, huge and dressed in a black suit. When he saw me approaching, he said, "Hello, ma'am." I greeted him back with a small smile. He was a big guy, and yet he still managed to not draw too much attention to himself. I guessed that was a good quality for a security guard to have.

As I stepped directly in front of the gold-framed doors they slid apart automatically, allowing me into the short corridor between the doors I had just stepped through and what looked like a second door entrance, surrounded by an enchanting glass encasement. The thick glass displays on both sides of the corridor held colorful, large artificial flowers, glittery ornaments, and little lights that cast an inviting glow over the area, reflecting off of the gold-tinted tiles. *Trust The Lost Cantrell to have an entrance within an entrance*, I thought as I made my way down the corridor toward the next entrance doors. As I took my last step toward them, about a foot away, they automatically slid open too, just like the first set of doors. It felt like a warm welcome for some reason. Like the hotel was saying, "Come on in." But my warm and fuzzies were quickly forgotten when I finally laid my eyes on the magnificence of The Lost Cantrell's lobby, all gold trimmings and crystal chandeliers and ivory leather sofas. It was splendid, and I was so mesmerised by it that it was only when I heard the bellhop's greeting to my right that I stopped staring, with my mouth slightly agape, at my surroundings.

"*Bonjour*. I am Daniel. Welcome to The Lost Cantrell. Le Cantrell Perdue." He said it all with a mild flourish, and I immediately caught on to the fact that he was probably of genuine French heritage and not just putting it on for the job. The Lost Cantrell was known to have its employees use French greetings when guests first arrived, but Daniel was very natural about it, and even his English words were laced with an obvious accent. With his neat navy-blue uniform, dark brown eyes, and dark hair, he looked young. Younger than my 24 years.

On the same side that Daniel stood was the L'Annette Restaurant of The Lost Cantrell. Its sign wasn't lit up and its glass doors were closed, but it still looked like fine-dining perfection. I tried not to stare at it, at the restaurant that I wanted to work in so badly, and forced myself to focus on Daniel.

"*Bonjour*, Daniel. Uh, *je m'appelle* Ella." I smiled at him as I said it, and I knew that my French accent and pronunciation was terrible, but he didn't seem to mind. It was weird for me to be speaking French in the middle of New York but you know, when in Rome and all that.

I turned my head back to the lobby space.

"Beautiful, *n'est-ce pas*?" Daniel said next to me. When I turned back to him he had a smile on his face, and it calmed my nerves a little.

"Yes, it is, Daniel. Very beautiful," I replied.

"Would you like to book a room here at The Lost Cantrell, Miss Ella?" Daniel asked.

"Um, no. I'm here to apply for a job actually. The kitchen help job." I reached into my slightly oversized handbag that carried my resume folder and pulled it out. "I'm here to drop off my resume."

"Ah, I see. So we may be workmates soon, yes?" He was so darn friendly that I couldn't help but smile again.

"I hope so, Daniel."

"Well, you may make your way to Miss Bernadette at the reception desk for further inquiry and information," he said as he held out his arm toward the reception area. It was clear he said that a lot, like some kind of rehearsed performance.

I looked over to the reception area on my left where a young woman with long, curly auburn hair was stationed, looking down at something.

I turned to head over there when I heard Daniel say, "*Bonne chance*, Miss Ella. Good luck."

"*Merci*, Daniel, "I replied, then I made my way quickly toward the front desk.

The young auburn-haired woman looked up at me with dark-green eyes as I approached her desk.

"*Bonjour*. Welcome to The Lost Cantrell. My name is Bernadette. How may I help you?" she said with a stiff smile. Her accent was American. Definitely American.

"*Bonjour*, Bernadette. My name is Ella-Cherie Silver. I'm here to drop off my resume for the kitchen help position that was advertised on the hotel website."

"Oh. Okay," she replied as she looked down at my resume in my hand, resting on the desk surface.

"Monsieur Cantrell, the owner of this hotel, reviews all applications and candidates himself. But he is busy at the moment. You can leave your resume with me, and I will be sure to let him know that you came in, and I will see to it that he receives it." She smiled again. It was not quite as stiff as the last time but certainly not as pleasant as Daniel's.

I was hesitant. I hated leaving room for error. What if she didn't give it to him? If he was ultimately in charge of picking his employees, then I wanted to make sure that he got it before the deadline. I couldn't leave it in the hands of someone else, regardless of how efficient they seemed. If you want something done right then you better do it yourself, right?

I was just about to politely let her know that I could come back at a later time when Mr. Cantrell was not as busy when her eyes suddenly cut to her left, and she smiled genuinely this time.

"Looks like you'll be able to hand it to him yourself."

I followed her eyes and saw a tall, slim man with salt and pepper hair, dressed in an impeccable suit. He was headed toward us, his strides long and strong. The huge lobby space gave me enough time to study him as he made his way to the front desk, an air of authority surrounding him. I was immediately intimidated, and all of the calmness that Daniel's welcoming smile had brought to me dissolved under the stoic expression of The Lost Cantrell's owner.

"Monsieur Cantrell, I'm so glad that you're out of your office now," Bernadette said cheerfully when Mr. Cantrell had reached us and looked over at her questioningly. "Your presence is needed here."

And that was when Mr. Cantrell turned his dark brown eyes on me, and I felt instantly smaller. Literally. I am not a short woman. Not by any standard. I am five feet seven inches. Barefoot. In the heels that I was wearing, I was about a solid five feet eleven. Yet there I was, staring up at Mr. Cantrell, feeling completely out of my depth. I guessed that he was way over six feet tall. Way over. He looked down his nose at me with a bored, blank expression, and it scared the heck out of me. Why did it scare me? Here's why: There was no way he could have known what I was there for. Bernadette had not told him that I was there, obviously for fear of interrupting the boss while he was busy. For all he knew, I was an inquiring potential guest, and yet the way he was looking at me, neutral and uninterested, was hardly befitting of what I would expect the owner of a supposed hospitality establishment to be like. So, in that moment, I concluded that that was either Monsieur Cantrell's natural demeanour around everyone, including guests, or he was a mind reader and already knew that I was nothing but a lowly job-seeker. Either way, it did not bode well.

"Bonjour. I am Monsieur Hector Cantrell, the owner of Le Cantrell Perdue. How may I assist you?" He had more of an English accent, which surprised me. I thought he would be definitively French.

I cleared my throat and responded. "*Bonjour*, Monsieur Cantrell. My name is Ella-Cherie Silver. I am here to apply for the kitchen help position. I have my resume right here." I lifted the folder containing my resume off the desk surface slightly to draw his attention to it. He glanced at the folder briefly and then back to my face.

"Miss Silver," he said slowly before continuing on, "we use an online application system for the recruitment process here at The Lost Cantrell, so as to limit unnecessary movement in and out of the establishment. Candidates need not come in unless they are called in for an interview. You must use the online application form provided on the website." He turned a look of mild irritation toward Bernadette as he said, "Bernadette should have informed you of that as soon as you made your inquiry."

I hoped that she wouldn't be in trouble because of me, but when I looked over at her, she was more than just a little unbothered by his words. In fact, she even shrugged slightly as she said, "She's already here. Doesn't make sense to send her away," and went back to staring down at her computer screen. I noticed Monsieur Cantrell's eye twitch a little as he watched Bernadette return to her screen without a word of apology at all. Then he turned back to me with a sigh, took my resume folder from my light grasp, opened it up, and began scanning over it. Relief washed over me. This was good. At least he was looking at it.

It felt like forever before he finally looked back at me, and I held my breath, waiting anxiously for his words. Preferably an invitation for an interview.

"Thank you for your interest in the position, Miss Silver, but it appears you are overqualified. I cannot move forward with your application," he stated plainly. Then he closed the folder and held it out to me.

I stared at him. Was he serious?

"Overqualified?" I repeated in question.

"Yes." One word. Not enough.

"I don't understand." I blinked up at him,

genuinely confused.

When Monsieur Cantrell realized that I hadn't taken my resume out of his hand yet, and quite frankly I had no intention to, he put it down on the desk and stood even straighter, which was something I would not have thought possible.

"Let me explain, then," he said. "This job is for kitchen help. The general job description of kitchen help here is to assist our head chef in whatever preparation he needs done before meals are served, as well as to clean up the tables and kitchen after serving. This includes tasks such as washing the dishes, sweeping, peeling and chopping of vegetables, and so on." He looked at me pointedly then, as if he had said something that should have explained his rejection of my application. I simply blinked at him again, which made him release another sigh. "You are a qualified chef, Miss Silver. A graduate of The Crest Institute of Culinary Arts, according to your resume. This is not a job for a chef. You are overqualified."

That explained it.

Never had I thought that graduating from one of the top culinary institutes in New York would be a disadvantage to me. The Crest Institute of Culinary Arts had a good name. It made the list of top Culinary Arts Schools internationally every year, without fail. That's why I had worked hard to get into it. I thought that I would graduate and get a good job at a top restaurant immediately after, but that wasn't the case. New York was competitive. Sure, there were lots of job opportunities in smaller restaurants, diners, and cafes. But I didn't go to culinary arts school for four years and obtain a Bachelor in Culinary Arts for that. No. I wanted a job in a Michelin star restaurant. Just like the one-Michelin-star L'Annette Restaurant at The Lost Cantrell.

But to eventually get a top chef or sous-chef job, you needed experience and to get experience, you needed a job in a top restaurant. See the problem? I needed a job in an upmarket, high star restaurant. There was no shortage of qualified chefs looking for that kind of job too, though. Like I said: competitive.

So the whole situation was new to me. In most cases when I would apply to a job at a top restaurant or hotel, I would be one of the least qualified applicants due to my lack of relevant experience. So hearing the term "over-qualified" being used on me in a place as grand as The Lost Cantrell was obviously surprising, at the very least. I didn't know whether to pat myself on the back or cry at the irony of it all.

"I don't mind washing dishes, Monsieur Cantrell. I really don't. And wouldn't it be to the hotel's advantage, anyway, to have a qualified chef at the wage of general kitchen help?" I pointed out. I was trying hard to convince him to at least give me an interview.

He looked at me and lowered his chin a little. "Be that as it may, it still would not sit well with me." Then his eyes softened ever so slightly as he said, "You may think that you are content with general kitchen work now, but I assure you, Miss Silver, that this blind enthusiasm will not last long. Ambition is a powerful force, and it does not allow for contentment." Then he lifted his chin up again and said the words that were in line with the general response that I had gotten from most of my applications to top establishments. "Good luck with your future endeavors, and I hope you find a

position more suited to you. Good day, Miss Silver."
He turned away from me and made his way around the
semi-circle shaped front desk and entered behind it to
stand next to Bernadette. He had basically dismissed
me. He was going about his business, while I stood
there looking like a nerd trying to get in with the "cool"
crowd…and failing of course.

I had been rejected. Again.

Not again. Not again, I thought.

I stared at my resume folder that Monsieur Cantrell
had left on the desk surface, and I shook my head
lightly, my disappointment slowly turning into
determination and a refusal to accept yet another
rejection. Then I looked up at him again, and he was
speaking to Bernadette as if I wasn't even there.

No. Not this time. Not that easily.

I let out a light exhale and began speaking before
my nerves had any chance of interfering with my
newfound courage.

"I'll prove myself," I said softly, but clearly loud
enough that Monsieur Cantrell and Bernadette heard
me, because they both looked up, as if they were
surprised that I was still standing there. "I'll prove
myself," I repeated, a little louder.

"Miss Silver…" Monsieur Cantrell began, and I
knew where it was going.

"With all due respect, Monsieur Cantrell," I cut
him off quickly, watching as his head snapped back
ever so slightly at my interruption, "we both know that
working here as kitchen help is just as good as working
at a no-star restaurant as a chef. The Lost Cantrell is a
big deal. So I'm willing to work my way up." I looked
him in the eyes and added some grit to my voice so I

didn't sound whiney when I said, "But I have to start somewhere, sir. And there's no better start than here for me. All I'm asking for is a shot at an interview." Then to maintain my respectfulness, I added, "Sir."

Bernadette turned her head slowly to look at Monsieur Cantrell with her eyebrows raised. I got the distinct feeling that no one had ever interrupted him before, let alone argued a point against him. Especially not someone who was looking for a job. He stared at me with his mouth in a thin line and his expression skeptical. Then he turned that same skeptical eye to Bernadette, who shrugged again and said, "I like her."

My nerves were all over the place again, and I kept looking back and forth between the two of them. Bernadette liking me didn't seem like a significant enough factor. However, I didn't have enough time to dwell on it because Monsieur Cantrell suddenly snatched up my resume from the desk, turned away, and made his way out from behind the reception area, heading back in the direction he came from before, without a word.

I stared off after him, too surprised to say anything. Until I finally heard Bernadette's voice say, "You asked for an interview, right?"

I blinked at her, still surprised by Monsieur Cantrell's sudden departure.

"He wants you to follow him," Bernadette said slowly, catching on to my confusion.

"Oh, right!" I exclaimed, already hurrying off in the same direction that I had seen Monsieur Cantrell head off in, but I just about managed to turn around and call out, "Thank you!" to Bernadette, who simply smiled in return.

I followed Monsieur Cantrell through a door that read *Monsieur Cantrell* in gold lettering. *No question as to who the office belongs to.* He closed the door behind me, then went to stand behind the large desk that was toward the back wall. It was made of the same beautiful deep, dark wood that the front reception desk was made of, but the rest of his office was certainly not as warm and inviting as The Lost Cantrell's lobby. It was a fairly large office, with a brown leather double sofa to the far right of the desk on the same wall side as the office entrance door, and rows of high windows along two of the walls: one row on the back wall behind the desk; and the other row on the wall to the left of the desk. They allowed for ventilation without letting people outside see into the office. There was also a large, fully stocked bookshelf in the corner but, besides that, the office was plain. No photos or paintings or anything. Just plain. It surprised me because Monsieur Cantrell obviously must have had excellent taste in décor if he had anything to do with the lobby design. It did not make sense for his office to look that way.

All of the windows in his office were open, letting in the cold late-March air. So yeah, his office was also cold. Plain and cold. Just plain cold.

"Take a seat, Miss Silver," he said, still standing behind his desk, with my resume resting on top of the shiny wood surface.

I sat down in the chair opposite him on the other side of the desk and waited while he stayed standing and looked over my resume again. Then he finally took his own seat and looked straight at me with disinterested eyes.

"Since you are already here, I have decided to

conduct your interview now."

"Thank you, sir," I responded, after clearing my throat.

He pulled out a clipboard from his desk drawer, as well as one red ink and one black ink pen. He scribbled something on the top sheet of paper in black ink and then looked up at me again.

"Let's begin," he said, completely neutral. I saw him flick his wrist quickly over the paper as he wrote...in red ink this time. I assumed that the red ink was for negatives. *I already have one negative before the interview has even started. That must be a record.*

"We have already established that you cannot follow simple instructions, otherwise you would not be here right now. So, I will leave out the question as to how well you can." He glanced at me briefly when he said this, and I had no response because, technically, he was not 100 percent wrong. I figured that was what the excess amount of red ink was all about. *Not great, but I can salvage this.* I looked directly at him and sat up a little straighter in the chair, determined to impress Monsieur Cantrell with my responses. And by the end of the interview, I was sure that I had. I managed to answer the rest of the questions smoothly and confidently, and Monsieur Cantrell seemed to have run out of snide, snarky comments.

"Thank you for your time, Miss Silver. We will be in touch to inform you of the result of your interview. Please note that I discuss all candidates with our Head Chef before any decision is made, as he plays a major part in the decision-making for hiring kitchen staff. Good day," he said, as he stood from his chair and held out his hand to me. Ever the professional.

I smiled at him politely as I took his hand, shook it, and said, "Thank you, sir. Good day to you, too."

Then he walked over to the door, opening it to indicate that we were totally done, and I exited his office feeling way more calm and collected than I had barely twenty minutes before. Bernadette was no longer at the front desk when I looked over, but Daniel was still at his post, and as I approached him, heading for the hotel doors, he cheerfully said, "See you soon."

All I could say, because it was the only thing that I knew for certain, was the same thing that I had said to him earlier, "I hope so, Daniel. I hope so."

Daniel nodded his understanding, then I made my way out of the beautiful Lost Cantrell, praying for just a shot at the opportunity to work there.

Chapter 2

It was a Monday. It had been exactly a week since my interview at The Lost Cantrell and, in short, I was going a little nuts. I kept my cell phone close to me at all times during that week, even more than usual, and I checked my email constantly. I wasn't applying for any more other jobs either. Quite frankly, after seeing the inside of The Lost Cantrell, I didn't want to work anywhere else. In fact, the only time I was able to even think about anything other than The Lost Cantrell was in the evenings and on weekends when my roommate and best friend, Stacey, was home, because she always had something to talk about. Also, she had sort of, kind of banned any more talk or focus on the kitchen staff job. I might have unintentionally been driving her nuts too.

"Look, Elz, I love you and all, honey, but if you bring up that hotel one more time, I'm going to lose it," she had said on Saturday night, without even looking at me. We had spent the day in, lounging on the sofa and chatting. Stace had been writing something in her notebook for work. Some new marketing strategy or something. She worked at a marketing firm in Midtown, and she loved her job. Actually freaking loved it.

"I know. I'm sorry. It's just…I really want this job, Stace." I leaned my head back on the couch, letting out a frustrated sigh. I hated being unemployed, but I hated the idea of being employed at the wrong place even more. I wanted to work somewhere where I would love my job just like Stace did. Somewhere that would eventually help me to achieve my goals. And I just knew that The Lost Cantrell was that place.

Stacey put down her pen and looked over at me this time.

"I know how much you want this, but worrying about it isn't going to help or change the outcome. It's either they're smart and they'll call you, or they're idiots and they'll pick someone else." She looked to the side and tapped her chin with her index finger as if in thought then said, "Kinda like the guys I meet in the club." Stace gave me a playful wink, and I laughed at her comparison. She swept her long, straight, blonde hair to one side as she leaned in and gave my hand a reassuring squeeze.

"Everything is going to be okay, Cher," she said, using the nickname of my middle name that only she and my mom used. "One way or another, you're going to be a successful chef. No matter what happens with that hotel, whether you get the job or not, you are going to make it. We won't have it any other way." Then she let go of my hand, clearly done with the heavy convo, and continued in her usual breezy tone, "Trust me. Stacey-Ann Hartfeld is never wrong." Her bright blue eyes were sparkling, like they always did, with barely contained mischief.

"Never? Really?" I asked skeptically through a laugh.

"Never," Stace said, as if she actually believed it. Then she quickly added, "My dating life and judgment in men don't count."

We both burst out laughing at that. The fact was that Stacey-Ann Hartfeld, as picture-perfect-pretty and smart as she was, seemed to always get it wrong with men. Always. From when she first arrived at my high school back home in Minnesota, where I was born and raised, to when we decided we both wanted to move to The Big Apple together for college, Stace had always picked the worst guys to like. She always said, "I give good love to bad boys, Cher. I need help." And it was true. She always fell for the worst of them. Every time.

I had known and been best friends with Stace since we were fifteen, when she and her dad had moved to Minnesota from Indiana. We had hit it off immediately, and even my family loved her. That was the thing about Stace, she was like a little slice of home for me. It wasn't easy being away from my parents and sisters for so long, pursuing my dreams. They were all back in Minnesota. Stace made it bearable. Our little brownstone apartment in the mostly student-filled area of Reign Hill was warm and cozy. Home.

"Well, you'd better not be wrong this time, Miss Hartfeld, coz I need this to happen," I said to her when our laughter had finally died down.

"It'll happen. Now, relax and don't worry about a thing. Even if you don't get this one, something else amazing will come up for you." Stace was always so encouraging. I thought on her words for a second.

"You're right. I'm done worrying," I said firmly, sitting up. Then I gave Stace a grin and asked, "Junk food and a movie?"

"Junk food and a movie," she replied, grinning back at me. That was Stace and I in a nutshell. Junk food for dinner was our idea of being rebels. I jumped up from the sofa, once again feeling like a carefree being. But like I said, that was Saturday, and when Monday rolled around, all of that "done worrying" stuff went right out of the window, and I was back to being crazy over "that hotel," as Stace had chosen to call it.

Stace was at work so my mind had no distraction. It was eleven a.m., and the only thing that I could do to keep myself busy was what I loved, and that was being in the kitchen. I was baking cupcakes and icing them as intricately and accurately as if they were going to be served to the Queen, when my cell phone rang. I was startled for a second, causing me to jump and ruin the cupcake masterpiece that I was working on. Yeah, I was so deep in concentration that the sound of my own cell phone ringing on the counter startled me. What can I say? Cooking did that to me. I reached for my phone, expecting to see "Mom" in the caller ID. She called almost every day just to chat because she found texting too impersonal. When I glanced at the screen, however, it was not home calling. In fact, it was a number that I didn't know, and my heart started beating a mile a minute as hope swelled inside of me. I answered the call as calmly as I could.

"Hello?"

"Miss Silver?" a female voice asked.

"Yes?" I was still unsure, so my answer sounded like a question.

"You are speaking to Bernadette from The Lost Cantrell Reception. Would you be able to come in today at two p.m.? It is in connection with your application for the kitchen staff position."

I didn't think it was possible, but my heart started

beating even faster. "Yes, of course. I'll be there." I managed to speak calmly, and I was surprised by it.

"Fantastic. We look forward to seeing you, Miss Silver. Good day." Then Bernadette cut the phone without waiting for me to answer. I stared at my phone screen, breathing in deeply and hoping that I hadn't dreamt up the call. I put my phone down on the kitchen counter slowly, carefully. Then...I lost it. I danced around the kitchen and squealed in the most immature way possible, and I didn't care. They had called! The Lost Cantrell had actually called me back! I jumped up and down on the spot and squealed some more, my royalty-worthy cupcakes forgotten. It was only when my over-excitement had died down that I realised that Bernadette hadn't actually explicitly said that I had the job.

****

I once again found myself jumping out of a taxi at The Lost Cantrell drop-off area, feeling as nervous as ever. It was 1:50 p.m. I had a point to prove. Just in case they had merely narrowed the candidates down and this was a second interview or a test run in the kitchen or something, I wanted to start it off the right way. The best employees are always early, right? I walked by the big security man again, and he greeted me in much the same way he had the week before. He looked even bigger this time. "Hello," I replied, smiling.

As nervous as I was, I still noticed how beautiful The Lost Cantrell's entrance corridor was...again. Seeing it once wasn't enough. I stepped into the lobby, sneaking a quick peak at L'Annette, and was immediately greeted by a cheerful Daniel. "Ah!

Bonjour, Ella! Good to see you again."

"Hi, Daniel. It's good to see you again, too," I replied. He gave me a nod, smiling wide, and I smiled brightly in return, then turned to head over to the reception desk. I had taken just one step before I turned back to Daniel, my lips pursed in thought. *Why not?*

"Hey, Daniel? Um, I was called in today, but I have no idea why. Not really. If you happen to know why, I don't want you to tell me. But could you just wish me good luck again? Like you did before my interview last week. Please?"

As you can see, I was a talker. Bordering on blabbermouth. Daniel looked perplexed for a moment before he answered with his token smile. "*Bon chance*, Miss Ella. Good luck."

"Thank you, Daniel," I replied, instantly feeling a little less nervous. I wasn't superstitious or anything. Not in the least. But there was a certain calm that came from knowing that at least one employee at The Lost Cantrell was definitely in my corner. I proceeded to the front desk, where Bernadette stood, staring down at her computer screen just like before. She looked up with a smile as I got nearer. "*Bonjour!*" I greeted awkwardly, but with enough enthusiasm to cover up the awkwardness.

"Hey! You're early. That'll make a good impression. I'll let Monsieur Cantrell know that you're here." She picked up her telephone receiver and pressed a few digits. I noticed that she had greeted me informally this time. No "*Bonjour*" or formalities. It relaxed me even more. *Maybe she's in my corner, too*, I thought. Bernadette spoke into the receiver in a professional tone. "Monsieur Cantrell, Miss Silver is here." She listened for a second and then put the receiver down softly, smiling at me again. "He'll be right out," she said, before looking back at her computer screen.

"Okay. Thank you," I responded on an exhale. It was probably only thirty seconds or so, but it felt like an hour before Monsieur Cantrell came out of his office and headed over to us at the front desk. I was wearing shorter heels that day, just in case a test run in the kitchen was on the cards, and I found myself looking up at him at an even more neck-straining angle.

"Miss Silver, welcome back, and thank you for coming in," Monsieur Cantrell said as we shook hands.

"Of course. Thank you for calling me back in. I'll take any excuse to see this lobby," I responded with a nervous laugh. *Stop babbling, Ella.*

Monsieur Cantrell cleared his throat and attempted a small smile, but it looked more like a grimace. "Yes, well…" Monsieur Cantrell obviously found my rambling annoying. "Miss Silver, in your interview you expressed a passion for the professional kitchen. And passion cannot be taught. That is why the job is yours," he said with his chin lowered, and then he added, "If you still want it, that is." Then with a slightly amused expression on his face, he said, "Hopefully once we discuss the details of the job duties and remuneration in my office, you will accept the position with the same blind enthusiasm that you had before."

I stared at him for a second, letting it sink in and swallowing hard before I answered. "I…I got the job?"

Monsieur Cantrell looked surprised by my question. "Of course. What else would you be here again for?" he responded.

"Uh…"

That's all I managed to get out before Monsieur Cantrell turned to Bernadette and said, "We'll be in my office if my attention is required for anything." Then, just like the last time, he turned and headed in the direction of his office without another word to me. This time, however, I didn't need Bernadette to tell me to follow him. I kept up with his long strides, excitement pushing my pace. I had gotten the job! I, Ella-Cherie Silver, would be working at L'Annette Restaurant in The Lost Cantrell! I couldn't believe it. I guess I should have used common sense. Why else would they have called me in, right? I just never thought that my luck would be that good. Well, not without an uphill struggle. I had immediately assumed that this was a second interview or a kitchen test run with some other shortlisted candidates because I didn't expect anything to come easy. I never had. Yet there I was, soon to be an employee at The Lost Cantrell. *I need to believe in myself more.* That was my thought as I entered Monsieur Cantrell's plain, cold office.

Once we were both seated, I listened impatiently as he explained what my duties and work stations would be, and also told me how much I would be paid, which I gawked at. The job even came with health benefits and free first floor overnight hotel room stays when needed. *Are all five-star hotel kitchen-staffers this well-rewarded?* I thought as Monsieur Cantrell went on. All I wanted to hear was the question as to whether or not I was taking the job…so I could say "yes" over-enthusiastically.

"So, do you accept the position, Miss Sil—?"

"Yes, sir. I would love to work here, sir," I said

quickly. I had interrupted him again, but he didn't seem as surprised by it this time. He handed me my contract from the drawer at his desk and spoke while I looked it over.

"As the contract states, you will start April 1. For today, I will introduce you to our Head Chef and the rest of your workmates in the kitchen." He gave me just a few more minutes to finish reading the contract and sign where I needed to before he stood and walked over to his office door, opening it and striding out with a simple, "Come along, Miss Silver," before I even responded.

I left my contract on his desk and followed him out, attempting to match his stride. We headed for the L'Annette entrance, and my pulse quickened. I was about to finally step foot inside one of New York's finest restaurants and in just a couple of days, I would be working there. Monsieur Cantrell pushed L'Annette's glass doors open and, as I stepped in behind him, I took a deep breath. It was as exquisite in décor as I thought it would be. The small glimpses and glances that I had taken through the glass doors before hadn't even come close to doing it justice. There were gold and crystal chandeliers hanging from the ceiling. The tabletops all had white, gold-trimmed tablecloths, with shiny silver cutlery and neatly folded white napkins. The chairs also had an intricate gold design on the back of them, tying the whole theme together. I took it all in in the space of a few seconds because Monsieur Cantrell wasn't exactly sightseeing.

"The kitchen is this way," he said, turning and heading for a plain white door that was in a corner of the room. We entered the kitchen to find it bustling with activity and preparations. When the staff noticed Monsieur Cantrell enter, they all stilled and greeted him in French, their attention fully on him.

"Hello, everyone. I know that I usually only come in just before serving, but I wanted to get this done now. I won't take up much of your time." He clasped his hands together before continuing. "Now as you know, we were in need of one more kitchen assistant fairly urgently due to our increase in business. After carrying out interviews and discussing all of the candidates with Chef Fords, we selected the most suitable candidate for the job, and that candidate is Miss Ella-Cherie Silver here," he said as he stretched out a hand in my direction. "Please join me in welcoming her as a new addition to L'Annette and Le Cantrell Perdue."

I shook hands with each of the staff members who were on duty as they all introduced themselves to me. There was the Head Chef, Chef Graham Fords, whom I was more than a little excited to meet. He was a big deal and a top chef who had worked all over the world and was highly respected. He was one of the main reasons that I had wanted the job in L'Annette so badly. To work in the same kitchen as Chef Fords was an achievement in itself. He was pale and chubby with a round, clean-shaven face, gray hair, and a kind glint in his eyes. He shook my hand firmly and said, "Welcome, Miss Silver. Looking forward to having you in the kitchen."

His words, in his strong English accent, were like music to my ears, and I smiled widely. "Thank you, Chef," I responded. In the kitchen with Chef Fords were his two assistant chefs, Melany and Jeff, one other kitchen help staff member named Catherine, and a couple of line cooks named Tom and Arnold. I immediately knew that I would call Arnold "Arnie" once we were used to each other. In my family we were big on nicknames. What else can I say?

Jeff, Catherine, Tom, and Arnold were friendly and welcoming, smiling as they introduced themselves. Melany, on the other hand, was a tad bit on the side of stand-offish. By tad bit I actually mean a whole lot. Her blonde hair was cut into a pixie style under her toque blanche, and her pale blue eyes looked me up and down as she shook my hand without a smile. She didn't seem interested in socialising or making courteous small talk with me like the others, but she wasn't being directly rude either. Just kind of disinterested. However, I was too excited to dwell on her lack of enthusiasm for my presence. I had enough enthusiasm for the both of us. No, I had enough enthusiasm for the whole friggin' hotel.

Monsieur Cantrell's voice cut through our chatter suddenly. I had no idea that he was still there, simply observing our short interaction with each other. "Chef Fords, you can expect Miss Silver here officially from the first of April, working the two p.m. to ten p.m. shift as needed, yes?"

"*Oui*, Monsieur," Chef Fords answered casually.

Monsieur Cantrell gave everyone a nod and then turned to leave with yet another use of his seemingly favorite sentence for me, "Come along, Miss Silver. I'll see you out."

I hesitated, stopping Monsieur Cantrell before his long strides took him any farther. "Um, may I stay for a little while longer? Please. I won't be in the way, I promise. I just want to observe the kitchen work before I start officially." I said it all quickly, hoping for a "yes."

Monsieur Cantrell lifted his eyebrows in question to Chef Fords, who easily responded with, "I don't mind at all. Gives her a chance to get a feel for the job." Chef Fords smiled at me in his cheerful way, and I knew that we would get along great then and there.

"Very well," Monsieur Cantrell said. "I will leave Miss Silver in your capable hands, Chef. Good day to you all."

After Monsieur Cantrell strode out and Catherine handed me a hair net that matched her own, I stood in a corner of the kitchen where I wouldn't be a nuisance. I had only planned to stay for a few more minutes, to watch, listen, and get a feel of the L'Annette kitchen before my start date, but eventually I was offering to help with tasks. A few minutes turned into hours, and by the time I was leaving The Lost Cantrell, having learned and done many of my future duties, it was already 5:45 p.m. and just about L'Annette's opening time. I arrived at our brownstone after 6:30 p.m., thanks to the unkind traffic, and my feet were practically throbbing from the three hours of work that I had done…in heels. They may not have been that high, but they were still heels.

I stepped in the door and was immediately met with a full-on rant from Stace. "Where have you been? Why weren't you answering your phone? I had no idea where you were, and I couldn't get in touch with you. Where is your phone? Is it on you? Were you just not picking up? Don't do that. I thought you had been kidnapped or something. Your cupcakes were all over the place..." Oh yeah, Stace was dramatic too. She went on like that for a few more seconds before circling back to, "Where have you been, Cher?"

I didn't have the mental energy to explain every detail to her in that very moment, so I just kicked off my shoes and said, "I got the job, Stace. That's where I was. The Lost Cantrell. L'Annette. I got the job."

The annoyance that was on her face just moments before disappeared in a second, and I was suddenly in her arms as she hugged me, dancing around and squealing her congratulations. So I joined in, because I obviously hadn't done enough celebratory squealing and dancing yet.

Chapter 3

I had been working at The Lost Cantrell for three whole weeks, and I loved it. I had started April 1, just like my contract stated, and the job was as amazing as I thought it would be. I mean, my duties only included tasks such as washing dishes, cleaning the kitchen, taking out the trash, and chopping vegetables, just like Monsieur Cantrell had said, but I still loved it because being in the L'Annette kitchen was exciting.

On top of those duties, I also occasionally did room service runs and helped out at the bar when needed, like during serving time when all the prep was done and all the waiters were busy. I had a fixed shift at the hotel from two p.m. to ten p.m. Monday to Friday and weekends off, unless extra help was needed for something. L'Annette opened up for sit-ins for both guests and non-guests of the hotel from six p.m. to nine-thirty p.m. for dinner and from seven a.m. to nine a.m. for breakfast for guests of the hotel only. In between those times, room service was available to hotel guests. Waiters came in an hour before each opening time on shifts, and everything was done according to a very strict schedule.

It was a rule at the hotel that the guests were to go to their rooms unaccompanied and remain uninterrupted after check-in. Daniel would only assist them with their bags up to their floor, but he never went to the room unless instructed to do so specifically.

"Le Cantrell Perdue is very exclusive, Miss Silver," Monsieur Cantrell had told me on my first official day. "Our guests come here for privacy. We must be like little elves, yes? Only the results of our hard work must be seen, Miss Silver, not so much our presence."

Even housekeeping was limited to after the guests had checked out unless, just like with Daniel, the cleaning ladies were specifically instructed to clean a particular guest's room throughout their stay. My room service instructions were exactly the same. I was to knock on the guest's door and announce that the room service order had arrived, wait for the guest to acknowledge me, and then let them take their order into their room themselves before wheeling the tray away. I was never to take it in for them unless, you guessed it, I was instructed to. I know it seems like a lot, but it's what made The Lost Cantrell so exclusive. I assumed that some of the guests who stayed there were probably famous people who didn't want to be seen much, even though I hadn't seen any famous people yet. I guess that was the point. At the end of the day, it worked. The Lost Cantrell, in every way, ran efficiently like a well-oiled machine.

I had phoned Mom and Dad and my sisters, Rose and Jasmine, the same day that I had gotten the call for the job. Mom squealed over the phone with me, and Dad gave his classic, "That's my girl." Duncan and Blossom Silver are the kind of parents that every kid needs, and I love them dearly. They owned a little flower shop back home that brought in some money and allowed them to work their own hours. It obviously wasn't bringing in tons of cash, but they loved it and were comfortable enough financially.

Rose, my older sister, was 27. She was an optometrist and ran her own practice as a partnership with a fellow optometrist that she knew from university. She had been paying my half of the crazy rent for the brownstone that I shared with Stace. Since I had graduated, she had basically been paying for all of my necessities to lift the pressure and stress from Mom and Dad. She was amazing like that. She was kind and helpful in every way, and that's why she had been nicknamed "Angel" by all of us. We actually called her Angel more than we called her Rose. I was excited to tell her that she wouldn't have to pay my living costs anymore and that I actually had a job and could hustle for myself like an adult should. When I told her, her response was, "You know I love helping out when I can. I didn't mind at all. But I'm so happy for you, Elz. You deserve it. If you ever need anything, though, you know I'm here. Don't hesitate." Yeah…Angel.

Jasmine, my younger sister, was twenty-one and still in university back home. She was a Business Administration student in her final year. Jaz had graduated high school a year early because she was smarter than average, so she had started at university early too. She was strong-willed, sarcastic, and blunt almost to the point of seeming rude sometimes. We had nicknamed her "Sweetheart" and then shortened it to "Sweety." The nickname had been given to her sarcastically, of course. When she was about eight years old, she had made one of her typically blunt comments and Mom had said, "Wow, you're a real sweetheart, aren't ya?" It had stuck.

Sweety was just as excited to hear about my new job as everyone else was. "Finally! Now Angel can focus on giving *me* cash. You've been hogging the finances," she joked. Mom and Dad paid most of Sweety's tuition, but Angel chipped in there too. With me off Angel's back, she could use all the money that she had been spending on me on something else. She was already spread so thin helping out Mom and Dad and Sweety, so I was glad to be making her burden lighter.

I laughed at Sweety's comment, regardless of the truth in it. Personally, I loved her sense of humor and sarcasm. In reality, she had a heart of gold and was full of compassion. She just didn't like the idea of people seeing that side of her all the time because she didn't want to be taken advantage of. "Seriously, Ellzy, congratulations," Sweety said sincerely. "Don't forget us when you become a big-name chef and all."

I had a big grin on my face as I said, "Never." I knew that Sweety was only kidding, but I still felt the need to reassure her that family always came first, no matter what.

Overall, I had been feeling a whole bunch of good emotions over my first three weeks at The Lost Cantrell. I loved my job already, and my family had been as supportive as they always were. It was great.

I had made quite a few new friends who worked at the hotel too, like the cleaning ladies, Maria and Iris, the bartender Joe, and a couple of the waiters, one of whom was a real charmer named George. They were all nice and fun to be around. Actually, just about all of the staff that I had met were warm and sociable. Even Bernadette, who had been a little reserved in the first few days, was more talkative with me. I had taken to calling her "Bernie." She didn't seem to mind. In fact, she might have even liked it.

I had learned in my first week that Bernie was actually Monsieur Cantrell's daughter. I guess that's why she wasn't intimidated by him like everyone else was. She never called him "Dad" or anything in public, just "Monsieur" like the rest of us, even when she spoke about him. It was weird to me, and I didn't understand it. But then again, it wasn't for me to understand. It was their dynamic and theirs alone.

I also learned that even though Monsieur Cantrell was known to be a stern man, he was very well-liked by his employees and guests. I kind of liked the guy too, to be honest. Even with his stoic personality, he was pretty cool.

The only person that I couldn't quite click with was Melany. She just always seemed irritated to have me around and avoided me or gave me one-word answers when she could. She was stand-offish in general, but she had become all the more so ever since she had heard me telling Catherine and Jeff about my culinary arts qualification and what it was like studying at Crest. Melany had one too, from a different culinary arts school. When I complimented her on the achievement, because I know that it takes a lot of work, she said, "Well, it's nothing fancy like a culinary arts degree from Crest but, you know, it's something." It was a snide response, no doubt about it. She barely looked at me when she said it, and then she walked away. I knew from that moment that she was definitely not interested in being friends at all. I could take a hint.

I did my best not to get in her way and kept

conversation with her to a minimum and only in relation to what was needed in the kitchen, because I knew that was what she wanted.

Beside from ice-cold Melany, I was happy and had been well-received by the rest of the hotel staff. I was so comfortable, in fact, that I had developed the habit of asking myself what I had to lose by doing something new or out of my comfort zone. It made me more confident. It made me better at my job. Okay, so I know that I was only kitchen help, but I did my job well, and that was what mattered. If the role of kitchen help was all that I could get at The Lost Cantrell, then I would be the best kitchen help in New York City. And I believed that I was.

My mind was set on positive thoughts only, and everything was going great...until it wasn't going so great anymore.

****

My very first screw-up happened after I had been working at the hotel for about a month and a half, the day Monsieur Cantrell asked me to cover a small part of Iris's room prep routine. I was hovering around the kitchen at about five o'clock, having done most of the meal preps already and waiting for Chef Fords to give me something else to do, when Monsieur Cantrell walked in, headed straight for me.

"Miss Silver, unfortunately Miss Lopez has had to rush out to attend to an urgent family emergency. I need you to cover her room preparation for a guest arriving at six o'clock. I have the room requirements here." He held up a crisp, white sheet of paper. "You are to have prepared the room before his arrival, but not so long before that the ice melts entirely. "This explains everything." He handed the sheet of paper over to me.

I scanned through the requirements. The guest had a "special" whisky order that was prepared by Joe. "What's special about his order?" I asked.

"What's special about it is that it is special," Monsieur Cantrell answered pointedly. "Now, I trust that you will carry out the duty well. If you have any questions, I will be in my office." Then, in his usual custom, he walked away without another word.

I waited for him to exit the kitchen before I leaned on the counter in the corner near the sink and began to look over the list. Truth be told, it could barely be called a list because it was so short.

After reading through the requirements in detail, I understood the "ice" reference. The guest was one Mr. Zeke Gage, who was staying in the hotel's top floor penthouse suite, and liked having a glass of his specially formulated whisky on the rocks in his room upon his arrival. His requirements were minimal, especially compared to what Iris had told me some guests required in their rooms.

I headed over to the bar to make sure that Mr. Gage's drink order would be timetabled in and ready for me to take up to his suite by five-fifty p.m. so that I could be back down by six p.m. when he would just be checking in.

He, like almost all the guests at The Lost Cantrell, wanted to enter his suite unaccompanied and didn't want anyone on his floor once he checked in, so it was important that I was out of there before he went up. Timing was everything at the hotel, and Monsieur Cantrell emphasized that.

I waited in the kitchen, performing any small tasks

that Chef Fords needed done until five-forty-five p.m. struck. I practically power-walked to the reception to get the spare penthouse suite keycard from Bernie, headed quickly to the bar with my room service tray, collected the glass of whisky from Joe, and made my way swiftly to the golden elevator doors that would take me up to the penthouse suite. I was right on time to make it in and out of Mr. Gage's suite in a flash and get back down to the kitchen in time for the six o'clock sit-ins.

The elevators at the hotel were just as extravagant as the rest of it, with their mirrored walls, gold accents, and roominess. I tried my best, as I always did when making room deliveries, to keep still and not dance a little to the elevator music. It was always a struggle. I found a compromise and just tapped my foot instead.

I had never been to the penthouse suite before, and when I heard the soft "ding" announcing that I was on the thirtieth floor where it was, I braced myself for more hospitality décor excellence. I stepped out into the hallway and made my way to the door that was a few feet away directly across from the elevator. I unlocked the door, pushing it open slowly, and then paused for a short moment to take everything in. It was as I expected. The Lost Cantrell penthouse suite was excellent. Excellent in its simplicity and charm. The neutral colors and plush fawn-colored carpet made it the perfect combination of homely and luxurious.

I closed the door softly, wheeled my serving tray to the side slightly, and walked across the spacious lounge area to the small coffee table near the floor-to-ceiling glass doors leading to the balcony. I placed the drink on it, on one of the custom coasters laid out, as the instructions had stated, and then turned to leave, looking around the room at the open doors leading to the bedroom, guest bathroom, and separate kitchen area as I walked to the door.

I took all the grandeur in for another moment before reaching for the handle and pulling the door open, and that's when my timely leaving process was interrupted. Interrupted because I was startled. And I was startled because I almost came head-on face-to-chest with someone's body. Someone's tall, male body. I took a step back quickly so that we wouldn't bump into each other, and then I looked up into his face. He was young. I estimated early thirties maybe.

The man stared down at me with a neutral expression, and his body was tensed. He had dark hair and crystal blue eyes. Was this Mr. Gage? It had to be. If it was, he was definitely early.

"I'm...I'm sorry," I stuttered. "I was only expecting you to be checking in at the front desk at six o'clock. Um, are you Mr. Zeke Gage?"

It was not the best welcome to give to a guest, that was for sure. I hadn't even greeted him. I was flustered, and I knew that I had messed up in a major way. The rule was simple: No staff on the floor after guests checked in, let alone in their room. He must have been startled too. Now, there was just a heavy silence. He didn't answer my question, and his eyes narrowed slightly as he asked, "Who are you?" His voice was calm, low.

"Oh, sorry, sir. I'm Ella Silver. I was in charge of your room prep for today. I'm sorry you found me up here. I must've mixed up the times somehow." I knew that I hadn't, but I decided to just comply with the old saying "*The customer is always right.*" Maybe it would make him go lighter on me, because the bottom line was that Mr. Zeke Gage was early and I was screwed.

He looked down at my nametag and then, to my surprise, he took a step forward, forcing me to step back farther into the suite. His eyes swept slowly around the room from left to right before he closed the door quietly and looked back at me again. All he had on him was a large, black duffle bag. Definitely not the standard rich person's luggage, in my opinion. I clasped my hands together in front of me, coming to the realization that neither of us was speaking and the silence was getting eerie.

Maybe he noticed my discomfort or maybe he was just as uncomfortable as I was because he finally put his bag down to the side of the door and spoke.

"I like to come in here undisturbed and...alone." He was a slow talker. "Hector..." he began, and then caught himself as if remembering that I was an employee. "Monsieur Cantrell knows my requirements. This...situation shouldn't have happened. He needs to be made aware of that." He said everything very matter-of-factly. His tone was still calm, and he had noticeably relaxed from when he had stood in the doorway, but he appeared nowhere near at ease...and neither was I.

"Of course, Mr. Gage. I'm so sorry about this situation," I apologised again, imitating his wording. "It won't happen again."

He nodded once and then pulled the door open for me to leave. I grabbed my tray as I said, "I hope the drink is to your liking."

"I'm sure it will be," he replied.

It was only when I had wheeled my tray past him,

one foot still in the suite, that I realized that making Monsieur Cantrell "aware" of the "situation" basically meant that Mr. Gage intended to rat me out and make a report. He was well within his rights to do so as a guest of course, but I feared what that meant for me. Monsieur Cantrell expected efficiency without excuses, and I didn't need any negative reports coming my way after just over a month of working there. For all I knew he would fire me for this, practically sending me back to Broke-town in Irrelevantville. I couldn't let that happen.

My tenacity had worked before to get me an interview and ultimately a job at the hotel. Maybe it could work again. Maybe I could appeal to Mr. Gage's softer side. *What do you have to lose, Ella?*

I turned back around and looked him right in his eyes, which seemed to be turning a prettier shade of blue each second. He narrowed them again, and I let out the breath that I had been holding in and started talking before I could chicken out.

"I need this job, sir. It's my dream to work here. When the position opened up, it was all I thought about." I breathed in and continued. "I'm not asking you not to report this, Mr. Gage. I completely understand why you would. I'm just asking that, if or when you do report it, you leave room for me to keep my job. Honestly, I kinda…" I paused, unsure if I wanted to say the next part, but saying it anyway. "I kinda feel like a winner when I'm here. I'd like to keep feeling that way." That was the best that I could do.

Mr. Gage looked uncomfortable again and he didn't acknowledge anything that I had said. Like I said before, I could take a hint.

"Okay, have a good evening, Mr. Gage." I stepped away from the door so that he could close it and turned toward the elevator, slowly wheeling my trusty tray with me. He still hadn't responded to me, and he didn't close the door immediately, but I eventually heard the soft click of the door closing behind me. I entered the elevator and headed down, dreading what waited for me on the ground floor once Monsieur Cantrell heard about the "situation."

I stepped out of the elevator into the lobby, and my steps faltered when I spotted Monsieur Cantrell behind the reception desk with Bernie. He was on the phone, listening intently to whoever was on the other end, and then his eyes fell on me. The look on his face was pure annoyance, and the thin line that his lips had formed gave his usual stony expression an even harsher edge. I knew in that moment that Mr. Gage had already reported me. Monsieur Cantrell motioned for me to come over as he spoke into the phone and then put the receiver back into its cradle. I looked down at my tray. I couldn't leave it there looking out of place in the lobby, and I couldn't wheel it all over the place with me either. I also definitely could not leave Monsieur Cantrell waiting too long, so a trip to the kitchen to drop it off wasn't happening, even though that would have been the best solution. But I had already messed up, and I didn't want to give him any other reason to scold me.

Daniel, clearly noticing my predicament, came over from the entrance door to wheel the tray to the kitchen for me. I thanked him with a look of sincere gratitude, and he smiled at me knowingly.

I walked over to the reception as if I were walking the plank. When I got there, Monsieur Cantrell said in a low voice, "In my office. Now."

I looked over at Bernie, and her face held an expression of genuine pity as she mouthed, "Sorry" to me. I had no idea why she was apologizing. Maybe she figured that I was possibly about to get fired. I gave her a tiny smile just so that she would stop looking at me like I was a puppy that had just been kicked, and then I followed Monsieur Cantrell to his plain, cold office. As soon as we were inside, he didn't even wait for us to sit down before he turned to me and began his lecture.

"Monsieur Gage is a very, very important guest here. He stays here frequently and maintains his booking in the penthouse suite. He is a particular man when it comes to his privacy. For you, Miss Silver, to be found not just on his floor but inside his suite is an almost unspeakable blunder when it comes to his requirements. Most guests would expect me to relieve you of your position for such carelessness."

I didn't say anything. What could I say? That Mr. Gage was early? The fact was that the customer was always king, whether they deserved the title or not. All I could do was wait for what was coming, whatever it was.

"Luckily for you, Miss Silver, Monsieur Gage is not like most of the guests here. He made it very clear that he does not wish for you to lose your job and that his report is merely to ensure that you do not make the same mistake with a less-understanding guest. It is a courtesy to you, believe me, that you be made aware of the fact that the guests here are of a very high standing and are used to getting their way. They will not hesitate to have you fired if you fumble like you did today. Mr. Gage knows this, has seen it happen, and he simply asked that I relay that information to you, even though I should not have to since it is a standard rule here that our guests be undisturbed and unaccompanied to their rooms." He sniffed and turned his head slightly to the side to give me a sideways glare before ending with, "Like I said, a courtesy."

His face turned even sterner then as he said, "A courtesy, Miss Silver, which will only be extended this once. Something like this should never happen again. Is that clear?"

Relief flooded my body. "It won't happen again, Monsieur. I'm so sorry. I thought he would only be checking in at the reception desk at six o'clock. I promise to budget my time better next time, if I ever have to do room prep for a guest again. I'm sorry." I said everything hurriedly, but I wanted him to know that I meant it.

He cleared his throat in his usual way, and his expression softened. "The fault is not entirely yours to carry, Miss Silver. You were merely the face of the inefficiency because you were physically present there. Mr. Gage was indeed earlier than his usual six o'clock arrival time, and it was Bernadette's duty to inform him to lounge in the lobby until you came back down. In reality, she is the one who could have prevented all of this mess, and she did not. I assure you that she will receive even more of an earful than you did, and some."

He looked irritated again, but in the way that only Bernie could irritate him.

It made sense then that Bernie had apologised to me, since she had let Mr. Gage up before I had managed to come back down, which put me in the "situation." I wasn't angry with her, though. Not at all. I knew that she hadn't done it on purpose. In my short time working at the hotel, I had learned that Bernie was both fairly disorganized and forgetful. Not all the time, but enough for it to be noticed. I had also learned that Bernie could be sweet, funny, and helpful, and those qualities mattered way more to me than her cluttered, goldfish tendencies.

"I'm sure Bernie already feels bad enough about this whole thing, Monsieur. I know she'll probably be more careful next time, too. Maybe you can spare her the further embarrassment," I said softly.

Monsieur Cantrell gave me a look of utter disbelief. "Spare her?" he asked. "Spare her? What kind of employer would I be if I treated my daughter differently and *spared her* every time she did something wrong? A bad one, that's what kind. Bernadette is employed here just like everyone else, and the rules are meant for all employees, myself included. No exceptions, Miss Silver."

"Yes, Monsieur," I responded quickly. He made a valid point, and I had already used up one lucky charm that day by keeping my job so I was not about to push my luck by arguing with the man. "I'll just be heading back to the kitchen now. They'll be needing me eventually."

The truth was that during serving time the chefs and cooks took over, and there wasn't that much for Catherine and me to do, even though we were asked to assist here and there. Our work was mostly preparation before serving and cleanup after. I just used the kitchen as an excuse to get out of there and get back to where I was most comfortable before Monsieur Cantrell could change his mind. "Thank you, Monsieur," I said as I turned to leave his office.

"Wait, Miss Silver." His voice stopped me, interrupting my getaway plan.

"You are to continue with the room prep and service for Monsieur Gage from now on."

I couldn't help but frown at him. "After what happened today, Monsieur? I would think that you wouldn't want me to…"

He held his hand up dismissively as he interrupted me midsentence. "I know, Miss Silver, but Monsieur Gage would prefer it if the same person tends to him. He is not keen on having different people in his private space. He would rather have just one staff member tending to his floor during his stays. He requested this himself. It is his usual rule. Normally Iris tends to his floor without making any contact, but now he obviously knows that it was you who was in his suite, so he wants to keep it that way. Less traffic, easier accountability, yes?"

I nodded quickly, not wanting to appear as if I were not a team player, even though I didn't want the role of tending to Mr. Gage's floor.

I assume my nod was a sufficient enough response for Monsieur Cantrell because he carried on. "Monsieur Gage's requirement is very simple. He takes a glass of his special whisky on the rocks every day at six p.m. unless he states otherwise."

"What about on weekends when I'm not at work?" I asked.

"He rarely stays here on weekends, but if ever he does, I will deliver his order myself."

The idea of Monsieur Cantrell doing room service himself was so surprising that my mind stuttered for a moment. I guess the penthouse suite really did come with crazy benefits.

I finally got my words together. "Yes, Monsieur," I replied, and then a thought crossed my mind and I just had to ask, "Uh, but if I'm the only one tending to his floor, does that mean that I have to do housekeeping too, if he requests it? I mean, that's not exactly in my job description."

"No, no. The suite will only be cleaned when Monsieur Gage checks out, so you need not be concerned about that, Miss Silver. That duty will remain with the housekeeping staff. He usually only stays for a week at a time," Monsieur Cantrell replied, pulling a sigh of relief out of me. There was no way that I would have managed extra work outside of my usual duties, whether I got paid for it or not.

"Okay, great. That works." I was rarely ever that casual when I was speaking to Monsieur Cantrell, but there were times when I had nothing better to say. He didn't seem bothered by his employees being a little informal with him sometimes anyway. The keyword there being "sometimes."

"Well, that will be all, Miss Silver."

"Thank you, sir."

I left his office and quickly headed to the kitchen. I went through the motions, but all through the rest of my shift I thought about the guest that I had basically been assigned to. He had done as I had asked and let me keep my job. I appreciated that. I was grateful, but I wasn't entirely comfortable with his request. I understood his reasoning, in a weird kind of reclusive way, but I wasn't overly keen on having the burden of such a particular guest solely on me, especially the "very, very important guest" who could afford to stay in the penthouse suite of The Lost Cantrell regularly.

All I could hope for was to not mess up with him again, and to definitely not find myself face-to-chest with him again either. So basically, I needed to work like the quiet little elf that Monsieur Cantrell said I should be.

Chapter 4

The next day I did my best to just try and get back into the normal flow of things. The "situation" had happened on a Monday, and Mr. Gage was staying for the week, checking out on Saturday morning. So it was Tuesday and my first official day as Mr. Gage's floor-handler. To say that I was dreading to take his order up and see him again after my blunder was an understatement. The idea of it made me queasy. The only thing that kept me from openly grumbling to everyone about how much I didn't want the burden of facing Mr. Gage again (whom I had practically begged to let me keep my job—I know, cringe right?) was the fact that Bernie had it worse than me. Monsieur Cantrell had given Bernie somewhat of a parental punishment for her mistake, so she was working in the kitchen with us for the remainder of the week as the manual dishwasher, while Monsieur Cantrell occasionally manned the front desk. I felt bad for her, especially when she broke a nail while washing up a couple of plates that had come back from a room service order. She almost looked as though she would burst into tears for a second. How she had managed to break a nail under her rubber glove was beyond me. Bernie wasn't a brat, not in the least, but I knew in that moment that physical labour was not her forte.

I stepped toward her as she looked over her broken

nail. "Hey. Why don't you take a break and I'll finish those up," I offered. Relief spread across her face at my offer, but then she looked down and shook her head.

"No. This is my punishment. I need to learn to be more careful." She looked back at me. "Thanks, Ella, but I can handle it." Bernie then gloved back up and went straight back to work, a look of determination on her freckled face. I respected her for it, because it was clear that she wanted to face the consequences of her mistake, regardless of the fact that she was the owner's daughter, and only child for that matter. Monsieur Cantrell might have been stern, but Bernie was his soft spot, whether he admitted it or not. Everyone knew it. She could have tried to use his affection to her advantage and gotten out of her punishment, but she hadn't done that, and I was impressed by that show of maturity. I gave her shoulder a quick squeeze then went back to busying myself with small tasks.

Once Bernie's mood picked up, the atmosphere in the kitchen became as light as it usually was, and everything was moving smoothly again, but I couldn't stop myself from constantly looking up at the wall-clock nervously as Mr. Gage's room service time approached. The minutes raced by and before I knew it, it was already time for me to take his order up.

Once I was on the thirtieth floor, standing in front of the suite's door, I allowed myself a moment to calm my nerves before I knocked on it softly. I didn't hear any response, so I waited…and waited some more. Then I lifted my hand to knock again and that's when the door swung open slowly. Mr. Gage stood there, looking at me with that neutral expression again, but he didn't speak. It was then that I realised how very handsome he was. Handsome in a dapper way, too. I dropped my hand quickly and gave him my best classic hospitality worker smile. "Bonjour, Monsieur Gage. Your order." I looked down at his drink. "Your top secret whisky on the rocks. Again." I laughed nervously. *Really, Ella?* My blabbermouth tendencies were becoming a problem.

He still didn't say anything, but simply raised an eyebrow at my "*again*" statement. I cleared my throat out of discomfort, and that's when he picked up the glass and said, "Thank you."

I smiled again and replied, "You're welcome, Mr. Gage." Initial formal French greeting done and dusted, I could stick to English with him now. I turned around with my trusty tray and headed to the elevator feeling a lot less nervous about the arrangement. He didn't close the door immediately, just like the last time, but eventually I heard the door quietly click shut...just like the last time.

I got back downstairs and finished my shift in a much lighter mood than before, and so it went the next day. I took Mr. Gage his drink at six o'clock on the dot; he simply said, "Thank you," and I replied, "You're welcome." Everything went smoothly, and we both said and did just about the exact same thing as before. Until Thursday, when I said, "Good evening, Mr. Gage. Here's your drink." And that's when the non-talkative Mr. Gage said, "Again."

I was so shocked to hear him say anything else other than "Thank you" that my head shot up at just that one word. He might as well have read a whole speech, in my opinion. He had a look of amusement on his face, and I realised that he was actually making reference to the comment that I had made earlier in the week. I smiled up at him, glad to know that he at least had a little sense of humor.

"Again, yeah," I said with a laugh.

He took the glass and said, "Thank you...Ella."

Hearing him say my name was just as unexpected as him using an extra word during our encounter. *Thank you, Ella.* I played it over in my head again before giving him my usual, "You're welcome, Mr. Gage."

He gave me a small smile as I turned to leave. Well, it looked like a small smile to me at least. I made my way back down to the lobby, my mind solely on the guest who had surprised me, by simply saying my name.

****

Time dragged on slowly the next day, and the usual energy drain that I felt on most Fridays was kicking in swiftly. By the time Mr. Gage's order was due, my mind was solely on my bed and sleep. And I didn't even care which one came first.

I knocked on his door, already pasting my smile in place. He opened up, dressed in a crisp white shirt, fitted black trousers, and formal black shoes that looked as if they cost more than I earned in a month. Come to think of it, I had only ever seen him in different variations of a crisp white shirt, and formal trousers up to that point. He was a strange one. I guess he liked the look. It definitely suited him.

"Hello, Ella," he greeted. *My name again.*

"Good evening, Mr. Gage. Here you go."

I waited for him to pick the glass up like he usually did, but he didn't. Instead he pulled the door open wider and said, "Would you like to come in?"

I figured my tired mind was making me hear things. "Uh...um. Excuse me?"

"Would you like to come in?" he repeated calmly. I stared at him with my mouth open, figuratively clutching my pearls and what not. I mean the guy was a looker, no doubt, but that did not excuse what I assumed he was implying. I looked him straight in his eyes and squared my shoulders slightly.

"Mr. Gage, I appreciate you not getting me fired and all, but that doesn't mean that I would do anything indecent because of it." I tried to be polite while still getting my point across, because the situation was already awkward for me and needed to be handled delicately. Mr. Gage, on the other hand, didn't seem to be phased at all. In fact, he looked amused again, for the second time in as many days.

"I assure you, Ella, I have no sinister intentions. None at all. I just want to talk to you...for a little bit."

I was so taken aback that all I could do was stare at him. It was an odd request. We didn't get paid to chit chat with the guests. "Talk about what exactly? And anyway, we staff are not allowed to fraternize with guests at all," I pointed out, and it was true.

"I'm aware of that, so I won't take up much of your time." He looked down then back up at me, appearing almost sheepish. In that moment, he came across as maybe a little shy even. "I'm not always a very sociable person. Especially outside of work. I could use some practice."

I nearly laughed at that. The conversation was just getting weirder by the second. "You want to practice your social skills on me?" I asked, tone full of skepticism.

"Yes. And I would like to learn a few social skills, too." He smiled that "too-small-to-really-be-called-a-smile-but-I-can-see-it" smile of his, and I felt a part of me cave. "You seem to like to talk, so…"

He shifted from the doorway to make room for me to enter the suite, and I side-eyed him. Truth be told, I didn't get any bad vibes from him. But then again, didn't people say that most sociopaths hid their true nature well? I stood there, undecided. If he was a serial killer, he couldn't hurt me in the hotel where so many people would be looking for me, right? Plus, he had spared me my job. I figured that I could do him the favor of talking for a minute. I pushed my tray past him into his suite and followed, then I stood in place awkwardly just inside the room. There was no way that I was going to sit down, even if he offered me a seat. *This must be how some supposedly smart girls wind up in trouble.* It was too late for me to change my mind though, because he had already closed the door behind me. I looked around the room just to avoid making eye contact with him now that I was in his space.

The first thing that I noticed was how neat everything was, given the fact that the room wasn't receiving any housekeeping. I thought that guests would let loose once they checked in, especially when they knew that they would be undisturbed. Zeke Gage's room, on the other hand, looked almost unused and unoccupied.

My discomfort must have been clear yet again because he broke the silence, without asking me to sit down. "So, Ella, where are you from?"

I looked over at him. "Uh…Minnesota. I'm from Crownsvale, Minnesota."

"What made you want to move to New York?"

"I don't know. I grew up in a small town, and it was great and all, but I just wanted to see what it would be like in a bigger, busier place, you know? So my best friend, Stacey, and I just said, 'Let's do it,' and here we are! Roommates in New York!" I stretched my arms out in the classic "ta-da" pose purely out of nervousness.

One corner of his mouth turned up in another almost-smile. "You said that this is your dream job. What made The Lost Cantrell so special?"

"I mean, it's The Lost Cantrell," I replied with a shrug. "I got my degree from The Crest Institute of Culinary Arts, and L'Annette is a top restaurant here, so this is an amazing start for me. Being here just feels right. Even with the ten o'clock knock-off time," I joked. Truth be told, I had gotten lucky with my shift hours, and I knew that.

"Congratulations," Mr. Gage said. "From what I've heard it's an achievement to even get accepted into Crest. You should be proud."

We were both standing, facing each other with an appropriate distance between us, but I still felt like he was right in my face when he said that. "Thank you." I looked down, embarrassed by the compliment. I was probably blushing a little, and I was glad that my warm brown skin wouldn't show it much. "Uh, what about you? Where're you from?" I asked, genuinely curious.

"Here," he replied with that low, deep voice of his.

He kept his eyes on me. *One word?* Maybe he really did need to practice his social skills. I blinked at him a couple times, thinking that maybe he would say more. He didn't. I guess it was on me to try and get him to talk more.

"Here? As in, New York?"

He had an amused look in his eyes as he slowly replied, "Yes, Ella. Here. As in, New York."

I tilted my head at him, so many questions going through my mind. "But if you're from here, why stay in a hotel? Why not just get an apartment or something?"

"I'm from New York, but I don't live here anymore. I haven't for a while. I just come here on business, occasionally."

Before I could ask him anything else, he moved to the door, picked his drink up off the tray and said, "Well, Ella, I won't keep you any longer. Wouldn't want you to get in trouble." Then he pulled the door open for me to leave with a simple, "Thank you, and I hope you have a good evening." So abrupt. I didn't hesitate though.

"You too, Mr. Gage," I said as I wheeled my tray out. I turned around to smile at him then headed straight for the elevator. Once I was inside and heading down, I released a breath. "That wasn't so bad," I said out loud. I had gotten through the week like a trooper and could look forward to everything going back to normal.

****

Upon getting back to work the following week, rested and rejuvenated, I remembered that Mr. Gage had checked out on Saturday. I had told Stace about my strange interaction with the mysterious guest, and she had found it weird too. "Did he give you any serial killer vibes?" she had asked.

"Not really, but he is kinda odd though."

Stace's brow furrowed a little at my answer. "Well, just be careful next time, Elz. Especially if your boss says that this guy is a regular there. I mean, you don't know the guy, and him inviting you into his room just to talk"—Stace made air quotes with her hands on the word "talk"— "is totally inappropriate."

She was right, but I didn't feel like he was a threat of any kind. "I'll be careful, Stace. I promise."

Obviously Stace had nothing to worry about since Mr. Gage was gone. The sensible, professional part of me was relieved that I wouldn't have to deal with another awkward conversation with him, but the curious part of me was a little disappointed too. A part of me wanted to know more about the man. Just a little part of me. But by the time Friday came around again, I was perfectly fine with not knowing because everything was back to normal and I was at ease. I hadn't slipped up in any way, and Bernie was back where she belonged, in the comfort of the lobby at the reception desk. The usual routine was restored, and my nerves were back at a reasonable level...until the following week on Monday when Monsieur Cantrell approached me yet again. He didn't come to me unless he absolutely had to so I knew, as I watched him take his long strides in my direction, that he had a task for me to do. As usual, the kitchen always seemed so much smaller when Monsieur Cantrell was in it.

"Miss Silver, you are to continue with the room service of Monsieur Gage's suite this week, exactly the same as before."

"He's back?" The question was out before I regulated my tone, and I hoped that I didn't sound too eager.

Monsieur Cantrell's eyes narrowed ever so slightly. "Yes, he is." He looked me over for a second before his face went back to its usual neutral expression. "He checked in a little earlier today. You know the schedule, yes?"

"Yes, yes, sir," I replied quickly.

"Very well," he said. And then he was gone, marching away to find someone else to intimidate, no doubt.

As I watched Monsieur Cantrell leave, taking his imposing presence with him, I wondered if Mr. Gage would still want to be social with me. I couldn't help but admit to myself that I didn't mind if he did.

****

Standing outside Mr. Gage's door, I smoothed my hands down my white shirt and dark, navy-blue slacks before knocking. The uniform that we kitchen help staff wore was hardly flattering, but it had never bothered me until that very moment. Was I actually concerned about what Mr. Gage thought of my appearance? *Wow. I need a date.*

Mr. Gage opened the door wearing a crisp black shirt this time, top button left casually open. I guess he had decided to switch it up. Looking him over, the thought popped into my head yet again that the man was a pleasure to look at. His dark, wavy hair made the clear blue color of his eyes stand out even more.

"Ella." That's all he said.

"Good evening, Mr. Gage. Your drink," I said, smile in place. He didn't seem to be in a very talkative mood, but then his mouth turned up in that small smile, and he pulled the door open wider for me to enter. I slowly entered the room, and he helped me out by pulling the tray in as I pushed it and putting it to the side of the door. I stood and waited with my hands intertwined in front of me.

"How are you, Ella?"

"I'm good, Mr. Gage. How are you?"

"Fine. Thank you."

Then…silence. Both of us just standing there. I could practically hear nonexistent crickets in the background.

The lack of conversation quickly became weird, so I blurted out the first thing that came into my head. "I'm glad you're back. It's nice to have you again. Have you here again, I mean. We must be doing something right if you keep coming back." I gave a nervous laugh after my awkward blabbering because, of course, the moment wouldn't be complete without my classic nervous laugh. *For crying out loud, Ella,* I thought, feeling embarrassed that I was so bad at making simple conversation when it came to Mr. Gage.

My embarrassment, however, was short-lived because when I looked at him, he was smiling. Genuinely smiling. No teeth showing, but certainly more of a smile than his usual. It even crinkled his eyes at the corners a little. It definitely qualified as a smile in my opinion, and it made him look more approachable.

"Thank you, Ella. I'm glad to be back. I'm very…comfortable here. It's familiar to me." He answered in that slow-paced way of his. "Did anything interesting happen in your life during the course of the week?"

So, it turned out that he was in a sociable mood after all. As surprised as I was by that, I was still trying to get over his smile. His really friendly smile.

"No, nothing interesting. Just the same old." I realised then that, although I loved my quiet life, I may come across as boring to him, and I didn't want that. "But, uh, I'll be heading back home to Minnesota next week, just for a couple of days, for my little sister Sweety's graduation so...yeah," I said quickly. I had been genuinely surprised when Monsieur Cantrell had agreed to let me go for my sister's graduation, especially since I had only been working at the hotel for barely two months. He hadn't even hesitated. Like I said, sometimes he could be a cool guy.

"You have a sibling?" Mr. Gage asked, looking interested in whatever I would say next.

"Yeah, two actually. Two sisters. One older and one younger. Sweety is the youngest one, and Angel is the eldest. And I'm right in the middle."

He angled his head to the side a little, then said, "Sweety and Angel. Your sisters have very interesting names."

I laughed out loud at his comment. "No, those aren't their real names. Those are just nicknames. Sweety's name is Jasmine Amora, and Angel's name is Rose Adorlee."

"I see. And do you have two names as well?"

"Kinda. Mine is sort of joined together. My full name is Ella-Cherie, but I just go by Ella."

"Ella-Cherie," he repeated. "It's a very lovely name."

The combination of him saying my full name that way (which no one ever really did), complimenting me on it, and looking straight at me with those pretty blues had me feeling a little bit flushed and a lot nervous. "Thank you," I managed to say, avoiding eye contact with him.

He suddenly walked over to the door, picking his

drink up on the way, and pulled it open. "I hope you enjoy your sister's graduation." He shifted the tray slightly so that it would be easier for me to push it out.

Abrupt again, I thought as I headed out the door and simply said, "Uh, okay, thank you."

Before I had even wished him a good evening, he started speaking again. "I'll be informing Monsieur Cantrell of a change in my requirements. I would like to alter the arrangement. There will be no need for you to come up here at six o'clock anymore."

No need for me to come up at six o'clock anymore? "Oh…okay." I had no idea what had brought about the change, and I felt a little disappointed.

"Have a good evening, Ella."

"You too, Mr. Gage." I gave him a bright smile, hoping it didn't look too fake, and tried to keep the disappointment out of my voice. I shouldn't have been feeling any in the first place. But on my way down to the lobby and throughout my shift I wondered what could have possibly made Mr. Gage not want to talk anymore, and why on earth it even mattered to me anyway.

****

The next day I went in to work slightly less enthusiastic than my usual self. I knew that it was ridiculous for me to feel any disappointment at all over Mr. Gage putting a sudden halt to our short conversations, which we had technically only had twice, but it didn't stop me from feeling that way. It just felt a little like rejection. In fact, I was still semi-moping about it when Monsieur Cantrell walked into the kitchen and headed straight for me…again. All I could think was, *What now?*

"Miss Silver…" he began, then exhaled through his nose before continuing. "You are to carry on with the room service for Monsieur Gage, however you will now be taking his order up at nine fifty-five every night, and no longer at six o'clock."

I was confused at first. *I'm still going to be doing that? And at nine fifty-five p.m.?* That was just five minutes before my knock-off time. I said, "Yes, Sir" despite my confusion, and Monsieur Cantrell turned to leave. "Sir," I called out, stopping him before he could exit the kitchen. "Why did he change his order time?" I asked.

"Excuse me?" Monsieur Cantrell actually seemed surprised by my question.

"Why did Mr. Gage change his schedule from six o'clock to nine fifty-five?"

Monsieur Cantrell stared down at me blankly then finally answered, "Because he is a guest, and he is allowed to change his mind if he likes."

I simply nodded, knowing full well that that was as good an answer as I would get from him. He then left without another word.

I exhaled slowly, and for the remainder of my shift it felt as if I was counting each second. When I finally went up to Mr. Gage's suite, I was back to my upbeat self. He opened the door, looking as well put-together as he always did.

"Good evening, Mr. Gage," I said.

"Zeke. You can call me Zeke. Please."

I can call him Zeke. How…familiar. "Good evening, Zeke."

"Good evening, Ella."

I entered the room and, as usual, we remained

standing while we talked. Awkward silences occurred here and there, but he tried to be more talkative. It was ten oh-five p.m. when I realised that I had stayed past my knock-off time, and that's when a thought crossed my mind. *Maybe that's what he wanted. For me to be able to stay longer and not need to rush back to the kitchen. Maybe he likes our conversations that much.* I wanted to ask him if that were the case, but I didn't. Instead, I cleared my throat before saying, "I should go. It's past my time to head home. Plus, Stace worries about me when I'm even a minute later than usual so..." I trailed off.

"You can use my driver," he said casually. Yeah, no way was that happening. I wasn't that trusting. Maybe he saw the look on my face because he quickly added, "You can let your roommate know."

I shook my head. I needed to be smart. And letting a stranger know where you lived, no matter how comfortable you felt around them, wasn't smart. "It's really not necessary. I'm not leaving that much later than I normally do. I'm fine with catching a cab." Then, because I didn't want him to feel bad, I said, "Maybe next time."

He walked me to the door slowly. "Goodnight, Ella," he said.

I smiled. "Goodnight, Zeke."

Chapter 5

In the weeks that followed, I realized that I had officially formed a social routine with Zeke Gage. One week on and one week off, according to his stays. Each time our conversations got slightly longer and yet, still, I barely knew anything about him. He knew a whole lot about me though. What can I say? I was a talker.

After I had returned from Sweety's graduation in Minnesota, he had asked, "How was your sister's graduation?" I had then launched into a full-on chatter of how amazing it was to be back home, and he had listened intently, looking as interested as he always did.

I had even started sitting down on one of the couches and would have a drink with him. Well, I would have a bottle of water, but still. I would never be comfortable drinking at work, even though I had knocked off. He understood that. He understood a lot of things.

He even understood that our conversations were a gray area for me, especially in the beginning. Technically my shift was over, so I wasn't on the job, but I was still at my place of work. The thing is, I had started to actually enjoy our talks. It was a conundrum, really. But I was clearly willing to risk looking unprofessional, because every other week when Zeke was around, I would stay past my shift hours to indulge in some good, clean (albeit mostly one-sided) conversation with him. We didn't flirt or make any inappropriate comments, even though I was tempted to at times. I kept the conversation where he was comfortable with it. We just...talked. Then I would leave around ten-thirty p.m. and have the lobby to myself, avoiding any judgy eyes. But I always felt certain that Monsieur Cantrell knew something. He never said anything about it, but he started asking me things like, "Is everything going smoothly with your duties, Miss Silver?" and, "I hope everything is going well?" When I would say that everything was fine, he would simply nod, but his eyes held some skepticism. If he did know about the after-hour chats that Zeke and I were having, I was sure that he wasn't thrilled about it. I figured, however, that since I was doing the guest a favor it was cool, right? Okay, not really. It probably wasn't cool at all, but we can convince ourselves of anything if we want it enough, and I wanted to keep talking to Zeke. So I told myself that it was okay. I told myself that since all we were doing was talking, it wasn't totally inappropriate. By the time mid-July came around and we had been talking for two months every other week, I had completely lost any feelings of discomfort with both him and the situation. Zeke Gage was a part of my routine at The Lost Cantrell and I liked it that way.

I had always been a super-cheerful person, because I come from a super-cheerful family, but I had practically become an over-the-top prancing pony thanks to my budding friendship with Zeke. Well, it was a friendship to me.

Each night, I got chattier and, dare I say, bolder. I assumed that if we kept at it, he would have to get used to my talkative nature anyway, so why bother holding back? One warm July night, I was feeling particularly comfortable and cozy on the sofa in his suite, bottle of water in hand, and Zeke was relaxed too, so I let the mood lead the conversation and tried not to think too hard about anything.

"Hey, I haven't seen you in the restaurant before, and you haven't asked for any food to be brought up by me. What do you eat? And *when* do you eat? I'm starting to think you're a vampire or an alien or something."

He chuckled softly. Very softly. I still hadn't heard him laugh out loud yet. "I have breakfast downstairs in the morning, but for lunch and dinner I eat out."

"You don't like L'Annette's dinner menu specifically?" Unlikely. Who wouldn't like L'Annette's dinner menu? Only an ant-torturing, puppy-bullying heathen.

"No, that's not it. I'm sure I'd enjoy the dinner here. But I attend a lot of meetings throughout the day, sometimes at night, and it wouldn't make sense for me to be rushing back here every time I needed to eat. So I end up just grabbing something wherever I can from a food truck or takeout place. Sometimes I pick up extra to eat up here in case I get hungry again. Most of the time I just bring in my own groceries and make a quick meal. I'm always prepared." He smiled at me when he said that.

I couldn't believe we were actually talking so much. I couldn't believe *he* was actually talking so much. He rarely spoke more than two sentences at a time. He had already said so much in answer to my question.

"You can cook?"

"I can fry things up, yes. I'm no professional, like you are, but I won't starve if I have a few ingredients. Whether or not my cooking tastes good is another story entirely."

I let out a laugh. "So you stroll around the grocery store and everything?" I giggled like a teenage girl at the imagery in my head of him walking through the grocery store in his standard formal attire. It just didn't seem like something he would do. With the tons of money that he clearly had in order to be able to afford the penthouse suite regularly, he had struck me as the type to have an assistant do stuff for him.

"Is that hard to believe?" he asked with feigned offense.

"Yeah, it is actually. I can't imagine you pushing a shopping cart down the cereal aisle, you know what I mean?"

"You'd be amazed at what I can do, Ella. Grocery shopping is just one of my many talents. I'm full of surprises."

"I bet you are," I said on a laugh, enjoying the banter. We were actually joking around like old friends.

He smiled and leaned back in his chair, watching me, with one arm resting on the table next to him. His fingers tapped lightly on the surface. I watched him as well. His mannerisms were strangely adorable.

We sat there looking at each other, not talking anymore. That happened a lot with us. The silence was comfortable, but I started feeling self-conscious under his steady gaze so, to get him talking again, I decided to just go ahead and ask the question that had been on my mind for a while. I cleared my throat softly and went for it.

"So, um…what do you do? I mean, for work."

He didn't seem perturbed by the question, but he didn't make a move to answer immediately either, so I carried on. "It's just that when we have our conversations, it's mostly me, um, conversing. And that kind of defeats the purpose of a conversation. You never really tell me much about yourself, like what you do for a living."

I was being cautious, trying to choose the right words. He was a private person. I knew that some people didn't like talking about their work for whatever reason. Maybe he was one of those, so I didn't want him to close up on me.

When he finally spoke, it felt like an achievement on my part, because he said, "I'm a consultant."

Vague? Yes. But he had told me his occupation, and that was like him breaking out of his shell. I could work with that. It gave me leeway to ask more questions, and so I did.

"Consultant, huh? What kind of consulting work do you do? Like, what field?" I was excited to hear more about him, but I hoped it didn't show too much.

He looked to the side briefly as if he were thinking about my question, then he simply said, "PR."

I frowned at him. "PR? As in, Public Relations? You're a Public Relations Consultant?" I asked. I sounded like an inquisitive toddler, but I couldn't help it. His answer made no sense to me. I mean, he had told me himself that he needed to brush up on his social skills, so how would he deal with a job that required him to be an excellent communicator?

"Yes. I do some legal consulting, too."

Legal consulting. Now that was definitely something that I could picture him doing. "Legal consulting?"

He nodded, but I heard him hum a low, "Mmm-hmm."

"That sounds interesting. What does it entail?"

His mouth turned up on one side and he didn't break eye contact with me this time as he answered. "It's not that interesting at all, really. I make sure that my clients are safe, legally. That their businesses are safe when it comes to the law. Protected." Then almost as if it were an after-thought, Zeke said, "Protected in terms of the enforcement of the law."

I was so intrigued by him, and I hung onto his words, not only because his occupation sounded interesting, but also because he never spoke about himself. It was like a rare treat for me, listening to him speak…about himself.

"Wow. That sounds exciting," I said, wanting to know more. "So, how do you protect them? Your clients."

It was right then that I realised that I was actually getting used to him, because I knew the exact moment that he was done talking. I saw it in his eyes that he was closing up again.

"They ask me something, and then I answer with what I think is the best way forward," he replied. It sounded like a rehearsed line, well-practiced. He stood up then and said, "It's getting late, Ella."

I knew what that meant. We had been doing this for two months after all and, like I said before, I could take a hint. "It is. I'd better get going." I stood up and followed him to the door, which he had slowly made his way to and opened. I looked up at him, hesitant to leave. I knew better though. Zeke regulated our conversations and, when he was ready to stop, we stopped. "Goodnight, Zeke."

"Goodnight, Ella."

He held the door open for me as I walked out slowly. I didn't look back, but I heard the door close behind me. All I could think was, *Did the end of our conversation suck for him as much as it sucked for me?*

****

I was in luck the next evening when Monsieur Cantrell asked me to help Joe out at the bar. One of the usual bar servers was out, and L'Annette wasn't too busy for dinner, so I got to play bartender for the night. It was fun because Joe was a joker. I was taking orders and serving right at the bar, but only for the simple stuff. I left the complex concoctions to Joe.

I was drying a couple of just-washed glasses when I looked over in the direction of the restaurant entrance and saw a tall, built figure approaching the bar. A tall, built figure dressed in a crisp white shirt and fitted black trousers. I couldn't stop staring at him, not just because he was so darn good-looking, but because I hadn't seen Zeke anywhere else but in his suite. Seeing him inside L'Annette was unexpected, in a pleasant way. He sat down on the bar stool right in front of me, and I immediately caught the fresh, clean scent of his cologne. Zeke always smelled so good and, when I was around him, I did my best not to become one of those weirdos who sniffed people.

He rested his arms casually on the bar top and leaned forward. "Hello, Ella."

I was still staring at him like an idiot. "Uh, hi!

You're, um, here…in the restaurant." There was absolutely no reason for speech to be failing me at that moment, but it was.

Zeke smiled at me and said, "I decided to eat dinner in here for a change, so you'd be convinced that I'm not an alien or a vampire." He had a humorous twinkle in his eyes, and I had to laugh a little at the rare show of that side of him.

"I'll believe it when I see it," I told him, returning his humor. "So, do you want something to drink?"

He shook his head and leaned back. "No, thank you. I just came here for dinner, but then I saw you over here at the bar and thought I'd say hello."

My face heated slightly, but I still managed to maintain eye contact and reply with, "Well, I'm glad you came."

We were still just looking at each other in that awkward way that we always did when another tall body took a seat next to Zeke. We both turned to look at the man who had just sat down and, for the second time that night, I found myself staring. The man was strongly built and handsome, with skin the colour of deep mahogany.

He looked over at Zeke and simply said, "Gage."

Zeke nodded once at him and replied, "Smithson."

They know each other. I quickly jumped in to do my job. "Good evening, sir. I'm Ella. I'll be serving you tonight. What can I get you?"

The man that Zeke had called "Smithson" turned his dark brown eyes on me and threw me a cocky smile as he replied, "Hello, love." His gaze was intense and disinterested at the same time. He was British, I noted, with an accent similar to Monsieur Cantrell's and Chef

Fords', but it sounded even more emphasized to my ears. He casually ordered a brandy that had a price I tried not to gawk at.

"Single or double, sir?" I asked him.

"Single," he replied with a wink. Shameless flirt.

I smiled at him and said, "Yes, sir."

He took his wallet out and handed me the cash to pay for his drink. I got his change together quickly, placing it on the counter. He looked at it like he wasn't going to pick it up at first, but he eventually took it and put it in his wallet.

"I'm Colt Smithson, by the way. I have to introduce myself since Gage here has forgotten his manners," the man said to me.

I looked over at Zeke to gauge his reaction to the comment, and he appeared to be amused. I let out a light laugh. "It's nice to meet you, Mr. Smithson."

"Pleasure's all mine, Ella."

Picking up a clean glass, I got to work on his order while he and Zeke made small talk that was along the lines of, "I didn't know you were here in New York." I did my best not to listen in on their conversation but I failed because, well, I'm nosey.

"How's business?" Zeke asked Smithson.

"Slow. Not enough bad men to do business with," Smithson replied, taking a sip of the drink that I had put in front of him.

Zeke snorted and said, "You must not be looking in the right places."

Smithson tipped his head back as if weighing Zeke's statement before taking another slow sip of his drink.

"Are you sure I can't get you anything?" I asked

Zeke when their conversation had paused momentarily.

"No, thank you, Ella. I'll have my usual order in my usual way," he responded.

I was happy that we would be sticking to our routine, but I tried not to let it show. We did have company after all. When I looked over at Smithson, he was studying us, looking back and forth between Zeke and me with a critical eye. A little too critical. I cleared my throat and decided to start up a conversation with him just to escape his scrutiny. "So, how do you two know each other?"

He leaned back a little. "I've worked with Gage before."

"Oh, yeah? So, between you and me, is he any good as a consultant?" I asked conspiratorially.

Smithson let out a deep laugh. "I hate to say it, but the man's great at his job. Whenever I need any consulting done, he's the go-to guy."

"Good to know. If I ever need a PR or legal consultant, I know who to talk to," I said with a laugh.

Smithson slowly raised his glass to his lips and said, "Yup," before he downed his drink in one swift motion and took his wallet out again. "I think I'll head out. Let me get your tip."

I quickly shook my head. "We don't take tips here, Mr. Smithson."

"That's right. I always forget," he replied while putting his wallet away. "But I'd feel bad not leaving anything for you after such pleasant service, Ella. I have to give you some token of appreciation."

I didn't think that my service was any more exceptional than the other staff members at The Lost Cantrell. The hotel had an extremely high standard, and we were all expected to maintain it, without looking for any extra gratuity from our guests. "Really, it's not necessary. I couldn't accept a tip anyway. Hotel rules."

"Hmmm." Smithson pondered my words for a moment and then he finally said, "Well, you can't take money, but how's about this…" He pulled a thin gold chain that had been hidden under his shirt from around his neck. It had a small, round pendant on it that was made of gold and some kind of black stone. There was no discernible pattern on it, but it was very pretty.

Smithson held it out to me. "This is my lucky charm. I've had it for years. Now, it'll be your lucky charm."

I stared at him, waiting for him to tell me that he was kidding or something. He had to be, because my service hadn't been anything special. "Mr. Smithson, I couldn't—"

"Oh, come on, Ella," Smithson interrupted me. "Take it. It's just a cheap old chain, I promise. Not even real gold. But who knows? You might come into some money if you take it, you know, since it's lucky. That thought makes me feel better about not being able to tip you myself."

I stifled a laugh. "And how exactly do you know it's lucky?" I asked, side-eyeing him.

He chuckled and leaned in closer. "I'm here, aren't I? Alive and kicking."

I couldn't help but laugh then. "That is just about the worst argument in favor of calling something lucky. Like, ever."

His eyes held a spark of amusement as he said, "What do you have to lose by testing it out?"

"So, what are you saying? This lucky chain has the

power to make someone live longer? Keeps the owner...alive and kicking?" I joked.

Smithson's eyes never left my face. "Beats dying young, right?" He looked serious for a moment, but then he smiled again. I took the chain from his hand hesitantly, only because he didn't seem like he was going to let up.

"There you go!" he exclaimed when I took the so-called "lucky chain" from him. "Now, you wear that every day, Ella. Believe me, something good will happen."

I made a conscious effort not to roll my eyes at him because it would have been rude. Yes, we were having a friendly conversation, but it didn't change the fact that he was a customer, and possibly even a guest at the hotel, so I just smiled at him politely. Truth be told, it all seemed so silly to me, but I put the pendant around my neck anyway, tucking it behind my shirt, and decided that I would actually wear it every day. Not because I believed that it was truly lucky, but because I liked Colt Smithson and it clearly meant something to him. Also, Mom had always taught us to accept a gift graciously, and so I did.

"Thank you, Mr. Smithson," I said, keeping my polite smile in place. He stood from the bar stool. Zeke was sitting still, his expression unreadable for the most part, but because I had gotten to know him a little, I could tell that he was kind of tense and...annoyed. His brows had lowered into a slight frown, and his hands were clenched tightly around each other.

"Gage," Smithson said in lieu of goodbye, slapping Zeke on the shoulder.

"Smithson," Zeke replied, appearing normal again.

Smithson looked over at me and tipped an imaginary hat as he said, "Ella." I laughed at his antics as he continued speaking. "It was a pleasure meeting you but, alas, my room is calling." He pointed upward, indicating the hotel suites above us. *He is a guest after all.*

"Goodnight, Mr. Smithson. I hope you stay lucky."

He smiled wide. "I'm still here, right?" And with that, he left the restaurant.

I turned my attention back to Zeke. "So, you didn't look too thrilled when Mr. Smithson gave me the pendant." I wasn't asking. It was a statement.

He didn't deny it, just looked at me and said, "You should wear it. It was a nice gesture. People don't just give away their lucky charms, you know?" He smiled, and his eyes crinkled at the corners. He was back to kidding around with me, and I was relieved to see him lighten up again. I didn't ask him directly if he was jealous that Smithson had been a little flirty with me because that would push the friendship we had into inappropriate territory, though I couldn't help but wonder if that's what his reaction was.

Zeke stood abruptly, tapping the bar countertop once with his knuckles. "I think I'll have my dinner now. Like a normal human being."

I grinned at him. "I'll be watching you," I told him.

"I wouldn't expect anything less from you, Ella," Zeke replied. "I'll see you later." He made his way to a table at the far end of the restaurant and sat down.

For the rest of the time that I tended the bar, I watched Zeke. I watched him order. I watched him eat. I watched him pointedly look over at me while he chewed. *Not an alien, I see*, I thought with amusement.

Then, eventually, I watched him leave. I wasn't disappointed to see him go though, because I knew that our nightly chat was drawing near. Was I a little bit transfixed by the guy? Maybe. Yeah. But Zeke Gage was sort of a puzzle. And I like puzzles. I also liked how I felt when I was with him.

Chapter 6

I had never thought of myself as a social butterfly or anything, but I did like to be around people. I liked to talk to people too. That's why I used my breaks at The Lost Cantrell to chat with some of the other staff who didn't work in the kitchen. Bernie was one of my regulars. I would always pass by the reception and talk to her for a short while. The day after Zeke had come into the restaurant, I was hanging out with Bernie while she manned the front desk. I made myself inconspicuous so that it wouldn't look like Bernie was messing around when she should have been working. I stood a little to the side while we talked about stuff like our non-existent love lives and other "*girly things,*" as Stace would have called it. I was mid-sentence when the front desk phone rang. I stopped talking while Bernie answered the call. She spoke to the person on the other end of the line for a few seconds before apologetically saying, "I'm sorry, sir. We are fully booked and have no suites available at the moment. We should have some available suites the week after next."

Fully booked? I was surprised by that. I didn't see that many new guests checking in that week during my shift, but that was probably just because I was in the kitchen most of the time. But I also didn't see an increase in room service orders on the log or see a whole lot of guests milling around the lobby either, whether to go to the hotel gym or simply to get some fresh air. Don't get me wrong. The hotel was always well-occupied even when it wasn't peak season, but I just figured that I would be able to tell if we were fully booked, just from the likely heavier workload alone. As far as I could tell, our workload was just about the same. *Well, Monsieur Cantrell does always say that our guests like their privacy.* I was just glad that The Lost Cantrell clearly wasn't going out of business any time soon.

When Bernie ended the call, I looked at her with one eyebrow arched in question. "We're fully booked? Wow. Your dad must be rolling in money, huh? Just sayin'," I jested. Bernie just smiled shyly. The phone rang again before she could respond to me. This time it was the hotel's internal line.

"Hello, Monsieur," Bernie answered. She listened for a moment and then said, "I'll let her know right away." She put the receiver down and turned to me. "That was Monsieur Cantrell. He wants to see you in his office."

Why? "Okay. He say why?" I asked.

Bernie glanced in the direction of Monsieur Cantrell's office then back at me before saying, "Nope." Then she added, "Good luck."

I headed to his office, knocking lightly on the door. I heard him say, "Come in," and so I entered slowly, standing in front of him and waiting for him to offer me a seat.

"Take a seat, Miss Silver."

I sat down and watched him as he wrote something down on a piece of paper. Monsieur Cantrell was mostly old school like that when it came to taking down notes, and I didn't see him using electronics much.

He finally looked up and started speaking. "Miss Silver, Monsieur Gage will be staying here another week. I just wanted you to be made aware that you are expected to continue delivery of his order as per usual, according to his requests and instructions."

"Yes, Sir," I replied. *Zeke is staying another week?* I mentally high-fived myself for the rhyming thought while I considered the fact that it was the first time he would be staying two weeks in a row.

"Good. That will be all, Miss Silver."

Nodding, I stood up and bit down lightly on my bottom lip to try and stop myself from smiling too hard at the news that I'd be seeing Zeke for another week. I should have tried harder, because when I looked at Monsieur Cantrell again, he was looking back at me with a frown that rivaled even his most annoyed expression.

"Good day, sir," I said hurriedly, turning to leave. I was stopped short when I heard Monsieur Cantrell speak.

"Remain professional at all times, Miss Silver. It is important to know when to use your emotions and when to suppress them, especially here. Not everything is about…feelings."

I turned to look at him while he spoke. His eyes held a warning in them, and I immediately knew. I knew that he knew. He knew about Zeke and me talking late at night, and he could probably tell that I liked him too.

"Yes, Sir." It's all that I could say. He had read the situation perfectly, and he was right in telling me to be more professional.

He looked down at his desk. "Good. Good day, Miss Silver."

"Good day, sir."

I made my way out of his office feeling a little embarrassed by the whole thing. It felt like everyone was looking at me. They weren't. Embarrassment just has a way of making you feel that way. Long story short, it put a dampener on my mood. I went back to the kitchen before my break was even over and silently got to work on the prepping that needed to be done. My lack of talking must have stood out because Chef Fords came over to me while I worked in the corner and asked, "You all right?"

"Yeah, I'm okay," I replied.

He wasn't convinced. "You know what I do when I feel like I may be getting down about anything?" he asked me.

"What?"

"I cook," he said simply.

I chuckled at his answer. "But you cook all the time. You're literally always here in this kitchen."

"Exactly," Chef Fords said with a wink. "That's why I'm happy all the time, Ella."

A smile touched my lips, but only a little one. The man truly loved what he did. He was doing what he was meant to do, and it was inspirational to me.

"Look, you can call it the ramblings of an old man, but what I'm trying to say is that it's important to do what makes you happy. Do what excites you. As long as it's not hurting anyone or hurting you. Everything within reason, you know?" He added that last part as if his parental side had nudged him to not leave it out. "It's important to be happy, Ella. You're a ray of sunshine here, always smiling. Whatever you've been doing in your life so far, it's working. Don't lose that spirit. Don't change."

It was a heavy talk compared to how Chef Fords and I usually spoke to one another, but I guess he was just so used to seeing me upbeat all the time that my one glum mood concerned him. His words made me grin a little wider. *Don't change. Do what excites you as long as it's not hurting anyone.*

"Thank you, Chef."

From that moment, in true Ella fashion, I did my duties almost over-enthusiastically, because that's just who I am. Over-enthusiastic, a little talkative, and all about…feelings.

****

The following week, which I had dubbed "The Second Week of Zeke," L'Annette was bustling with customers and diners. Both the bar and the dining area had been full on Monday and Tuesday, and from the looks of the reservation log, Wednesday would be the same. I loved busy nights like that because it felt as if the air was practically alight with energy. It was so exciting and those were the moments that I craved at L'Annette.

I was doing my usual prep around the kitchen, looking forward to the full-house dinner sit-ins, when Monsieur Cantrell came in to see me. "Miss Silver," he said in greeting. "Monsieur Gage will not be taking any room service today. He has informed me that he is working on a very important business project and does not wish to indulge in any alcoholic beverage tonight or be disturbed."

"Yes, Sir," I replied.

Monsieur Cantrell left the kitchen without further word, leaving me with my thoughts.

Even though Zeke had told me before that he only came to New York on business, I still felt a little disappointed that we wouldn't be having our usual conversation over drinks. *All because of his project*, I thought, trying not to pout like a spoiled child. Before I could go into brat-mode, I checked the clock and realised that I didn't have time to think about not seeing Zeke because it was five forty-seven p.m. and just about opening time. I set my mind to focus on the task ahead and was giving myself a mental pep talk when Chef Fords came up to me. His normally friendly face was set in a serious expression. It usually was just before the dinner sit-ins.

"Hi, Ella. Listen, we're in for another really busy night tonight. We've been getting by all right, but I'm thinking we could do with another pair of hands in the front lines. Just to take some pressure off Melany and Jeff. So, I'm going to put you in charge of the Classic Seafood Risotto, yes?"

I blinked at him, hoping that I was understanding him correctly. "You want me to take a chef position tonight, Chef Fords?"

"That's right, and I know you won't disappoint me. You've seen how we do things here in this kitchen, and you know the standard I expect." The playful glint came back to his eyes for a short moment as he said, "And you are a qualified chef, right? Show us what you're made of, Ella." He gave me a quick wink.

I exhaled and said, "Yes, Chef. I won't let you down."

"All right then," he said as he turned to go back to

where Melany and Jeff were stationed. He spoke to them both for a minute, probably about his decision to give me a chef spot for the night judging by the glare that Melany shot my way. But I didn't care about her displeasure in that moment. All I could think about was the fact that I would be working as an assistant chef in L'Annette, even just for one night. It was my dream, a real opportunity, and there was no way that I was going to mess it up.

I was ready for action even before Chef Fords yelled out, "All right everybody, doors open in five! All ready?"

Everyone in the kitchen called out in unison, "Yes, Chef!"

From that second it was all systems go and, boy, did I go. I got to work on my allocated seafood dish and made sure to get every order out in time. I kept my focus in check even when the orders started to slow down as closing time drew nearer. Only when George informed us that L'Annette's doors had just closed behind the last of our diners did I lean against the counter and mentally pat myself on the back. It had been a good night. I hadn't messed up, not once, and I had even received some compliments from diners on my meals. The interesting thing was that, even though it had been a hectic shift, I didn't feel tired at all. In fact, I felt energized.

Chef Fords came to stand with the rest of us and said, "Fantastic work today, everyone. Great job, great service." Then he turned to me. "Ella, you really stepped up when we needed it. Great work."

"Thank you, Chef," I replied, allowing myself a moment to let the compliment sink in.

He looked around at everyone again and said, "Amazing work, all of you." He clapped his hands, and we all joined in. I felt like I was soaring. A compliment from Chef Fords was a huge deal. He had taken a chance on me, and I hadn't let him down. He winked at me, and I smiled at him, grateful for the opportunity that he had given me.

It took a minute, but the moment eventually passed. Catherine and I got to work cleaning up the kitchen. That was still my job description after all. *Maybe not for long*, I thought, smiling to myself.

Once everything was sparkling, I headed out of the kitchen, ready to get a good night's sleep in. I always left my handbag at the front desk with Bernie and when I knocked off, I would just grab it from there. Bernie was usually never there when I took it because she normally knocked off earlier than me, but she trusted me to not mess with anything in her absence. I was making my merry way to the front desk for my usual handbag pick-up when I was stopped in the lobby by the sound of Monsieur Cantrell's voice calling out, "Miss Silver." I watched him approach me from the direction of his office until he stood in front of me, as intimidating in stature as ever. "Chef Fords informed me that you played a bigger role than usual in the kitchen today?"

"Uh, yes, Sir," I replied, unsure of where he was going with the conversation.

"Did you enjoy it?" His eyes watched me with scrutiny.

"Yes, I definitely did, sir," I said enthusiastically. "I could do that every day." I knew that I was rambling again, but it was how I truly felt.

"Good to know." Monsieur Cantrell turned to leave, but stopped suddenly. "I hear you did very well today, Miss Silver. Chef Fords tells me that you maintained our high standard in the kitchen, and you held your own with a finesse and maturity that he has only ever seen in seasoned chefs. Fantastic work." He held out his hand to me and added, "Chef Silver." Then he smiled. A smile that reached his eyes and nearly, just nearly, brought tears to mine. It was just one of those moments that emotional movie scenes with hopeful background music were made of, in my dramatic mind at least. Monsieur Cantrell, owner of Le Cantrell Perdue, had called me, Ella-Cherie Silver, a chef. Not kitchen help, but a *chef.*

I held it together as I shook his hand and said, "Merci, Monsieur."

He nodded, still smiling, and strode back to his office with that purposeful walk of his, glancing around the lobby as he went. We employees knew that when he looked around that way, he was inspecting the area for any imperfections. *Monsieur Cantrell, ever the professional.* I stared after him for a few seconds with a smile on my face, feeling overjoyed at how my evening had turned out. If I was an over-the-top prancing pony before, I don't know how to describe my excitement in that moment. I wanted to shout my happiness from the rooftop. I wanted to tell my family and Stace. I also wanted to tell Zeke. More than I cared to admit.

I couldn't help but think that it would have been convenient for me to just send him a text message in this particular situation, but we had never actually exchanged numbers. More specifically, Zeke had never asked for mine, and I didn't want to force it onto him.

Like I said before, he regulated our conversations. We only ever talked during his stays.

I knew that I would be restless for the remainder of the evening if I didn't let him know somehow. *Maybe if I just go up for a second. Just to tell him the amazing news.* I promised myself that I wouldn't stay up there for long so as not to disturb him too much and, with that resolution in mind, I headed toward the elevators, putting the collection of my handbag on hold.

This time I didn't even bother trying to stop myself from dancing a little to the elevator music on the way up. I had to celebrate somehow after the day I had. I couldn't believe my luck. *Luck.* I raised my hand and lightly tapped the pendant that hung under my shirt, the one that Smithson had given to me. The so-called lucky pendant. I narrowed my eyes and shook my head, not giving myself the chance to even consider that the piece of jewelry was lucky in any way. *Nah. I don't believe in that.* I believed in reward for hard work, and I believed in blessings. Not luck.

I turned my thoughts back to Zeke as the elevator made its swift ascent. When I was finally standing in front of his door I knocked gently and released a slow breath to calm my excitement. He opened the door just a little and frowned when he saw me. He slowly pulled the door open just wide enough for his whole frame to be visible as he spoke. "Ella, what are you...?"

"Hey!" I chirped, ignoring his expression and cutting him off before he could dismiss me. "I know you're busy. I just wanted to tell you some news." He was still frowning down at me, looking more uncomfortable than I'd ever seen him. I studied his handsome face, hoping that the expression in front of me would change into a welcoming one. It didn't. He didn't even try to move the conversation forward by asking me what my big news was.

As I scrutinized his face, I was momentarily distracted from the whole purpose of my visit when I noticed a small red spot on his jaw. "You hurt yourself shaving or somethin'?"

Zeke ignored my question. "I had asked for some privacy tonight. I'll see you tomorrow, okay?" He didn't even bother to pretend that he wanted me there.

"Oh, okay. Yeah, sure. Tomorrow's good," I said, pasting on a smile. " 'Night."

"Goodnight, Ella."

I turned to leave just as the elevator dinged and its doors opened up to a pale-faced man wearing a black hoodie and washed-out blue jeans. *I thought no one else was supposed to be up here.* My confusion as to who the guy was quickly turned to panic when he pulled a shiny silver gun out from his waistband and pointed it straight at me. "Who the hell is this, Gage?" he yelled. "I don't do business with strangers, and you know that!"

Chapter 7

Zeke quickly stepped out into the hallway where I stood. I felt his hand grab my arm and push me gently to the side farthest from the man with the gun as he spoke to him. "Get in there. Now. I'll explain," Zeke told the guy, his body directly in front of me like a shield. I watched the man from behind Zeke. He looked back and forth between Zeke and me before finally putting his gun down but not away. He walked past us into the suite, eyeing me with suspicion all over his face the whole time. All the while I was frozen in place, trying to remember how to breathe.

Zeke turned to face me. "Ella, I need you to come in here, okay? I'll explain everything."

I looked up at him, unable to speak. He pulled me slowly into the suite, and I let him. Shock, apparently, made me cooperative. The trance that I was in, however, soon faded when the room erupted in male voices. That's when I looked toward the glass doors leading to the balcony and saw them. It was a group of men, including the pale guy who had just walked in before us, surrounding one other man who was on his knees, bloodied and hunched forward but still conscious. I inhaled sharply and stumbled backward. Zeke held me upright and whispered, "Ella, it's going to be all right. Everything's going to be fine."

All the men were looking at me, mumbling to each

other in hushed voices. One of them, a large black man with a beanie on, decided to address the me-shaped elephant in the room. "Who's the broad, Gage?" he asked.

"Watch your mouth," Zeke warned the man. "She works with me." *What?*

"How come we don't know her then?" The man in the beanie wasn't letting up.

"You questioning me, Dirk?" Zeke asked him. His voice was low and calm. The man looked down, seeming intimidated, and didn't answer.

Another voice piped up, "No disrespect, Gage, but I thought we dealt with Organisation members only." The voice came from a man with dusty-blond hair.

"I'm glad you brought that up, Sy, because she is a member. If any of you were higher up the ladder, you'd know that," Zeke stated in a matter-of-fact tone.

Member of what? What is he talking about? What is happening? I was beyond confused and way past terrified.

Zeke turned to me and said, "Ella, do you have your pendant with you?" I just stared at him. "The special pendant, Ella. Are you wearing it? Do you have it on you?"

The pendant I got from Smithson? I nodded in response. I saw a flash of relief pass through Zeke's eyes. "Good," he said. "Show them."

I had no idea what this was all about, but I did as he said while the men all watched me. I slowly lifted the pendant and placed it over my shirt so it could be clearly seen. The men all visibly relaxed.

"So are you going to introduce us, Gage?" Sy asked after the brief silence.

"Not yet," Zeke replied. "That'll happen formally at the next meeting. Right now she's here to observe, that's all. Let's get this over with."

They all turned their attention to the beaten man, disinterested in my presence now. "I don't know if he can take much more without this becoming a casket situation, if you catch my meaning," Sy said to Zeke. The bloodied man began to breathe heavily in panic, one of his eyes swollen shut.

Zeke walked over to him, grabbing the man's chin and tilting his bruised face upward. "No, I don't think he can. And what use would he be to us then, hmmm? I'm sure he's learned his lesson." Zeke leaned in closer to the man's battered face and asked, "Haven't you, Bill?"

The man managed to get out a weak, "Yes," in response, the thorough beating he had received clearly a hindrance to his speech. Zeke let go of Bill's chin and took a step back, his hand now smeared with blood. "Good." He looked at the other men and said, "Get him to The Doc and get him cleaned up. And don't get any blood on the carpet."

He turned toward me but stopped mid-stride and faced the men again. "Don't ever bring a problem like this to the hotel ever again, do you understand me?" His tone was threatening. They all nodded silently. "Good. You know the way out," he said to them as he came to stand by my side.

I watched as the men all left the room, two of whom had helped Bill to his feet and were now practically carrying him out. I noticed that there was a thin black plastic sheet on the floor where Bill had been kneeling, probably to ensure that no stains were left in the suite. *Stains. Blood stains.* Mixed in with my fear, I felt guilt. Guilt for not helping Bill. Guilt for not even trying. I had no idea who he was, but I knew that he was a human being. *But how exactly can I be of any help to him in this situation? These men are probably all armed.* That logic kept me from trying to be a hero for the stranger.

As Sy walked past me he said, "Nice to meet ya. Lookin' forward to the formal introduction." I didn't respond. I couldn't. My mind was racing with too many unanswered questions. *Who are these men? Are any of them guests here? Surely I would know at least one of them if they were, wouldn't I? How the heck did they get up here if they aren't guests? And how do they plan on getting out unseen?* I heard a soft ding as the elevator announced itself. *They're using the elevator? There's no way they won't be seen coming out of the elevator. Someone will see. Please, please let someone see.*

When all the men had left, Zeke turned to me and spoke calmly. "You did good, Ella. Real good. I'll explain everything, I promise. Just let me get cleaned up first, okay?"

I still wasn't able to get any words out, and he didn't wait for me to respond before he made his way to the guest bathroom. I tried unsuccessfully to stop the trembling of my body. I wasn't shaking like a leaf; I was shaking like a whole tree in a storm. My mind was stuttering, misfiring. My body wanted to do so many things. Pass out, scream, stand still. Eventually, my body and my misfiring mind pulled themselves together and agreed that the best thing to do was run.

I turned on my heel, bolted out the door, and took

off toward the stairs. There was no way that I was going to risk waiting for the elevator to come back up. I reached the top of the staircase and propelled my body forward, filled with adrenaline. I was running like there was a gold medal in store for me if I kept at it. The burn in my legs became insistent, but I had to get downstairs and alert Monsieur Cantrell and the security about what I had seen. When I had gone down about two flights, I heard thumping footfalls behind me, heavy and quick. *Zeke.* He was coming after me. I tried to pick up speed, but it was as if the faster I went, the closer he got. Why on earth did I ever think that I could run down thirty flights of stairs?

By the time I had gone down another flight, I knew that I wouldn't make it to the ground floor before he caught up. And I was right. Zeke grabbed me from behind in a bear hug hold, pinning both my arms to my sides. That's when I finally screamed. I screamed like my life depended on it because, obviously, it did. Zeke, on the other hand, was whispering. "Shh. Ella, it's okay. Everything's going to be okay. I won't hurt you. No one's going to hurt you. Shh…"

Then he let go of me. I didn't waste a second of time. I took off again, forcing the aching muscles in my legs to keep working and telling myself that if I survived this ordeal, I would definitely spend more time in the gym. It was only when I reached the next floor that I stopped, because I realized that there were no sounds coming from behind me anymore. No sound of shoes hitting against the floor. No sound of a gun being fired at me. No sounds that indicated that anyone was in hot pursuit of me in any way. In fact, the only thing that broke the silence was my heavy panting from all the running I had done. Zeke, it seemed, was no longer chasing after me. *What if he just decided to take the elevator and catch me on a lower floor?* That was a real possibility.

I stood in place, completely undecided. My options were all pretty lousy. It was either keep going down the stairs and risk running into Zeke if he had used the elevator, or head back up the stairs and risk running into him anyway if he had stayed put. The only thing that I knew for sure was that I couldn't stay there like a piece of confused furniture. *Come on, Ella. Think.* I was obviously way closer to the penthouse floor than I was to the ground floor. I blinked my eyes a few times as I weighed my options. In the end, I went with the idea of going back upstairs. The decision came about mainly because I knew that there was no way that I would make it down thirty flights of stairs without collapsing somewhere along the way. I just wasn't fit enough. Also, if Zeke was still up there, it would mean that he really had stopped chasing me. It would mean that maybe he was willing to let me go even though I had seen something that I shouldn't have. *Maybe he was telling the truth when he said that he won't hurt me.* It was exactly that kind of naïve thinking that had put me in this situation in the first place, but I made my way slowly back up the stairs because, like I said, my options were all lousy. Whatever I did, I was just buying time.

I was about to reach the landing where Zeke had grabbed me and the thought of it happening again set my nerves on edge. I looked up as I took my next step, ready to tackle more muscle pain, but then I froze. Zeke was sitting on one of the stairs right at the top of the flight, his elbows on his knees and his head bowed. *He hasn't left.* He sat so still that it looked as though he were sleeping. I was holding my breath, unsure of whether or not he had heard me. I had been panting so heavily all the way up that I would have been surprised if he hadn't. I started to back away, slowly and quietly.

"I'm not going to hurt you," he said, with his head still bowed. Then he raised his head, looking me right in my eyes. "I won't hurt you."

I watched him as I contemplated running down to the next floor and using the elevator the rest of the way. *I can make it if I go now.* Zeke spoke again and broke through my thoughts. "Please trust me, Ella. Come up to the room, and I'll explain everything. Please."

His voice was as calm as usual, but the look on his face told me that he needed me to comply more than he was letting on. Obviously, I didn't trust him. Not anymore. He was clearly into some shady stuff that was nowhere near legal or moral. But my options were not great in that moment and since he had stopped coming after me, I figured maybe he didn't want to kill me after all. So I climbed the stairs cautiously, having decided to give him a chance to explain.

****

I didn't enter the suite when we got to the door. I wanted to be able to make a run for it if Zeke was lying about not hurting me. We had trudged up the stairs in complete silence, and I was done waiting to hear what he had to say. I faced him. "Explain," I demanded with a shaky voice.

"I need to make a call first." He pulled a cell phone out of his pocket.

"To whom?" I asked, getting even more nervous.

He didn't answer me as he tapped the screen a couple of times and lifted the phone to his ear. "Hector, we have a problem here. Come up to the penthouse suite." Zeke didn't wait for a reply before hanging up.

What does he want with Monsieur Cantrell? I didn't want Monsieur Cantrell to get pulled into my mess. "What do you want from Monsieur Cantrell?"

"To talk," Zeke replied.

"He won't get dragged into this, right? He's not in any trouble because of me? He won't get hurt?"

Zeke looked at me for a second before answering, "No. He's not in any trouble. Just want to talk to him."

He turned his back to me and faced the elevator doors, his arms crossed in front of him. He looked like a bodyguard on duty. I turned to face the elevator too, nowhere near as composed as Zeke was. A minute later, the doors opened up and Monsieur Cantrell stepped out. He stilled when he saw me standing there, confusion and surprise dominating his face. Then his expression changed as the realization hit him that I was the "problem" that Zeke was talking about.

"What happened?" he asked with a stiff voice.

"She saw us," Zeke answered simply.

"What did she see?"

"A lot. Too much."

Monsieur Cantrell's face visibly blanched when he heard Zeke's answer. *Wait, Monsieur Cantrell is a part of this?* I didn't have enough time to register the shock at the fact that Monsieur Cantrell was aware of the unsavory activities in his hotel because my attention was caught by what Zeke said next.

"I won't let them hurt her, Hector, but she has to join. At least, for now."

What is he talking about? "Join what?" I asked Zeke. He ignored me. "Join what?" I asked again, directing the question at Monsieur Cantrell this time. He ignored me too. I looked back and forth between the two men, hating that I was the topic of discussion but not a part of it.

Monsieur Cantrell spoke up then, but he was still only addressing Zeke and didn't answer my question. "I kept the hotel nearly empty like you requested, in order for you to conduct Organisation business as discreetly as possible. This should not have happened, Gage. Especially not with the care we took. The girl should never have been involved." He sounded agitated, but what stood out the most to me was how nonchalant he was about Zeke's…work. *He knows what Zeke does up here. He knows. He even helps him to do it discreetly.* I didn't know what to do or how to feel because I was still in shock. It was like my entire time at The Lost Cantrell had been one big theatrical act.

Zeke responded calmly but with a stern voice. "I know that, Hector, and that's why I told you to make sure that no one came up here tonight. You told me you would take care of that. I wasn't expecting Ella this evening, and I never conduct violent business up here. Things just happened to get out of hand with the men this time. Believe me, I'm just as pissed off about this as you are. Probably more."

My thoughts went back to the stairs briefly, and I instantly regretted going up to the room again with Zeke. *I could have gotten away and been in the clear right now.* As I considered running for a second time, Monsieur Cantrell found his words and asked Zeke a question that had me focusing on them again.

"I'm assuming she has to go with you right now?"
What?

Zeke answered, "Yes."

No! "I'm not going anywhere with you," I told Zeke firmly. They both ignored me. Again.

"I have your word that she will be kept safe? I would feel responsible if anything happened," Monsieur Cantrell said before glancing in my direction and adding, "I hired her. I…feel responsible."

"I understand. You have my word. I'll keep her safe," Zeke replied.

Monsieur Cantrell gave a sharp nod of his head and said, "Very well. You cannot use the lobby exit obviously."

"I know. I'll take her out through the passage," Zeke responded.

What passage? Seriously, what are these guys talking about? I was tired of being confused. I felt drained from all of the anxiety that I had experienced in the minutes since the ordeal had started. "Please can one of you just tell me what's going on?" I asked. My voice was shaking again.

Monsieur Cantrell looked down and didn't answer me. Zeke spoke up. "I'll explain everything soon, Ella. But we need to go now."

I felt him gently tug me toward the elevator, and that's the moment that my panic kicked in. I began to cry out loudly to Monsieur Cantrell. Surely my boss was not about to let some dangerous man take me away, was he? "No! No! Don't touch me!" I pushed Zeke away, shouting loudly as tears streamed down my face. "Monsieur, please! Please! Don't let him take me! Please!" I pleaded with him, begging him to save me. I was terrified. So terrified that my whole body shivered like I was out in the freezing cold.

I don't know how long I was pleading and screaming for, but it felt like forever, and to no avail. I heard Zeke trying to calm me down again with his quiet, soft whispers. Monsieur Cantrell, however, was still speaking in his classic neutral tone. He kept repeating, "Miss Silver," over and over to try and get my attention. When he realised that it wasn't working and I just kept crying, he decided to continue with his sentence. "Miss Silver, you need to go with Monsieur Gage now. It will be all right."

I couldn't believe what was happening. I didn't want to. I decided to carry on with my attempt to appeal to their better nature. I wanted to get them to pretend that the whole mess had never happened. So I kept on crying. Then I begged and cried some more. I cried until a hard voice and callused hands pressing against my cheeks snapped me out of it.

"Enough, Ella! That's enough!"

I looked up into Monsieur Cantrell's dark brown eyes. His brows were drawn together, and he looked so distressed that it gave me pause. Also, he had never called me by my first name before. Not ever. He had always been very formal and professional with me. His actions and words in that moment took me by surprise because they were so far from formal. He was holding my face in his hands, and he softened his voice as he said, "You need to be strong now, my girl. Strong, do you hear me? Be strong, and you will be fine. Everything will be fine." He looked over at Zeke, who was standing behind me, and added, "It has to be." Then he wiped the tears from my face gently with the pads of his thumbs. "Go now," he said, dropping his hands abruptly.

I was breathing a little hard but, besides that, Monsieur Cantrell had succeeded in calming me down. Maybe it was the look on his face. The look that told me that he was as afraid as I was of how everything would turn out. Maybe it was the almost-fatherly affection that he had shown me. Who knows? Whatever it was, it worked. Zeke pulled me gently toward the elevator again and, this time, I let him. I walked backward slowly and never turned toward Zeke while he guided me through the open doors. Instead, I watched Monsieur Cantrell the whole way in. Watched him as he stared back at me, even as the elevator doors slid closed, with a look that held the obvious sadness and sympathy that he felt.

Chapter 8

My second screw-up had officially happened. Yet
again, it had happened because I was at Zeke Gage's
door at the wrong time. I stood next to Zeke while he
sent multiple messages from his phone, wondering how
he planned on getting out of the hotel unseen, yet we
were taking the elevator down to the ground floor. The
only exit there was through the lobby and, even though
it was late, there was still a chance that someone would
be around.

"What do I say if someone sees us?" I asked him.

"No one will see us," he replied, sounding so sure
of himself.

Before the elevator reached the lobby floor, Zeke
pulled out a small, black gadget from his pants pocket.
It looked like a little remote control, but it only had
about five buttons on it. He pressed one of the buttons
while we were still going down and I noticed that when
we eventually reached the ground floor, the elevator
doors didn't automatically open for us. *That's new,* I
thought as we stood in the motionless elevator. Zeke
looked over at me and asked, "You ready?"

I wasn't ready for anything that had happened that
night and I probably wasn't ready for what was to
come, but I nodded my head anyway. Zeke then pressed
another button on the mini-remote and turned around to
face away from the doors.

"What are you...?" I stopped before completing my question because, from the corner of my eye, I saw the mirrored back wall of the elevator parting vertically down the middle, each side sliding away from the other in the same way the elevator doors would.

The parted wall opened up to what looked like a corridor. It was short and narrow, but well-lit. *The passage.* Zeke held his hand out to me and said, "Come on."

I took his hand, staring wide-eyed down the passage and feeling like I was in some spy movie. *Stuff like this really happens? No way.*

We slowly walked down the short corridor toward the door at the end of it. Zeke walked in front of me and pulled me along behind him because the space was too narrow for us to walk side by side. When we reached the door, he pressed his remote again. The back wall of the elevator began to close back to its concealed state at the same time that Zeke manually opened the door in front of us. The door opened inward toward us and revealed yet another obstruction. It was another door, but this one was more advanced. It was metal and looked quite thick and heavy. It had a small screen at the top of it, and Zeke pressed his hand into it for about five seconds. I watched with fascination as the screen appeared to scan his hand before the door suddenly snapped open, dragging on the ground with a slightly noisy scratching sound. A cool breeze hit my face as the door opened to the alley where we took the trash out for the hotel. Zeke ushered me out into the alley, and I stood in the open air, still puzzled by all that I had seen. *How does no one notice a random door in the alleyway?* That question was answered as soon as it popped into my head when the door closed again, revealing the perfect pattern of bricks on its outer side. It closed tightly shut and not one thing looked out of place, matching seamlessly with the rest of the alley wall. The trap door was camouflaged on a level that was bordering on impossible. So impossible, in fact, that I was starting to question if we had come out of there at all. I stared at the wall and touched the area where the hidden door was, and the bricks felt real. *Are they real?*

Zeke interrupted my moment of awe by touching my arm gently. "Ella, we need to go."

I turned and followed him, still a little stunned. Okay, that's not true. I was *a lot* stunned. Actually, I was so stunned that I didn't even notice the sleek, black car parked in the alley until its lights turned on. A man with blond hair got out of the driver's side. He was tall and bulky, his suit straining to contain his muscles. The man was a tank. He was also scary. Until he opened his mouth to speak.

"Hey, Mr. Gage," he greeted. Then he looked at me and smiled a little awkwardly. "Ma'am. How are ya this evening? I'm Chris, and I'll be your driver from now on. Uh, indefinitely." He sounded Southern, but I couldn't tell from which part.

I looked up at him, getting undeniable gentle giant vibes from him. "Hello, Chris," I replied. "I'm Ella."

"It's nice to meet you. Let me get the door for you, ma'am," he said as he walked over to the back door on the right side of the car. He pulled the door open for me, and I found that I instantly liked him and wanted to smile at him in spite of my situation.

"Thank you, Chris," I said as I got into the car.

Zeke came in after me, and I scootched sideways on the plush leather seat to make space for him.

Chris got back into the driver's seat and inquired, "Where to, boss?"

"The apartment." That's all Zeke said. He was obviously still being vague about everything around me, but I didn't have time to dwell on that fact because the word "apartment" reminded me that Stace was probably waiting up for me at our brownstone like she usually did. I needed to get in touch with her. *My handbag.* I had left my phone in my bag, which was still behind the front desk in the hotel lobby.

"I left my bag in there," I announced loudly before the car pulled off. "It has my phone in it. Stace will freak if she doesn't hear from me."

Zeke exhaled through his nose and pulled his phone out again. "Where's the bag?" he asked me.

"I left it behind the front desk."

Zeke tapped on his phone screen a few times and then got out of the car. He casually walked down the alley and stood inconspicuously on the corner. A few minutes later Monsieur Cantrell handed him my purse and quickly disappeared around the corner again. Zeke came back and gave me my bag without a word, and I took my phone out as the car began to move, immediately dialing Stace's number.

She picked up after just two rings. "Hey, Cher! You on your way home yet?"

Her voice was such a comfort, just like she was. It occurred to me that there was no way that she would accept me not coming home all night without a reasonable explanation. It just wasn't something that I would do, and she would figure out that I was in some kind of trouble. *I'll probably be gone for even more than one night.* I closed my eyes and did what I thought was best. "Hey, Stace. Yeah, I'm on my way home right now. I'll see you soon, okay?"

"Alrighty! See you in a bit."

I cut the call and peeked up at Zeke innocently. He was looking at me with narrowed eyes. "She was going to get suspicious if I slept out all night unexpectedly and didn't show my face," I said in my defense.

He sighed. "Change of plans, CP." I gave them my address and we made our way there, none of us speaking.

But after three minutes of silence, I was ready to interrogate Zeke. "Can I get that explanation now?"

"Soon, Ella. Let's just get everything in place first."

It was as if he was trying to get out of giving me answers, and I felt my anger bubbling up to the surface like lava. "You keep saying that you'll explain everything, but you still haven't explained anything. I want to know what is going on. Now. Or, I'm telling you, you'll have to kill me to shut me up about what I saw tonight. I will sing it from the rooftops." I was all talk. I obviously didn't want him to off me, but I was done with him giving me the run-around. I wanted the truth.

Chris's hazel eyes glanced at us through the rear view mirror, clearly showing how interested he was in our conversation. Zeke sighed again then licked his lips and started talking. "I'm part of an organization. An organization that manages certain activities."

"What kind of activities?"

"Criminal activity. For the most part. The

Organization ensures that everything runs smoothly and that everyone gets a piece of the pie, so to speak."

"What's this organization called?"

"It doesn't technically have a name. Safer that way. Everyone just calls it The Organization or The Org."

"How many of you are a part of this organization?"

"Thousands. It's a large network, Ella. We have members all over the world."

"And you manage every member in it?"

"Yes. Sometimes I delegate but, ultimately, everyone checks back in with me."

"So you're the boss of this whole thing?"

Zeke didn't answer me for a while but eventually he replied, "No. I'm not the boss of the whole thing. The Official is."

"The Official?"

"Yes. The Official. He's in charge."

"Does he not have a name either?"

"That is his name."

"I mean a real name, Zeke."

He gave a half-smile at my obvious annoyance before he answered, "Not that any of us know, no."

I paused my interrogation to take in everything that he had told me. It was all so crazy to me. *Criminal activity?* "What kind of criminal activity is The Org involved in?" I just had to ask. Zeke looked uncomfortable with the question, but I didn't care.

"It may be best if you don't know the details, Ella. It's not very...pleasant," he replied.

"My opinion of you right now cannot possibly get any lower, so don't worry about it," I stated pointedly.

"It's about plausible deniability."

"I don't care about that. I've already seen what I

saw. Tell me what criminal activity you're into."

Zeke said, "Okay," as if he were resigned to it. "The Organization is involved in just about everything. Drugs, guns, gangs. You name it."

"So you're basically just a network of criminals then?"

"No. Not everyone in The Org is a criminal. Some members are cops, judges, feds, medical professionals. We all work together." When he saw the look on my face, he added, "Peace in disorder, Ella. Calm amidst chaos. That's what most institutions are. Deceiving."

I stared at him. There was clearly so much I didn't know. "How do law enforcement officers benefit from being members? Just by taking bribes?"

"They do receive payment, yes. A salary of sorts. All members do. But there are other perks for them when they work with us."

"Like what?"

"Well, for example, when a member goes rogue in any way or a non-member gets in the way of our business, we find a way to hand them over to one of the law enforcement officers in our network, without it linking back to us of course. They get what appears to be a clean bust, and we get rid of a problem. Makes them look like they are actually doing their job right and keeps our members in line."

"So you basically set them up?"

"Basically, yes."

"What's to stop them from snitching on the rest of you in The Org? I mean, if they are going down, why wouldn't they take you guys down with them? Maybe even get a deal out of it for a lighter sentence or charge." Clearly, the fruits of my crime-drama viewing labor had paid off in that moment.

Zeke raised his eyebrows at my question. "We have our ways of making sure that they're not comfortable with turning rat. Fortunately, it's only ever been lower-level members who broke the rules, and lower-level members don't know enough to say enough. But any member would know better than to snitch, even when they're on the outs with The Org."

That sounded more than a little threatening. "You guys really have this crime thing down, huh?" I asked rhetorically.

Zeke answered anyway. "We try." He smiled a little, and I realised that the statement was his attempt at humor. I snorted out a laugh despite my anger at the whole situation and looked out of the tinted window, noticing the familiar infrastructure that was about a five minute drive from my apartment.

I dropped my head into my hands and inquired, "What am I supposed to tell Stace about why I'm going away?"

"I already worked that out with Hector. Everyone will be told that you are going away for a short chef internship at the L'Annette Paris branch, and you have to stop work here from tomorrow in order to prepare for your trip and start your new position on time. After your apparent excellent performance in the kitchen this evening, it will be plausible. Hector will say that he wants to give you the chance to expand your skills in an even faster paced restaurant because of the potential you showed tonight, and the offer has a time limit on it. He'll handle the finer details."

So Zeke had eventually heard about my "excellent performance" from Monsieur Cantrell, only because they had to devise a plan to explain my sudden absence for as long as this mess took to clear up. It definitely wasn't the way that I had wanted him to hear my news, and I almost laughed at the irony of it all. I had wanted to tell Zeke so badly but, in that moment, it didn't even matter anymore. However, I had to give it to them, it was a good plan. Very believable. I had heard about young chefs who showed potential being given the opportunity to train at the L'Annette branch in France, so it would seem fitting that Monsieur Cantrell would find me suitable for the position. It was an explanation that the staff would believe. I just wished that the story was true. I wished that I had actually been offered an internship in France and that I wasn't being taken away to who knew where. I leaned my head back against the headrest and exhaled slowly through my nose.

Did I mention that I had always been fascinated with how quickly things could change in a second? I did mention that, didn't I? Well, this was a classic example of that. I was a normal girl from a good home and all I wanted to do was cook, but in a split second I had become caught up in a secret criminal organization. Boy, things really could change in a second.

****

Chris parked the car around the corner from our brownstone apartment, and we all walked the short distance to my home away from home. It felt so awkward having Zeke accompany me because I had no idea how I would explain his presence convincingly to Stace, but I was even more surprised that Chris had come along too. I got the feeling that he wasn't just the chauffeur but doubled as extra security as well. Maybe not for Zeke, but he was definitely guarding me. His body was so close to mine as we walked that I kept bumping into his side, and he was looking around constantly as if he were expecting an ambush. He was making me even more nervous. "Are you guys expecting something to happen? You both seem kinda jittery," I said to the two men, one walking on each side of me.

Zeke glanced at me and answered, "Until you're a confirmed member and it's announced officially at a formal meeting, the men may not be fully comfortable with what you saw tonight. They all may have seemed satisfied with my explanation, but you never really know with those guys. We just want to make sure that if anyone tries anything stupid, we see it coming."

We reached the steps of the brownstone, and Zeke and I made our way up to the front door. Chris stayed at the bottom of the steps on the sidewalk, scanning the area and clearly not interested in entering the apartment with us.

I pulled my keys out of my purse and fumbled with them a little before unlocking the door. Even though we had a solid plan in place, my stomach still fluttered with fear and anxiety. We walked into the apartment together and as soon as we did, Stace called out, "Is that you, Ellzy?"

"Yeah, it's me, Stace," I called back.

We entered the living room just as Stace jumped up from the couch that was in front of the TV. "I'm thinking we can do a rom-com tonight, Cher. I'm in the mood for some romance. What do you...?" She stopped mid-sentence when she spotted Zeke standing behind me. She had never met or seen Zeke before, and her surprise at seeing a stranger in our apartment was obvious.

I began to make clumsy introductions. "Uh, Stace, you know the guest I'm always telling you about? Zeke Gage? This is him." Then I looked at Zeke as I said, "Zeke, this is my best friend, Stacey. I've told you about her too."

"It's nice to meet you, Stacey. I've heard a lot of good things about you." Zeke sounded so charming, and I noticed that Stacey relaxed slightly after he spoke. *For someone who was so terrible at socializing with me he sure is doing all right with everyone else.*

Stacey walked over to us slowly, her bright blue eyes keen with interest. "It's nice to meet you too. I didn't know we were having company tonight or I would have tried to have something prepared for you before you got here," Stace stated politely. She then looked at me and opened her eyes wide in a mock accusatory and questioning expression. I knew Stace well enough to understand that the look translated to, "Why the heck didn't you tell me he was coming?"

"Oh, don't worry about it, Stace. Zeke's not staying. He's just, uh..." I faltered, not knowing what else to say.

Luckily, Zeke did. "My driver and I needed to know where exactly Ella lives so we don't get lost when we come over tomorrow to take her to the airport for her to catch the earliest possible flight."

"Airport?" Stace questioned with a worried frown.

I quickly jumped back into the conversation then because I didn't want her to think that there was some kind of emergency back home in Minnesota. "Yeah. I, uh, I've been offered a prestigious internship by Monsieur Cantrell." I paused before adding, "In Paris."

"Paris? Paris, France?" Stace asked, staring at me in utter bewilderment.

"Yup. And it's such a great opportunity, Stace. I, um, I got it because I stepped up in the kitchen today. I actually prepared some meals, and I impressed everybody so much that Monsieur Cantrell offered me the opportunity right there. The thing is, it has a time limit on it, and I have to leave tomorrow. In the morning."

A plethora of emotions flashed across Stace's face as she considered my words. "How long will you be gone for?"

"Um, a couple of months probably. Yeah, two months tops. It's not forever, Stace. It's just a short internship. I'll definitely learn a lot from it though."

Stace looked between Zeke and me before asking him, "So you'll be taking her to the airport tomorrow? That's why you came here tonight? To see where we live?"

"Yes," Zeke answered in a flat voice.

"Couldn't you have just used GPS for that tomorrow?" It was obvious that she was becoming suspicious of the whole situation.

"We could have, yes. But I didn't want to risk it. Ella needs to be at the airport in good time, and I want to make sure that nothing is left to chance. I have a good memory, and I trust it more than GPS." Zeke gave her one of his small smiles to indicate that he was being humorous, but Stace just stared back at him with an unamused expression.

"I don't know. This is extremely short notice," she stated with a shake of her head. I could tell that she didn't trust Zeke.

"I know, I know. But I want to give it a try. I'll be back before you know it," I told her softly.

She gave Zeke a side-eyed glance before asking me, "Are you *happy* about this, Ellzy?"

"I am. It's a big deal. I'm so happy, Stace." A lie. A big, obese lie. And I was a terrible liar.

Fortunately for me, Stace was a bad lie-catcher. So she simply smiled wide and hugged me tightly. "Then I'm happy for you too, Cher." She pulled back and looked into my eyes, and for a second, I thought she would call me out on my dishonesty. Whatever she saw there was giving her doubts again. She didn't look convinced at all anymore. "I still wish this wasn't so sudden. I'm working tomorrow, and I don't know if I'll be able to get the time off to go to the airport with you. There's this stupid meeting—"

I cut her off in the middle of her rant. "Stace, it's okay. I understand. I don't expect you to come to the airport with me anyway." *Because I'm not really going to Paris.* "Zeke and Chris will help me out, okay?"

"Who's Chris?" she asked with narrowed eyes.

Zeke spoke up again. "Chris is the driver I mentioned before. He's right outside. Let me get him. Maybe it's best if you meet him too, so you know everyone who will be with Ella tomorrow. Would that make you more comfortable, Stacey?" Zeke was laying the charm on thick.

"I guess," Stace muttered, still seeming unsettled.

Zeke went to get Chris and when the two men walked into the apartment together a minute later, Stace was immediately distracted by the driver's imposing frame. From the way her eyes went wide at the sight of him, it was clear that she was more than a little interested in the guy. Chris had become the perfect tool to put a stop to Stace's scrutiny of me in a heartbeat. Her focus had shifted almost entirely to him.

He greeted her with a polite, "Ma'am."

"Hi," she breathed out. "I'm Stacey. You're Chris? The driver?"

"Yes, ma'am. Chris Poller. I'll be driving your friend, Miss Silver, to the airport tomorrow and helping out with anything else she may need before she leaves."

"Okay. Well, please get her to the airport safely."

"Yes, ma'am."

"Stacey. You can call me Stacey. I'd like that better."

Chris gave a shy smile. "Yes, Stacey," he said, like the gentle, cuddly giant he was, and Stace's instant attraction to him was tangible. Chris, too, appeared to be struck by Stace's classic good looks and charm. Their eyes stayed locked for a brief moment, and it was the corniest but cutest thing ever.

Stace turned back to me and said, "Okay, Ellzy. I guess I can live without you for a couple of months. It's gonna suck being alone in our apartment though."

"Well, Chris here can check up on you regularly when you're home, if you like?" Zeke offered. "He has a lot of free time between drives. I'm sure he can stop by and make sure you're okay. Right, CP?" I knew what Zeke was doing. It was an excellent strategy. Distract the love-starved girl with a juicy piece of man-meat in the form of Chris. It worked magically by the way.

"I can do that, yeah. If the lady wants me to," Chris stated slowly.

"I really, really want you to," Stace responded

quickly. Chris, the poor man, blushed a little.

"Then I'll stop by to check in, ma'am. I mean Stacey."

She smiled wide after he spoke, and her eyes twinkled like they usually did when she was excited about something. "Okay. That works for me. Now we've reached a happy compromise. I'm still going to miss you like crazy though, Ellzy."

I reached for her hands and gave them a squeeze. "I know. I'll miss you too. But I'll be back real soon, and everything's going to be fine," I assured her, even though I wasn't assured of anything myself.

Zeke cleared his throat and announced, "I guess CP and I will head out now. It was a pleasure to meet you, Stacey." Everyone said their goodnights, and I walked Zeke and Chris to the door while Stace busied herself in the kitchen.

"You don't seem too bad at conversation anymore. Why's that?" I asked Zeke from the doorway as he stood just outside. Chris waited on the sidewalk, clearly back in bodyguard mode.

"I guess our late-night chats made me better at it," Zeke answered with a wry smile.

"Or you were just putting on an act the entire time."

"It's not like that, Ella. I can converse just fine when I'm reasonably detached from someone or when I'm familiar with the person I'm speaking to, but I do need help with learning how to speak to people that I…like." He looked me right in my eyes again, just like when he had been sitting on the hotel stairs, and I couldn't help but feel that he was being sincere. I hated the fact that him saying he liked me mattered to me.

Yup, I definitely need to get a date when this is all over.

I cleared my throat like it would clear the awkward air too. "Uh, well, I guess I'll see you tomorrow then," I told him.

"Yes, seven a.m. We need an early start."

I was about to close the door when a thought occurred to me. "Hey!" I called out to Zeke just as he turned to go down the front steps. I lowered my voice so that Stace wouldn't hear what I said next. "Is Zeke Gage your real name? I want to know who the man I'll be stuck with for a while is. The real you."

His mouth turned up in a lopsided grin. "Yes, Zeke Gage is my real name. I didn't lie to you about that, Ella."

I had my doubts. His name sounded a little too cool to me to be real, but I just responded with, "Good. Goodnight, Zeke."

"Goodnight, Ella."

I closed the door behind me and went to find Stace, who was still milling around in the kitchen. We spent the rest of the night chatting and fell asleep on the couch together at some point. We only went to our different rooms around two a.m. and, as I watched her close her door, I began to think about how I had taken the small things for granted and just how much I would miss our normal life.

Chapter 9

The next morning went by in a flurry of packing and goodbyes. I called my family back home and my friends at The Lost Cantrell to tell them all the same lie. They had mixed feelings about me leaving but were mostly excited for my "trip." My completely made-up trip. The thing is, it's easier to lie when you don't have to look into someone's eyes. With Stace, it wasn't so easy.

"We'll talk every day, right?" she asked me as we stood outside while Chris put my luggage in the car.

"Of course we will, Stace."

"And you won't be gone for longer than two months? Two months, tops?" Her brow was furrowed in worry.

I held her gaze even though I wanted to cry. Stace loved me like a sister, and I loved her that way too. She wasn't clingy. She was just fiercely loyal and caring. It scared me to think that I wouldn't see her again. I wanted to tell her what was really going on, but I couldn't. I didn't want to drag her into it and endanger her life, so I lied again. "It won't be more than two months, Stace. I promise. It may even be less. Who knows? It's just a temporary internship."

We hugged then for what felt like ages and when we finally let go, Stace's eyes were shining with tears. "See you soon, Cher," she said quietly.

"Yeah. Soon," I replied.

I kissed her on the cheek and quickly got into the car where Zeke was waiting for me, because I knew that if I stood next to her any longer, I would probably burst into tears. Chris started the engine and pulled away from the curb slowly. Stace waved at me from the bottom of the front steps as the car drove away. I stuck my head out of the window and waved back, memorizing every detail of her features in motion, just in case it was the last sight of her that I ever had.

****

"So where are we headed?" I asked in the car, setting my mind on tackling whatever came next.

"To my apartment," Zeke replied, typing something on his phone.

"Where is that?"

"State Isle."

"State Isle? As in, here in New York?" *State Isle, the neighbourhood that caters to the elite and very wealthy only?*

"Yes."

"Wait, you have an apartment here in the city?" I wanted to make sure that I heard him correctly.

"Yes, I do. It's a condo actually. I own a lot of property in a lot of different places. Real estate is always a good investment."

I shook my head in disbelief at the new information that he had given to me and the casual nature in which he had revealed it. *Is he serious?* "I don't care about investment advice, Zeke," I told him. "I'm wondering why on earth you stay at The Lost Cantrell if you can just stay at your own apartment. For free."

"My condo is a safe haven for me. A quiet place

that I can escape to whenever I want. I conduct business at The Lost Cantrell most of the time. I stay there when I'm working, so it's not very private. And I like to keep parts of me private. The condo is one of those things. Only a handful of people know about it. And now, you'll be one of those people."

"You're a really secretive guy, aren't you?"

"Maybe," he replied.

"You know I'm adding this to the list of lies you've told me, right? You said that you didn't live in New York," I said accusatorially.

He looked down at his hands and said, "I'm sorry for lying to you, Ella. And I'm sorry for dragging you into this."

It was the first apology that he had given me since the whole ordeal had started, and he looked like he was feeling genuinely guilty. I decided to give him a pass, at least in that moment. I took some time to study his appearance. He didn't look as put-together as he usually did. His hair was mussed, and his shirt was slightly creased. "You look a little rough. Where'd you sleep last night?" I asked.

"Round the corner from your apartment," he stated simply.

"Round the corner?" I repeated.

"Yeah, round the corner. In the car. Had to keep a watch out for you." He looked down at me and must have seen the concern on my face because he added, "CP and I took turns looking out, so we both got some sleep in."

Despite the fact that I was technically in this mess because of Zeke, I felt bad that he and Chris had to sleep uncomfortably to protect me. "Thanks. For looking out for me, I mean," I mumbled.

He smirked at my begrudged gratitude. "It's a pleasure."

We remained silent for the rest of the trip and when the car came to a halt outside a fancy-looking apartment complex, the reality of my situation hit me with the force of a violent storm. *I'm alone in this.* I would be living with someone whom I barely knew. Yes, we had been talking for months at intervals, but not long enough for me to really know him. Clearly.

I didn't speak as we entered the complex and got into the elevator, making our ascent to the third floor where Zeke's condo apparently was. When we got there, Zeke unlocked the door of one of the apartments, numbered 310, and we walked into a space that looked like it was straight out of a pretentious real estate catalog. His condo looked modern. It was all style and aesthetics. Nice to look at but with no warmth. It wasn't a home. Not like mine and Stace's. No. It was just something pretty to sleep in. It had no feeling about it. I felt panic slowly rising in my chest.

"Let me show you to your room, Ella," Zeke said from behind me.

I tried to calm my nerves as Zeke, Chris, and I made our way to one of the bedrooms. When I saw it, I became even more despondent. It had no feeling or warmth in it either. Like the rest of the condo, the color scheme was basically white with a few black and silver accents.

Chris put my luggage down just inside the door of my new room and cleared his throat awkwardly before saying, "I'm gonna head out. If y'all need anything, you know where to reach me."

I had no idea where to reach him actually, but I assumed that the statement was primarily meant for Zeke anyway. Chris left us alone, and I felt Zeke still watching me as I looked around the room.

"Ella, are you all right?" he asked.

I realised then how loudly I was breathing. I felt like I was going to have a panic attack. "I want Chris's number. I want to be able to contact him," I blurted out. I don't know why I said it. If I were a psychologist, I would guess that I had begun to associate Chris with Stace since their little display of chemistry. Maybe I felt like he was my best connection to her during our separation, or some psychoanalytical explanation like that.

"Of course. I'll get that information to you. It'll be good for you to be able to reach him on your own if you need anything."

"Thank you," I said, trying to get my breathing under control.

"Can I show you around?" Zeke asked quietly.

"Yes, please," I replied, the good manners that I was raised with showing through even in my distress.

Zeke gave me a quick and to-the-point tour of the condo. It had two bedrooms even though he said that he had never intended to host any long-staying guests. He told me that I was the first overnight visitor that he had ever had there. "I've never had anyone spend the night before. I hope you'll be comfortable."

In the kitchen, Zeke showed me all the food that was available and where it was kept. There wasn't much of anything. I knew that I would have to be on top of the grocery lists because Zeke was certainly a minimalist kind of bachelor. He did have a good selection of alcohol though. He even had a six-pack of beer in the fridge, though he didn't strike me as a beer guy. I guess the saying about not judging books by their covers is accurate.

After he had shown me around, we ended up back in my designated bedroom where he promptly stated, "I'm going to take a quick shower. Make yourself at home."

"Thanks. I'll try."

He closed the door behind him as he strode out of the room, leaving me feeling painfully unsettled and alone. I felt like I was inside of a tiny, unyielding box. I needed a distraction, so I started to unpack my things, placing them into the wardrobe and various drawers. I even put a couple of framed personal photos on the nightstand—one of Stace and me, and another of my family. I stared at them for a while, feeling nostalgic after less than one day of being away from my normal life.

I took hours unpacking my belongings and trying to make the room look more homely. Zeke kept checking in on me, asking if I needed anything. Even though I was a little hungry, I told him that I was fine. Besides him occasionally popping into my bedroom, I didn't see much of him after mid-day. I heard him on his phone a few times, making some plan or another I assumed.

By the time I was done settling into my room, it was almost two o'clock in the afternoon. A sedated snail could have done a faster job but, in my defense, I spent a lot of that time zoning out and thinking about just how much my situation sucked. At that point, my stomach grumbled in protest, and I made my way to the kitchen to put something together from the little that was there.

I managed to make a simple pasta dish with the ingredients that were available, and I made enough for both Zeke and me. He ate with me at the kitchen counter, mostly in silence, and then washed up the dishes dutifully after saying, "Thank you, Ella. That was delicious." He then headed back to his room and left me alone again. I figured he wasn't used to the social norms that hosting encompassed. Or maybe he just thought that I wanted to be on my own. Either way, the atmosphere was far from what I was accustomed to, and I felt the panic coming back as I sat on my lonesome in the kitchen and watched time slowly drag on. I knew that I would break down if I didn't get a grip on it.

I jumped off the stool that I was sitting on and grabbed a beer out of the fridge. I did it for no sensible reason at all because I wasn't a fan of beer. I wasn't even a drinker, but I was scared and nervous, and I had nothing better to do. I just wanted something that would take the edge off. So I opened the beer and went to town on it.

The alcohol kicked in like a bullet train because I was a lightweight, but I was still stable enough on my feet to get another bottle out of the fridge after I was done with the first. I downed that one too before heading over to Zeke's huge display cabinet that showcased a variety of whiskies and brandies. There was even a wine rack on the side. I picked up one of the bottles and studied it. *This is probably the expensive stuff.*

"I see you've found the liquor," I heard Zeke say

from behind me.

I turned around to find him looking at me with one eyebrow arched, his eyes drifting slowly to the two empty beer bottles on the counter. "Yup. I have. You have a good selection." I narrowed my eyes at him. "You're not an alcoholic, are you?"

He chuckled low and replied, "No, I'm not an alcoholic. I'm a collector, that's all. A lot of them are vintage bottles."

"Oh, okay. Well, don't worry, I didn't open any of them. I was just looking."

"I wouldn't mind if you did. I send a lot of them out as gifts to acquaintances of mine anyway. And this is your home right now so you can open whatever you like." He smiled and sat on a stool at the counter, watching me intently.

His gaze made me feel self-conscious, so I changed the subject quickly, putting the bottle back in its place carefully. "I've never been to this neighbourhood before today. I'm looking forward to exploring it a little while I'm here."

Zeke shifted on his stool and leaned against the counter. "Eventually you can, yes. But right now, you need to keep a low profile."

"What do you mean?" I asked, walking over to him slowly.

"I mean you can't explore just yet."

"Why?"

"Because I'm trying to keep you safe, and I can't do that effectively when you're out there. Not yet, at least. Not until you're officially a member and the others trust you. You have to stay up here in this building until everything is in place."

"So, I'm a prisoner here?"

"No, Ella. You're not a prisoner. But I need you to stay underground. Everyone thinks you'll be in France for the next two months anyway. If someone who knows you sees you here in New York, our whole cover story will be blown. We shouldn't risk it."

What he said made a good amount of sense. It really did. However, the combination of the alcohol and the realization that my freedom was being taken away threw me over the edge, and I suddenly couldn't contain my anger anymore. "This is not fair! Do you even comprehend the ways that you have completely and utterly disrupted my life?"

"I know, Ella. And I'm sorry about that, but you have to be a part of this. Just for now. I'll get you out, I promise."

His words weren't enough for me in that moment. I hadn't given myself any time to truly let my frustration at his initial lies out, and now all I wanted to do was vent. "You promised me that your intentions weren't sinister! You said you were a consultant and that you just wanted to talk! You lied! About everything! What have you dragged me into?" My voice was raised to a volume that was close to yelling. I hated confrontation, but I needed to get everything out of my system.

"I never wanted you to get involved in this, Ella." He shook his head lightly. "Those men weren't supposed to be there. It was an unplanned visit. I only found out that they were coming up later on in the day, and that's why I told Hector that I didn't want you up there. And I definitely didn't expect them to bring Bill up in the condition that he was in."

"Why *was* Bill in that condition anyway?"

Zeke intertwined his fingers on the kitchen counter and was silent for a moment before answering my question. "Bill accidentally left out some key information on a deal, and it got one of our members badly hurt. All that was supposed to happen was for Bill to be taught a lesson in loyalty and the need for efficient communication so he never messes up like that again. But one of the guys lost his temper and took matters into his own hands, quite literally, before the situation could be handled properly and in a more appropriate environment."

"A more appropriate environment? So you're fine with the beating Bill got, just not with where it happened?" *Who is this guy?* "You're okay with beating people to death to teach them a lesson?"

"Not to death, no. I don't kill people, Ella. That's not my job. I've never done it before, and I never will. I simply play a managerial role. I mediate and make sure that everything is running smoothly."

I rolled my eyes at him. "Keep telling yourself that so you can sleep better at night, Zeke, but we both know that you were truly in your element last night. Like you enjoyed seeing that Bill guy hurting."

"It's just the job, Ella."

I snorted at him. "Whatever."

Zeke probably realized that the conversation wasn't going anywhere good because he simply sighed before saying, "You need to rest. We have a long day tomorrow."

"Don't tell me what to do. I don't feel like resting. In fact, what I want right now is another drink." After proclaiming that, I went to grab my third beer out of the fridge.

I heard Zeke sigh again. "You're going to feel like hell in the morning if you keep drinking like that," he told me.

I turned to face him, full scowl in place. "You know what, Zeke? You can *go* to hell in the morning. No, you can go to hell tonight. In fact, you can go to hell every single day of your life, 'til you die and actually go to hell! How's that?" I then sat very ungracefully on a stool with my back to him, but for a while after my tantrum I still felt Zeke's presence in the kitchen.

Finally he said, "Goodnight, Ella."

I didn't answer, taking another swig from my bottle instead.

The last thing I remember is downing the beer in my hand and then another, before stumbling to my room and falling asleep in a drunken pile on the bed.

****

I felt like hell the next morning. I groaned as I turned over on top of the bed and opened one eye slowly, trying to will away the throbbing in my temples. I spotted Zeke sitting on a chair in the corner of the room, reading something on his phone. He looked over at me when I stirred, and his face held an expression that barely concealed his urge to say, "I told you so."

I turned away from him, feeling embarrassed, but he didn't seem as bothered as I was by the situation because he walked over to the bed and stood directly in front of me. He handed me two white pills and a large glass of water that had been placed on the nightstand. He had obviously foreseen my morning suffering. I took them with no questions asked.

After drinking down the pills, I looked up at him and said, "Okay, I'm ready to cooperate now."

He smiled and replied, "Good. Let's get some food in you first."

****

Zeke prepared me a hearty, full English breakfast and added pancakes with fresh strawberries on the side. I was sure he had gone out at some point that morning to buy the ingredients because none of that stuff had been there the day before. Or maybe he had gotten Chris to do it. Either way, I was grateful.

After I had finished breakfast, and the pain pills that he had given me kicked in, I took a soothing shower and I started to feel a little less like a zombie. I got dressed in the comfiest clothes that I could find, tied my thick, frizzy hair up into a high bun, and walked out of my room to look for Zeke, who I found reading a newspaper at the kitchen counter.

He looked up when I walked in and asked, "Better?"

"Yeah, I'm good now. Thank you for helping me with my hangover."

"No problem."

"And I'm really sorry for blowing up on you last night. I was...I'm just scared."

"It's understandable. You have nothing to be sorry about, Ella. And I promise that I'll get you out of this mess as soon as I can. But while you're in it, I'll keep you safe."

To his credit, Zeke had been patient with me, and he was trying hard to be accommodating, so I told him, "I'm still sorry. You didn't deserve that. And I don't want you to, you know, go to hell."

He smiled at me, and there was a hint of amusement in his eyes. "Thank you, Ella. I appreciate that." He stood abruptly, checked his watch, and said, "There's a lot we need to get done before you're introduced to The Official and the rest of The Org members. We have to have your persona in place."

"Persona?"

"Yeah. You need to come across more…hard. You're a good person, and it shows. You'll stand out. We don't want that. So we have to figure out what your character will be when you're around members."

I blinked at him. "I'm not great at acting, Zeke. Or pretending. Or lying. What if they catch me out?"

"They won't. I'll make sure you're prepared, Ella." He picked up his phone and sent a quick text on it then asked me, "You good to go?"

"Go? I thought I couldn't leave this place."

"We're not going far."

"Where are we going?"

"To meet someone."

I looked down at my plain baby-blue oversized tee, gray fitted sweat pants, and fluffy slippers. "Um, maybe I should change first."

"No need. The person I want you to meet lives in this complex, just a floor down."

****

I stood anxiously next to Zeke as he knocked three times on the apartment door of whomever he wanted me to meet. It was on the second floor of the complex, which clearly catered to people who were on the right side of wealthy, so I figured the mystery person was rich too.

I was nervous but I was doing a good job of not

showing it. I quickly came to the realization that I had to be tough if I were to survive being a part of The Org. In fact, that's the only good thing that had come out of my grand performance the previous night. I had gotten all of the anger and frustration out of my system, and I was ready to put my big-girl panties on and deal with the reality of what was happening. Besides that, all my tantrum had earned me was a massive headache, an embarrassing morning, and a new-found dislike of alcohol that I felt to my very core.

No more drunken tantrums for me, I thought as I stared at the number 207 on the apartment door in front of us. A moment later, said door was answered by a woman who, to me, looked to be somewhere in her mid to late thirties. She had almost platinum blonde hair and the looks of an eighties pin-up. She arched one perfectly groomed eyebrow at me before saying, "Zeke. You told me you were bringing me a client, not an impossible mission."

"It's nice to see you too, Ethel," Zeke said with a smirk.

The woman ignored Zeke's sarcasm and asked, "So this is her, huh?"

"Yes. Ethel, this is Ella Silver. Ella, Ethel Demure. Top-tier member."

Demure? Sounds like a stripper's name.

"And no, I ain't no stripper. It's just what everyone would call me back in the day, and it stuck. I can barely remember what my real last name is," she stated with a snicker. "Anyway, it's nice to meet you, Ella. Come on in and make yourself at home."

"Thank you," I replied as we walked into her apartment. It was abundantly clear that she had different décor taste from Zeke. Her living room had colorful scatter cushions on the sofas, and there were even a few pictures in frames placed on the shelves. I liked the place already.

"Ella, Ethel here is a personal stylist. Almost every member who's higher up in The Org has dealt with her at some point. She's going to give you some new clothes and possibly a new look too," Zeke told me.

So this meeting is about making me more Organization appropriate.

"Possibly?" Ethel inquired. "No, honey, we are *definitely* giving her a new look."

I looked down at my outfit for the second time that day and, in my defense, what I was wearing wasn't at all an accurate representation of my general style. *I knew I should have changed.*

"How long will it take for you to get everything done?" Zeke asked her.

"Give us two hours. Maybe three. Depends on what I decide to do with her hair."

"All right. I'll be back in two and a half then. Let me leave you ladies to it," Zeke said, and turned to leave.

"You forgetting something, kid?" Ethel asked him before he reached the door. Zeke turned back around and walked over to her, placing a quick kiss on her cheek. It was a rare show of affection from him and as he strode back toward the door without another word, I remained in fascination at the interaction that I had witnessed between them. I got a maternal vibe from Ethel, and she and Zeke did relate with each other in a mother-son kind of way. I liked seeing that side of him.

After he had left the apartment, Ethel turned to me,

her green eyes looking me up and down. "I'm gonna be real honest with you, honey. You're cute and all, but you look like you have no style. At all. I mean, no one should look like this," she said as she gestured toward my clothes. "Not even at home. We've got a lot of work to do on you." She smiled slyly and drawled, "But luckily for you, I love a challenge. Follow me."

Ethel led me to one of the bedrooms, which she had transformed into a boutique-cum-office. Like Zeke's, her apartment also had two bedrooms, but she had made a business out of one of hers. I looked around at the multitude of clothes on rails and hangers, and I was immediately overwhelmed by the number of options that I had. Overwhelmed in a good way, I suppose. I mean, what woman doesn't like shopping, right? But I was overwhelmed regardless. All the clothes were stylish and looked expensive, and it was just a lot to take in. Don't get me wrong—I was good at pairing outfits together, but I was also used to shopping in department stores and I had been perfectly fine with that.

"As you can see, I cater to a certain kind of clientele," Ethel said as she watched me.

Rich clientele, I thought while I held a deep plum dress up against my body.

"I only allow very elite people into my home boutique," Ethel continued. "Everyone else has to go to my store in the middle of the busy city and get served by my girls. Needless to say, your boy Zeke's got some serious pull."

"Good to know," I responded with a small smile.

"So, what do you like so far?" she asked me.

"Um…" I liked comfort, affordability, and

whatever suited my body, but I knew that would sound unacceptable to this woman, so I didn't know what to say.

"Never mind," she eventually said with a wave of her hand when I didn't answer fast enough. "I'll have you looking like a high-street winner in no time. You don't have to know what you like. I'll figure that out for you." She winked at me and grinned.

"Thank you," I replied. I was being uncharacteristically unsociable, but only because it wasn't a normal social setting. Ethel was an Org member and if she became suspicious of me because of my tendency to blabber nervously, it would have blown our cover to pieces, so I kept my answers short.

We spent a significant amount of time "finding" my style, as Ethel put it. She picked out a lot of designer pieces for me. Her selection included high heels, coats for colder weather, a couple of evening gowns for specific member meetings and if I ever went out at night for a black-tie event, and she even added some lingerie that was sexier than what I usually wore. She did throw in a couple of casual outfits as well, but even those were designer brand names. The underlying excitement in her voice told me that she loved her job and I had to hand it to her, she knew what she was doing. She even gave me makeup and showed me how to quickly apply a full face. I had always preferred a more natural look, but Ethel said, "No female in The Org leaves the house without her face on."

The only thing that she didn't feel the need to change about me entirely was my hair. "You've got great hair. Thick and curly," she said as she ran her hands over it. "We can just accentuate that. Maybe put some wand curls in it, and you're good to go." She then went on to use a wand curler on my hair to demonstrate her point and, like its name suggests, it worked magic. I was officially runway ready. Well, besides the fact that I had put my old, comfy clothes back on.

"Can I get you something to drink," Ethel offered after all the styling was done.

"Yes, please. Just some water will be fine."

She brought me a cold glass of water with a slice of cucumber in it and sat next to me on the couch while we waited for Zeke. "So how exactly did you and Zeke meet by the way?" she asked. "I only have a general idea from what he told me, but I'm interested in the details." She took a sip from the glass of red wine in her hand and never took her eyes off me.

"Uh, at the hotel. The Lost Cantrell," I answered cautiously. I didn't like the direction that the conversation was going in.

"And you were working there, right?"

"Yes, I was."

"And how did you find out about The Org? How did he rope you in? And why?"

I shifted uncomfortably on the sofa. "Um…" I faltered.

A knock sounded at the door and Ethel smiled at me mischievously. "Saved by the bell, huh?" she said before getting up from the couch to answer the door.

A moment later, she and Zeke walked into the living room together. He looked at me and smiled. "You look lovely, Ella," he said quietly.

"Thank you. Ethel did a great job," I replied, trying to play down his compliment.

"Good? No, I did an amazing job," Ethel retorted.

"Which is more than I can say for you, Zeke."

Zeke raised one brow and asked, "What are you talking about?"

"I'm talking about the fact that this girl ain't one of us, and you've done a terrible job at hiding it. Doesn't take a genius to figure it out. Heck, I figured it out the second I opened the door and saw her standing there. What have you dragged this poor child into?"

Zeke kept his poker face on. "I don't know what you mean. Ella has exceptional skills that will be revealed in due time. I wanted her to join."

Ethel narrowed her eyes at him. "Boy, I've been on this earth for fifty-three years. You're not foolin' me, even on your best day. Trust me, lying to me won't get you anywhere."

Fifty-three? Wow. She looks good, I thought as my mind strayed from their conversation briefly.

Zeke exhaled slowly, confessing in defeat, "She walked in on a…an incident. So I had to get her involved. It was the only way to keep her safe. You know what happens to people who see things that they shouldn't."

I looked back and forth between the two of them, and I saw Ethel's almond-shaped green eyes go as wide as saucers. "Are you crazy?" she asked incredulously. She was doing that shout-whispering thing that people did when they were upset about something that they couldn't talk about publicly. "How could you drag an innocent civilian into The Org? It's obvious that she ain't built for this work. Zeke!"

"I'm going to get her out eventually. But for now, I need you to keep this quiet. Please, Ethel. She'll be an official member soon, and then the circumstances of her entry won't matter anyway. And I'll prepare her thoroughly for her talk with The Official. It'll be fine."

Ethel paced back and forth, shaking her head. "Fine?" she questioned, her disbelief at Zeke's calm demeanor evident in her tone. She studied Zeke's face then breathed out heavily. "Okay, Zeke. I won't say anything about this." She pointed a manicured finger at him. "But if anything happens to her, her blood is on your hands, not mine."

"I won't let anything happen to her," Zeke assured her.

Ethel looked over at me and shook her head again while she continued to address Zeke. "You'd better have a top notch acting class in place for her if anyone is going to believe that she's Org material. And she should never, *ever* open her mouth to speak. It's like a broadcast of her innocence."

Zeke's mouth tilted up on one side to form his classic, barely there smile as he said, "It's like you read my mind, Demure. I do realize that she'll have to talk much less than she's used to from now on." He turned to face me then and declared, "In fact, Ella Silver isn't going to be much of a talker at all."

Chapter 10

I learned soon after Zeke's statement about me not being much of a talker anymore that he didn't plan on cutting my tongue out or anything, much to my relief. He explained to me that my new persona would simply be of a very, very quiet individual. In fact, he wanted me to be so silent that people who didn't know me would have reason to assume me to be a mute. It was a tall order for me, but I knew that I could do it if it guaranteed my survival. I wasn't as bummed out about that as I was about what Zeke had told me after we left Ethel's place.

When we got back to his apartment, with several shopping bags labeled L'Ethel that were full of expensive clothing, Zeke sat me down and said, "I know Ethel said that she won't tell anyone about this, but it's important that you still keep as much as you can to yourself when you're around her. Don't ever be too trusting of anyone in The Org, Ella. And Ethel...she's loyal to The Official. Always remember that."

"Okay," I replied. I had hoped that Ethel would be an ally, especially since she was the only female in The Org that I knew up to that point and she was friendly enough.

Zeke must have seen the disappointment on my face because he sighed and explained further. "Here's the thing. Ethel was in a relationship with The Official at some point. Nothing ever came of it, but she still loves him, and he cares about her. If it were to come down to a choice between us and him, don't hold your breath on her choosing us. Do you understand what I'm saying?"

I got his point. "Yeah, I understand. I'll be careful about what I say around her."

"Good. Now, like I said in Ethel's apartment, I need you to come across as someone who doesn't like to talk. Limit your words as much as possible when we're around members." Zeke's lecture on how I was to behave went on for a while, and I took mental notes of what was expected of me. "You need to be confident, almost arrogant. Always make eye contact with everyone that you're in close proximity with, even when you're silent. Never look down at your feet, always straight ahead. And when someone greets you, just nod your head in acknowledgement. The only person you should always answer is The Official." *I really should have written all of this down.*

By the time Zeke was done explaining my new character to me, I knew that Org Ella and real Ella were complete opposites. "I want you to be a mystery to them," Zeke told me. "The fact that I've endorsed you will be enough to convince everyone that you're beneficial to The Org in some way."

"What if they want to know exactly what I can do? What will you tell them if they ask you?"

"I'll be vague. Like I said, you'll be a mystery. And your mystery will be your strength."

"So I guess being able to serve up a delicious meal doesn't count as being beneficial to a criminal organization, does it?" I asked jokingly.

"Not really, no. It was extremely beneficial to *me* yesterday evening though," he replied with a smile, returning my humor.

"Right," I said on a laugh.

The light moment we shared was like a cool breeze in summer because I was still extremely anxious, and I needed the reprieve. I bit my lip and tried to convince myself that if I just stuck to his guidelines, everything would go smoothly. Zeke, obviously noticing my worry, put a hand on my shoulder and reassured me. "You'll be fine, Ella. Everything is going to work out, okay?"

I hope you're right, Zeke, I thought, but I simply replied, "Okay."

"Okay," he repeated, then he dropped his hand from my shoulder and walked away abruptly, as was his way, in the direction of his bedroom.

I heard him speaking to someone over the phone and after a few minutes passed, he came back out looking like he meant business. "You're going to have to learn how to fight and how to defend yourself," he said. "I've scheduled some self-defense classes for you. You'll be taking them up here in the apartment. I'll shift the furniture around to create more room. Your first class is tomorrow."

"What makes you think I don't know how to fight?" I asked, feigning offense.

Zeke let out a low chuckle. "Do you?" he asked.

I didn't. "If you must know, Stace and I took a women's self-defense class together once." I knew that wouldn't count for much in The Org either, just like my being a budding chef, but I enjoyed joking around with him.

Zeke nodded slowly, and he looked as if he were holding in a laugh. *I would love to hear him laugh.* "Well, let's just brush up on whatever you already know," he said with a lopsided grin that still didn't quite qualify as a full smile.

Despite the fact that I didn't like the idea of fighting, I refrained from arguing. Given my situation, I knew that I probably would need to know how to protect myself. I listened carefully while Zeke continued to talk to me about what he had planned, and I went over the basics of my persona in my head like a diligent student.

"You should be ready to talk to The Official in a couple of weeks," I heard Zeke say. That snapped me out of my mental note-taking.

"I'll be meeting with him that soon? I thought I'd have more time than that. You know, meet some of the other members first," I said nervously.

"You won't be meeting with The Official," Zeke responded.

"I don't understand. You just said…"

"I said that you'll be ready to *talk* to him, not *meet* with him," Zeke interrupted. His eyes held the usual amused twinkle that they did when I expressed any confusion. "When I said I would introduce you to him, I didn't mean in person. He doesn't meet with members. He only ever talks to them over the phone. Different number every time. No one knows what The Official looks like except for his son, his son's bodyguard, Ethel, and me."

"Why?" I asked.

"Security. You can't kill a ghost, Ella."

I figured that I could learn a lot from The Official

when it came to my new character because he was definitely doing the mystery thing right. I considered Zeke's words. "You said The Official has a son?"

"Yes, he does. That's his only child."

"With Ethel?"

"No, not with Ethel. With his late wife. She died giving birth."

I was becoming more and more intrigued by the second. "Can you describe him to me? The Official?"

"Unfortunately, no."

"So he's just going to be a voice on the other end of the phone, and I won't even have an idea of what he looks like or anything?"

"Yes."

There was an awkward silence after his answer. "Is there nothing more you can tell me about him?" I asked, trying to get some information out of him about the leader of The Org.

"Not right now, no. But nearer the time for your conversation with him, I'll make sure you're prepared for his questions by giving you a general idea of his character. And I'll keep going over the cover story with you until it sinks in."

The Official didn't seem to be a subject that Zeke wanted to dwell on. He looked like he was getting increasingly tense with each question that I asked about the mysterious man who was in charge of The Org. Luckily for him, I still had loads of unanswered questions pending from the other night and, since The Official was clearly a secret in and of himself, I decided to get some answers out of Zeke that he could actually give me.

"Can I ask you something kinda unrelated?" I

inquired tentatively.

"Sure," Zeke replied, appearing to relax a little at my intent to change the topic of conversation.

"Would those men in your suite have wanted to harm me if I didn't have this pendant?" I touched my fingertips to the piece of jewelry around my neck lightly. I hadn't taken it off since the day that Smithson had given it to me, except when I showered, and after what happened in the penthouse suite, I didn't plan to take it off anytime soon.

Zeke glanced briefly away from me before answering. "Yes. You saw a lot."

"So the pendant is something that members get?"

"Yes."

I mulled over the new information Zeke had given me. "Why did Smithson give it to me then? Did he think I could be...like you guys? Did I give off underground criminal vibes or something?"

Zeke smiled and his eyes crinkled at the corners slightly. "No."

"Then why did he give me his pendant to wear in the first place?"

He looked to the side again then back at me. "He figured you would need it. Eventually," he said. "He could tell that you and I were becoming...friends. I guess he knew I'd probably get you in trouble at some point, especially since I hadn't told you what I was really involved in. He just wanted to make sure you were protected. Smithson doesn't like innocents being harmed." Zeke paused briefly before explaining further. "When a member of The Org, especially a top-tier member, gives a non-member their pendant to wear, it's considered an endorsement, which is almost like an invite. Granted, usual protocol requires that The Official is consulted with first, before any pendant is loaned. After The Official accepts the endorsement, the invited individual can wear the pendant of the member who endorsed them until their formal welcome event as a confirmed member where they will receive their own. So, as you can tell, our situation is a little out of the ordinary. That's why I need to keep you hidden away for a while."

I had to remember to thank Smithson the next time I saw him. He had practically saved my life. I cocked my head in thought as I considered something else about the pendant. "Is the pendant fake like Smithson said?" I asked.

"No. It's real. Gold and black sapphire."

I didn't even know that black sapphire existed. "Wow. So your organisation can afford to have its criminals walking around wearing real gold and black sapphire? Nice. I actually feel lucky to be joining now." My voice was dripping with sarcasm, but Zeke either ignored it or missed it completely. I honestly never knew with him.

"Not all members wear black sapphire, only the top-tier. The other members have different pendants from ours. Different kinds, depending on their rank. But yes, every member gets a pendant of a certain stone."

"So that means Smithson is top-tier, right?"

"Yes, he is."

"What does he do in The Organisation?"

Zeke was quiet for a while, and I knew that whatever was coming would be bad. "Smithson is a disciplinarian, of sorts. He handles problems. Problematic people."

"And how does he do that?"

"He gets rid of them," Zeke replied flatly.

"Gets rid of them?" I questioned.

"Yes. He gets rid of them," he repeated. Then he looked me in my eyes and added, "For good."

My mouth dropped open once I caught Zeke's meaning. "Are you saying that Smithson is a killer? He kills people?" I squawked.

Zeke exhaled through his nose and didn't directly respond to my question, but the look in his eyes was answer enough. "Smithson only eliminates problems within The Organization, members who become a threat to its functionality. He doesn't hurt innocents."

It made me sick the way he referred to members of The Org as "problems" and not people. *He assassinates people! He's an assassin!* My mind was screaming so many things, but I didn't say them out loud. All I could do was look at him in disgust. "So because they're a part of your organization they're not human beings anymore, Zeke?"

"Barely," he answered without hesitation. "You need to understand that The Organization is only for bad people, Ella. That's all we are. We're just a network of...bad people. Don't pity any of us. We deserve whatever retribution comes our way."

I stared at him for a moment longer before turning away to calm myself down. I didn't want to end up throwing another tantrum. Zeke didn't leave me alone in the room, but he stayed silent, giving me a moment to let the information about Smithson sink in. *Smithson, who I thought was so sweet after I met him. Up until just a minute ago.* I shook my head at my naivety. *So stupid, Ella.*

Once my initial dismay had eased up, I resigned myself to the fact that I would have to get used to seeing the negative side of the world, at least while I was in The Org. I didn't have any time to dwell on disappointments. I turned back to Zeke and asked, "What else do I need to know?"

After that, the rest of the conversation carried on smoothly, and that was probably only because Zeke knew that I had heard enough shocking news for one day. Later on, we ate dinner together. I did all the cooking again—not because Zeke expected me to or anything, but because I simply enjoyed cooking. As a chef, I found pleasure being in a kitchen, any kitchen, and it was almost therapeutic for me, especially given my predicament. I was relieved that I could still do what I loved, even though I was stuck in Zeke's apartment.

Surprisingly enough, as we ate, the atmosphere was pleasant despite the previous tension. Eventually, Zeke announced that we would both need to get some rest for the next day, and I knew that he was hinting at hitting the hay. Before we said our goodnights to each other, Zeke gave me both his and Chris's numbers so that I could communicate with either of them if I ever needed anything when they weren't with me.

Soon after that, I retreated to my room and I spent a while awake in bed, staring at the ceiling and thinking about my self-defense class that was planned for the next day. I also couldn't help but think about the type of person that I would have to become in order to make it out of my situation alive. I turned onto my side and forced my eyes closed. *Goodnight, Ella.*

****

I woke up a lot earlier the next morning and had breakfast, which I found laid out for me with a note from Zeke that read, "Enjoy." He was nowhere to be seen, and I figured that he must have gone out somewhere.

After I ate, I took a shower and dressed up in a T-shirt and sweatpants combo that would have probably made Ethel gag. I walked out of my room, heading to the kitchen for a glass of water, but stopped short when I saw Zeke in the now cleared out living room, standing with two people who I had never seen before. It was a man and a woman, both with dark hair and both wearing workout clothes.

Zeke and the two strangers all looked at me as soon as I stepped into the room, and I noticed the blue gym mat under their feet. I was sure that they were my trainers, and I immediately went into silent-mode because, judging by the yellow-stone pendants around their necks, I was also sure that they were Org members.

"Good morning, Ella. This is Viktor and Camilla. They will be training you in self-defense from now on, as I mentioned yesterday," Zeke said to me.

I nodded at them in greeting but didn't make a move to go to where they stood. Zeke held his hand out to me in a gesture for me to come over and I went to him, joining them all on the mat. He placed one hand gently on my forearm as he spoke to the trainers. "Like I said, nothing too strenuous. She's starting out, so go easy."

I noticed the woman, Camilla, frowning down in the general direction of where Zeke's hand made contact with my arm. "Go easy? Sounds like you have a soft spot for this one, Zeke," she said, looking up with a smirk.

I'm good at detecting vibes most of the time, and I knew immediately that she didn't like me. I could also tell that she liked Zeke. A lot. *Maybe she's jealous. Maybe she thinks there's something going on between Zeke and me.* Nothing could have been farther from the truth, of course.

Zeke didn't seem in any way affected by her snide comment. "Ella is going to be a very important part of The Org. I don't want her getting injured during training. So again, go easy," he repeated.

"Going easy isn't my usual style, but for you, Zeke, I'll try," Camilla said flirtatiously, taking off her pendant and handing it to Viktor. She put on a pair of grappling gloves and turned to face me completely, eyes full of contempt. "So, we hear that you've been endorsed by both Zeke and Smithson," she stated, looking me up and down critically. I had a good two inches on her, but she didn't appear to be intimidated by that. "They rarely endorse anyone, and neither of them has ever endorsed a woman," she continued. "So, tell me, what's so special about *you*, hmmm?" I didn't answer, just looked her straight in her eyes like Zeke had told me to do with members. "She deaf and dumb or something?" Camilla asked smugly, directing the question to no one in particular.

"I told you that Ella doesn't talk much," Zeke answered.

Camilla took a step back and said, "Oh, right. I forgot." Her flat tone made it obvious that she hadn't really forgotten. She just wanted to make fun of me. I didn't let it get to me though, because mean girls were nothing new. I just continued to look at her, barely blinking. It felt unnatural, but I knew that I was pulling it off pretty well.

Viktor spoke up then, causing me to look away from Camilla and into his much friendlier face. "It's nice to meet you, Ella. I'm Vik. And don't mind Cam. She can be a little intense sometimes." *Intense isn't quite the word I would use to describe her.* He held his hand out to me and I took it, shaking it firmly. "I'm looking forward to assisting you in getting the training you need," he added. "Obviously I won't be getting physical with you. That's what Cam is here for." *Great,* I thought sarcastically. He looked at Camilla and said, "Start slow."

"Sure thing," she said, but the look in her eyes screamed trouble. "Maybe you'll show us what's so special about you during your training," Camilla taunted. Then she added, "If anything."

I'm not one to retaliate. It was a very rare occurrence for me to do so, but on occasion it happened. Camilla was being unnecessarily rude to me, and my sister, Sweety, always said, "Never let anyone get away with being a jerk." So I chose not to let Camilla get away with it.

"If there's nothing special about me, and Zeke and Smithson still endorsed me, then where does that put you? You must be bottom of the barrel, huh? Just lucky to be here," I said calmly, my voice low in the same way that Zeke usually spoke. I knew that my words would sting her, and the narrowing of her eyes confirmed it.

Vik's eyebrows shot up, and he clearly wasn't one for reading the room because he clapped his hands together loudly once and laughed. "Guess she's not deaf or dumb after all, huh, Cammy?" he quipped.

Camilla, on the other hand, stood stone-faced and tense. "Let's get started, shall we?" she said stiffly.

I looked over at Zeke, whose face was practically a mask. I knew that I wasn't supposed to talk but Camilla had it coming. I still felt bad that I had already fudged up one of his rules though. However, my guilt was short-lived because Zeke gave me a small smile and winked at me when no one was looking. It was enough to give me some courage for my first training session.

Vik went to stand beside Zeke and began explaining to me what I should expect to get out of my classes. Camilla stood facing me, arms at her sides and her eyes a clear window into her obviously blackened soul.

Once Vik was done with his explanations, Camilla began to bounce lightly on the balls of her feet and said, "I was thinking we could start with a little lesson in anticipation."

I looked at Vik and then back at her, my brow slightly furrowed as I waited for her to give more details about what she meant. She didn't. What she did do, however, was punch me square on the mouth with her gloved hand. The force whipped my head back, and I fell over backward. The immediate metallic taste of blood in my mouth and the dull ache on my bottom lip was a strong indication that it had split open a little.

"Anticipation. Foresee your opponent's next move. Be ready for any eventuality. Anticipate a blow before it comes," Camilla stated nonchalantly.

Vik and Zeke's faces appeared in my line of vision as I lay on my back, and they both helped me up. Zeke looked so worried that I almost spoke up again just to give him some reassurance that I was fine, besides being a little stunned by the unexpected blow and my face hurting, of course.

Vik turned to Camilla with a scowl. "What part of go easy didn't you understand?" he demanded.

"If she can't take a punch, she'll crumble if a rival organization gets to her. I'm doing her a favor," she defended.

"You're out of line. You disobeyed my orders," Zeke told her, his voice eerily low.

When he said it, Camilla's eyes went wide as if out of fear. Even Vik looked anxious as he watched Zeke for a reaction.

"I'm sorry, Zeke," Camilla apologized, sounding like a child who had just been caught red-handed stealing a cookie out of the jar.

The tension in Zeke's shoulders that had been apparent since Camilla punched me in the face dissipated just a little, and he grunted his acknowledgement of her apology. Eventually he said, "Ella is no longer in any condition to train, obviously. We'll take a break from the classes until her lip has healed up."

Zeke was coming across as extremely overprotective and that, in turn, was making me come across as extremely weak. And the thought that anyone would see me as weak irked me. I was a whole lot of things, but I was certainly not weak. I shook my head and stepped back onto the mat that I had just been knocked off of. Zeke's brow furrowed but he said nothing.

Vik let out a low whistle. "She's a tough one,

Gage," he said with a grin.

"Yes, she is," Zeke agreed.

I needed them all to believe that. If I looked soft, I knew that I would become a target, just like Ethel said.

"Wait, she seriously wants to keep going?" Camilla asked, barely able to contain her excitement at the news that she would get to hurt me some more.

"Looks like it," Vik answered, putting a pair of grappling gloves on me. "Don't touch her face. Body shots only for this week," he added, glancing at Camilla with annoyance all over his face.

"No problem," she replied with a smug smile.

Vik cleaned up my lip before I continued with the lesson, and the rest of the class went exactly the way that I expected. Camilla whipped my butt like I stole the broom that she flew in on.

She pummelled my body until Zeke finally said, "That's enough." He came over and pulled me up from the floor where I had toppled a second time. "Are you all right?" he asked. I nodded my head, sticking to the silent act this time.

"You're one tough cookie, Ella," Vik said from behind Zeke. I smiled at him and immediately winced when I felt the sharp sting from the small cut on my lip.

"I still think that Ella will need a little time to heal up completely. Give her two days," Zeke told Vik. "And the next time you come here, don't make her bleed," he added, giving Camilla a stern look.

"I'm sorry, Zeke," she said again, but in a much flirtier tone this time.

They eventually said their goodbyes, Camilla batting her eyelashes at Zeke the whole time, and then the two of us were alone once again. Zeke walked over to me and put a hand gently to my face. "Are you sure you're all right?"

"I'm okay," I lied, just relieved to be able to talk freely once more.

"Let's see how bad that lip is," he said as he took me by the hand and led me to the guest bathroom. He sat me down on the edge of the tub and squatted in front of me, delicately tilting my chin from side to side and studying my injury. His eyes narrowed, and his jaw ticked as he assessed the damage.

"The cut doesn't feel very big," I told him after watching his reaction.

"It's not. It'll heal quickly," Zeke confirmed, but his expression didn't change. "Doesn't change the fact that Camilla didn't listen to my orders. I can't have that. Members have to follow orders."

His displeasure at Camilla's disobedience was evident, and I didn't say anything because I didn't feel like any words would help. We both remained quiet while Zeke further tended to my tiny cut, fussing over it as if it were life-threatening.

"She likes you, doesn't she? Camilla?" I eventually asked him.

Zeke snorted in irritation. "Camilla likes the idea of being loved. That's all. She wants any man who is willing." He shrugged and added, "And even those who are not. That's why she gets jealous so easily. She sees every other woman as a threat to her potential happiness. It's crazy. "

I went over his words in my head. "Have you two ever…you know?" I asked him, leaving my implication to hang in the air.

Zeke chuckled. "No. She's not my type. At all."

I don't know why hearing him say that gave me so much satisfaction, but it did. "I'm sorry for talking today. I mean, when I responded to her," I apologized.

Zeke looked into my eyes and gave me his classic lopsided grin. "It was a good way to establish your authority. You're most likely going to enter as top-tier, so it's important that the other members know to respect you. To be honest, I liked it."

I smiled back at him. "Yeah?"

"Yeah. But don't make a habit of breaking character."

"I won't."

We left the bathroom and as we stood in the hallway, Zeke said, "Just relax for the rest of the day, all right?"

"Sure. Thanks."

And that's exactly what I did. I grabbed a snack, watched TV, read a book, and took a nap because, after the beating that I had received that day, I deserved a little rest.

****

The next morning was a harsh reminder of what my body had been through the previous day. I rolled out of bed with a groan. The truth is that I only bothered to get up because I was starving. Otherwise I would have just lain there like a lump.

I threw on one of the cover-ups that Ethel had picked out for me to wear at home. The silk robe felt blissfully soft and comfortable, and I looked like a rich housewife. "Look at you living the dream, Ella," I mumbled to myself sarcastically as I studied my reflection in the dressing table mirror.

I trudged out of my room stiffly, my body

protesting and my feet dragging loudly because of the aches and pains from my training. "Looks like someone got to you before I could," a female voice said smoothly. I whipped my head in the direction that the voice had come from, startled by the unexpected sound.

There was a woman in the living room, sitting on the couch and facing the big screen TV, which was switched off. All I could see was the back of her head, flowing with lustrous brown hair. She must have been watching me on the sly when I first walked in for her to have noticed that I was hurting because she definitely wasn't looking at me anymore. It was eerie looking at the back of a stranger's head like that. I had no idea where Zeke was or if he was even home, so if the woman planned to do me harm, I had no help. I didn't speak, just stood in place with no clue what to do next.

Slowly, the woman rose from the couch and turned around. She was beautiful, with striking hazel eyes. She strode over, confident and comfortable in her high heels, and stopped in front of me. She was a tall woman, and her stilettos made her tower over me even more. "Mmm. So pretty. Be a shame to kill you," the woman stated flatly. *What?*

"That's enough," I heard Zeke say from the hallway, and a moment later he was standing next to me protectively. "I'm not fond of uninvited guests. What are you doing here?" he asked the woman.

"You know exactly what I'm doing here," she answered calmly. "I'm doing my due diligence."

Zeke looked more annoyed than I'd ever seen him. "There's no need for this."

"She hasn't been confirmed as a member, and yet she witnessed Organization activities. I think there's plenty of need, Gage."

"She'll be a confirmed member soon. I'd advise you to be civil."

"I only answer to The Official, so you can keep your advice." The tension was thick in the air and, even though their voices weren't raised, I could tell that there was some animosity between them. The woman suddenly turned to face me. "Do you know who I am?" she asked me. I obviously had no idea who she was but even if I did, I couldn't say anything because my persona was in play. "You can call me Al. Like the song. It's nice to meet you, Ella," she continued when I didn't answer her question. I looked her in the eyes, unblinking and silent. She tilted her head sideways, and it almost looked as if she were amused by me. "This is the part where you tell me that it's nice to meet me too," she drawled. I didn't say a word, but Al simply smiled. "So you're not a talker. That's good. I hate chatty targets anyway."

Zeke took a step closer to me. "You need to leave, Alissa," he told her.

Al moved away from me instantly, following Zeke's order as if out of deference. "Okay, Gage. I'll leave. But your girl has three weeks to get her own pendant. If she isn't confirmed as a member by then, I'll be back. And next time, it will be under orders from The Official."

Zeke didn't respond to her, but I could tell that he understood her statement, and so did I. She walked backward toward the front door quietly, grinning the entire time. "I'll see you around, cutie," she said to me with a wink. Al reminded me of a predator toying with its prey, the way she watched me and spoke. It was obvious that she enjoyed the game of cat and mouse. She looked at Zeke briefly and said, "Gage," in lieu of goodbye, then a second later she was gone.

Zeke turned toward me and placed his hands on my shoulders. "You okay? Did she try to hurt you?" he asked with concern.

"No, she was just talking. I'm okay."

"I'm sorry I didn't come to you sooner. I couldn't hear anything from my room."

"It's okay. She's probably just really stealthy, you know? Like, ninja certified or something," I said jokingly. Zeke didn't look amused at all though. "Zeke, I'm okay. Really," I reassured him.

He shook his head in annoyance. "I wasn't even aware that she knew about this condo," he said.

"So much for only a handful of people knowing where you live then," I stated.

"Yeah," was his only answer. He was clearly irritated by Al's intrusion. His brow was drawn downward, and his eyes were dark.

"Are *you* okay?" I asked him.

"Yeah, I'm good." But he didn't look good. Al's presence had definitely gotten to him.

"So, who is she?" I needed to know after her unexpected visit.

Zeke sighed before answering me. "Al is a top-tier Org member, but she operates independently from the rest of us. She works solely with The Official to keep everyone in line and everything in order. She basically does the same job as me." Zeke shrugged and then added, "Except she keeps order by eliminating threats, if need be."

Eliminating threats. Another assassin? "So, Al

does the same thing as Smithson?"

"Not quite. Smithson gets rid of criminals only, like members of The Org who are not cooperating. Alissa, on the other hand, gets rid of whoever she is instructed to by The Official, whether they are innocent or not." Zeke's jaw twitched before he continued. "Also, Smithson eliminates out of duty, but Al actually enjoys her job. She likes hurting people."

I noticed that he was avoiding the use of the word "kills" again, but obviously we both knew what he meant. I looked away from him, thinking about the woman whom I had just met and the confidence that she exuded. "She's good at what she does, isn't she?" I inquired, even though I knew what the likely answer to that question would be.

"Yes, she is. Some might even say that she's the best at what she does. Except Smithson, of course," Zeke said with a wry smile.

I snickered, then I shook my head at myself because it was twisted that we were joking about who the best assassin was. I looked up at him, serious again. "If The Official doesn't sign off on me joining, Al will be ordered to kill me, right? And if she's the best at what she does, I guess that'll mean I'm screwed?"

Zeke's brow furrowed even farther. "The Official *will* sign off on your membership. Don't worry about that." That's all he said before he turned around and headed to his bedroom, leaving me to ponder my possible end.

****

After the short break that I took to let my busted lip heal, the days that followed consisted of me going through training in the apartment with Vik and Camilla, who was still an ice-cold witch. I always ended up bruised somewhere on my body, but I had to admit that she was right about me learning how to take a punch. Each lesson started to feel less and less like torture. In fact, I was almost getting used to the pain. I had managed to swallow the bitter pill that was my situation, and I had dealt with my stress by facing my reality.

The only thing that hadn't eased up was how much I missed the people that I love. I only ever communicated with Stace and my family through video or online calls because I obviously couldn't call or text from my non-existent French phone number. Luckily, they didn't ask too many questions. They believed my story and I felt like an A-class douchebag for lying to all of them, but deep down I knew that it was for the best.

When I wasn't training or, to be more accurate, getting beaten up, Zeke left me alone in the apartment a lot. He was always rushing to attend some meeting or another, and to call him a busy man would be an understatement. So, because of my isolation, I spent the majority of my days just sitting around, cooking, reading books, or watching TV. I knew that my safety depended on it, but I was getting bored, and it was driving me a little crazy.

One particular day, the loneliness and inactivity just became too much for me to handle. I changed into jeans, a T-shirt, and sneakers, and made my way to the second floor. It was the first time that I had left the apartment without Zeke, and it was strangely liberating. A minute later I stood in front of Ethel's door, trying to figure out what I was going to say to her to explain my visit. I knocked three times, just like Zeke always did, and Ethel opened the door, looking at me quizzically when she saw me.

"Hey. Zeke didn't mention that y'all were stopping by today," she stated, glancing quickly down the hallway from side to side. "Where is he?" Even her surprise at seeing me standing at her door alone couldn't distract her from noticing my outfit and giving it a disapproving look.

"Uh, hi, Ethel. Zeke's not here. It's just me," I responded. She looked confused so I quickly continued. "I like to talk. And I haven't been able to do that since I saw what I saw. I also like company, but I don't have much of that anymore either. When Zeke's around, we do talk a little but he's not around all that much. You're one of the only other people who knows what's going on and who's been nice to me, so I just figured…I figured maybe we could talk. You know, hang out." I looked past her into her apartment. "Also, your apartment has color, so…" I trailed off, catching myself before I could ramble on further.

Ethel studied me, then she smiled wide with an amused shake of her head and said, "Come on in, honey."

She stepped to the side to let me in, and I practically pranced into her apartment, not waiting for her to ask twice. I texted Zeke to let him know where I was, and when he eventually came to get me a couple of hours later, Ethel told him that I could come over whenever I liked.

I had a great time and we had talked about almost everything, including our backgrounds. Ethel had told me that she was not, nor had she ever been, a stripper or escort. "The boys did like me though," she said saucily. "But I was way too classy for 'em. That's how I got the nickname 'Demure.' It just stuck." That was just one of her many stories. While I was with Ethel, I laughed more than any time since leaving my and Stace's brownstone, and I was a little disappointed to be out of her company after just two hours. However, I was still glad that I had at least made a new friend in the building and in The Org. I walked away from her apartment not feeling as lonely as I had before.

In the days that followed, I started going over to Ethel's regularly and, on one particular visit, I decided to get her to tell me about her relationship with The Official. We were sitting on her sofa having drinks like we normally did, and I asked, "So, have you ever had a serious relationship?"

She looked at me for a moment, then sighed. "It's no secret amongst top-tier members that The Official and I used to be a thing. But that was a long time ago. I'm guessing you asked me that question because you heard as much?"

I didn't bother lying. "I did. What happened?"

Ethel was quiet for a while before she spoke again. "He's a complicated man, The Official. That's actually what I loved about him. He wasn't boring or simple," she said, her eyes taking on a dreamy veil as she reminisced. "When we met, he had just lost his wife. She died from complications right after giving birth to their son. He wasn't interested in anything serious, and he definitely didn't want to ever get into another committed relationship again." Her eyes darkened. "He also made it clear that he didn't want any more children. So he...made sure that kids wouldn't be an

157

issue for us."

"Did you want kids?"

"At the time, yes. I mean, that's almost every girl's dream, right? A beautiful wedding, perfect husband and kids. I still think about it sometimes. But it wasn't meant to be."

"You never considered meeting someone new? Having kids with someone else?"

Ethel shook her head slowly, then sighed again. "I was in love with *him*. All I wanted was *him*. And even if I had started seeing someone new, I still wouldn't have been able to have children with them." She looked me in the eyes. "The Official, he took me to have a...procedure done. Irreversible."

I tried to hide my shock and disgust at that man for making Ethel give up something that she wanted just because *he* didn't want it, but I knew that I had failed when she gave me a sad smile and said, "Don't feel sorry for me, Ella. I was young and stupid and in love. But the experience made me stronger, tougher. I'm okay."

The whole topic honestly made me sick, and I knew that I had to change the subject before I told her how I really felt about what The Official had done to her. "What's his real name?" I asked, attempting to rein in my annoyance.

"His real name?"

"Yeah. He does have a real name, doesn't he?"

"Probably," Ethel replied with a wry smile.

"There is no way you actually called him 'The Official' in private. I mean, I understand kinks and all but come on, that is extreme." *She has to be lying about not knowing his name.*

Ethel chuckled. "I never called him anything. When we first met and in the beginning of our relationship, I asked him for his name, and he told me that it was 'The Official.' That's all he was willing to say. Eventually, I got used to it. He didn't give me a name, and I didn't need one from him. That's how much of a spell he had on me."

"And now?" I inquired. "Is the spell still there?"

She blinked at me several times as if my question had startled her, her mouth opening and then closing shut again. I lifted my eyebrows at her questioningly just as Zeke's familiar knock suddenly sounded at the door. Ethel shot up from the couch as if she had been previously trapped and then cut loose, making her way to the door to open it.

I shook my head at her evident relief. "Saved by the bell, huh?" I called out to her, repeating the words that she had said to me the first day that I met her.

She looked over her shoulder at me with an amused spark in her eyes and said, "Don't get cute, girly."

I laughed and got up from the couch just as she let Zeke in. "What's got you so tickled?" he asked when he saw my smiling face.

"Private inside joke between us girls, Zeke," Ethel answered for me.

The corners of Zeke's mouth turned up and he raised one eyebrow as if he was intrigued. "I see." He held his hand out to me. "Good to go?" he asked.

"Yup," I replied chirpily, taking the hand that he offered. "See you tomorrow, Ethel."

"Sure thing, honey."

Ethel opened the door for us to leave but before we could walk out, Zeke's phone began to ring loudly. He took it out of his pocket and looked down at the screen, sighing quietly. "I need to take this," he said, turning around and heading for Ethel's kitchen in order to take the call in private.

Ethel shut the door again, rolled her eyes and said, "Honestly, at this point, you two should just move in here. Y'all treat this place like you own it anyway."

I held in a laugh. I loved how dramatic Ethel could be. "I might take you up on that offer," I responded, pretending not to catch her sarcasm.

"Don't you dare," she warned me, unable to contain her laughter.

We were both still giggling when Zeke cut his call, but our smiles faded away when we saw the look on his face. "What's wrong?" Ethel asked, taking a step toward him.

There was a deep frown on Zeke's face, and he had a death grip on his phone. "That was The Official," he said stiffly. "He told me that he's ready to meet Ella. In person."

Chapter 11

So The Official, who never met with random members, wanted to meet *me*. I understood that it was obviously a change in his usual methods, but what I didn't understand was Ethel's semi-panicked reaction to the news. She had freaked out and shrilly told Zeke that The Official would figure me out if he saw me in person. I didn't get what the big deal was since I had my persona on lock and, in my opinion, I was pretty convincing.

Zeke had ushered me out of Ethel's apartment eventually, after calming her down, and we had gone back up to his condo in silence. Once we were in the living room, I asked him, "Why is Ethel so worried about The Official requesting to meet me in person?"

"Because it's not what he normally does."

"I know, but...maybe he's just interested in seeing me because I've been endorsed by you and Smithson, right? I mean, Camilla did say that you guys have both never endorsed a woman before. Maybe he's intrigued," I surmised.

Zeke exhaled slowly. "Maybe," was all he said before he went to his room without another word, leaving me to stand in the center of the living room awkwardly. He came back out a few minutes later with his cell phone in his hand again. "We fly out early tomorrow so it would be best if you started packing now," he stated.

"Fly out? Where are we going?" I inquired.

Zeke put his phone into his jacket pocket and replied, "Zimbabwe."

****

Zeke wasn't doing a very good job at hiding his tension. There was a constant tic in his jaw, and he was being even less talkative than his usual self.

I, on the other hand, was practically vibrating with excitement. Not because I was going to meet The Official, but because I was finally getting to leave the condo and breathe in some fresh air. It didn't hurt that I was going to travel to another continent, either. I had barely been able to sleep the night before after Zeke had told me the travel plan because I was looking forward to the trip so much. Maybe I liked a good adventure as much as the next person after all.

Not even the stern look on Zeke's face could dampen my spirits. He wore the same unwavering frown throughout our flight and, even though the private plane that we were on was the very definition of luxurious, he sat across from me as stiffly as if there were a cement block beneath him.

"Should I be worried?" I eventually asked him.

Zeke glanced in my direction. "No, you shouldn't be worried, Ella," he said.

"But *you're* worried," I pointed out.

"I don't like it when routines change, that's all."

I looked over at Chris, who was seated near the back of the plane with his eyes closed, dozing peacefully. "Chris doesn't seem worried," I said lightly. "That's a good sign, right?"

"Chris doesn't know the details of this trip. And

even if he did, it wouldn't be his job to worry."

I searched Zeke's face, keeping my eyes intently on his. "Be honest. Can this trip end badly for me?"

The tension in his jaw tightened. "No. I said that I'd protect you, and that's exactly what I'll do. With my life."

"But there's a chance that something bad might happen, right?"

"There's *always* a chance that something bad might happen. Right?"

He had a point. I turned my face forward, leaning back as I closed my eyes in the hopes that I would get some decent sleep before we landed at our final destination.

****

We arrived in Harare, Zimbabwe, around midday, and it didn't take long for the jetlag to settle in. We were picked up from the airport by a friendly driver named Mike, who seemed to know Zeke and Chris well. After introductions were made, Zeke informed me that Mike would be our guide and would basically drive us anywhere we needed to go while we were in Zimbabwe. Mike was a citizen of the country, judging by his familiarity with the area and, of course, his accent. I liked him. His personality was pleasant.

Mike drove us a few miles just out of the city to the Injabulo Ranch. It was a beautiful resort-style hotel, with two huge wood-carved elephant tusks just outside the entrance that were painted a dusty white colour to make them look like real ivory. The ranch was all greenery and clay pottery and, even though it was almost rustic in its themes, it exuded luxury and exclusivity.

Zeke had let me know very discreetly that The Official was staying at Injabulo, too, and I looked around at the few random people roaming the resort and wondered if he could be one of them. It made me nervous to think that he might be watching me and I wouldn't even know it.

Mike took our luggage out of the car with Zeke and Chris's help, and a porter came to quickly wheel it in on a golden cart. We checked into our rooms, Chris's suite being right next to ours on the fourth floor. I wasn't sure how everything would play out with Zeke and me sharing a suite because, unlike at his condo, we would actually be sleeping in the same room. I pushed the thought out of my mind, reminding myself that he had asked for a suite with two beds. *It won't be awkward. It won't be awkward. It won't be awkward.* I knew that Zeke just wanted to keep me close so that he could watch out for my safety more easily since I wasn't in the clear with The Official yet.

Chris headed to his suite, and we went to ours with the porter, whom Zeke must have tipped quite generously judging from the expression that crossed his face before he walked away, leaving us at the door with our luggage as we had requested. We entered the room, and I immediately liked the feel of it. It was cozy, with just about the same color scheme as The Lost Cantrell suites but more subtle in its luxury. It was homey and inviting.

"If you don't mind, you can take the bed farthest from the door," Zeke said politely. He didn't seem perturbed at all by the fact that we were sharing a room. I lifted my suitcase onto the bed nearest the window so that I could unpack my things. Zeke did the same on his bed. "I need a shower. You want to use the bathroom first?" he asked me.

I realized that we had never had the need to share a bathroom either, because both of the bedrooms in Zeke's condo were en-suite. "Uh, no. I'm good. You can go ahead. I'll shower later. I'm feeling a little jetlagged, so I think I'll just take a nap right now, at least for an hour or two," I replied.

"Okay," Zeke said with a nod. He double-checked that the suite door was locked before making his way into the bathroom and leaving its door slightly ajar.

Letting out a tired sigh, I kicked off my shoes, crawled onto the comfy mattress of my bed and, within minutes, fell into a much-needed deep sleep.

****

I woke up a while later, still wearing the jeans and T-shirt that I had arrived in, to find the curtains drawn and the low sun filtering through them, casting a dim orange glow throughout the room. I assumed that it was early evening on the same day that we arrived. I turned over and found Zeke sitting at the foot of his bed, fully dressed in a crisp white shirt and dark gray, fitted formal trousers.

He turned to look at me when he heard me stir. "Good morning," he greeted with a little half smile.

I tried to blink away my confusion. "Morning? What time is it?" I asked him.

"It's about seven-thirty a.m."

"I slept the whole of yesterday *and* through the night?" I questioned in surprise.

"Yeah. You must have been pretty tired."

"Yeah, I guess so. I'm sorry I wasn't good company. The jetlag hit me hard. I haven't traveled that much, and definitely never this far away from the States."

"It's okay. It's a good thing you got some rest actually, because we're seeing The Official this afternoon. At four thirty to be exact."

I sat up on my bed, the covers still unturned since I had slept on top of them. "Today?" I asked. "That's really soon."

"I know. But it's best to get it out of the way. There's no need to drag it on." Just then a knock sounded at the door, and I jumped a little from the unexpected noise. Zeke's mouth twitched slightly, but he managed to hide his amusement quickly enough for me to be unsure if I had imagined it or not. "I ordered us some breakfast. I figured you'd be up soon. I hope you don't mind," he said.

I cleared my throat. "Not at all. I'm actually starving. Thank you."

I jumped off my bed and went to use the bathroom, making sure to splash my face with cold water to fully wake myself up. When I was done freshening up, I went to sit on one of the stools at the counter in the suite's small kitchen area where Zeke had placed the room service order. The meal was huge and consisted of different sweet and savory pastries, a full English breakfast, a variety of sliced fruit, and a large jug of freshly squeezed orange juice. I couldn't wait to dig in, and I was grateful to Zeke for always making sure that I had a good start to my day when it came to food. It had kind of become one of his trademarks.

"Thank you, again. For ordering breakfast," I said, avoiding his eyes. He was trying to keep me comfortable under the circumstances, and I needed him to know that his efforts didn't go unnoticed.

"You're welcome, Ella."

I picked up a small tart and took a delicate bite of it, savoring the taste on my palate. After I swallowed the last bit of the delicious pastry, I dusted off my hands and broke the silence in the room. "Hey, you always make sure that I have the biggest, most decadent breakfasts. You're not trying to fatten me up, are you?" I joked.

He smiled and stated, "No, I'm not trying to fatten you up. I wouldn't want to change anything about you."

I stopped chewing the bite of food that I had taken and looked over at him. He had said the words so flatly, as if he were unaware of their impact. I stared at him for a few seconds while he ate and checked his phone, completely oblivious to the way my eyes were glued to his face. "Seriously?" I asked him. He looked over at me in confusion. "You wouldn't change anything about me?" I clarified.

His brow furrowed slightly. "Of course not. Why would I? Everything about you is..." He paused and averted his gaze, as if he was trying to figure out what he wanted to say, before looking back at me. "In my opinion, you're flawless."

My face heated, and I bit my bottom lip to stop myself from smiling like an idiot. *Flawless.* He had said it as if it were a matter of fact and not just an opinion. "No one's flawless," I told him, feeling embarrassed by such a strong compliment.

Zeke shrugged and said, "You are."

He went back to eating his breakfast as if the words that he had just uttered weren't the type of thing that women swooned over. "Thank you," I said quietly.

He looked over at me again and gave me a little closed-mouth grin as he chewed. "You're thanking me for being honest?" He looked genuinely amused.

I'm thanking you for being so ridiculously sweet. I didn't actually answer his question. I just smiled back at him and picked up my fork. We ate the rest of our breakfast mostly in silence. Zeke divided the majority of his attention between his food and whoever he was messaging on his phone, while I snuck a couple of glances at him and reached the realization that he looked kind of flawless to me too.

****

Later in the day, Zeke gave me some privacy to shower and change for our meeting with The Official. He said that he was going downstairs to "have a look around the resort," as he put it. When he finally came back up to the room, I was all dressed up and ready to get going. "Good to go?" he asked me.

"Uh, yeah," I answered hesitantly. Just as we were about to leave our suite, I asked him, "Do you have a gun on you?"

"A gun?"

"Yeah. Or a knife or something?"

Zeke shook his head slowly and said, "No."

"How will you protect us if things go sideways then?" I inquired nervously.

He chuckled at my question. "I have my ways," he said. When my facial expression remained completely serious, he put a comforting hand on my shoulder and looked me in my eyes. "Don't worry, Ella. I won't let anything happen to you."

I bit my lip anxiously but nodded in acknowledgement of his reassurance. Zeke took me by the hand and said, "Come on. Let's go."

We left our suite at four twenty p.m., allowing no room for us to be late for our meeting with The Official. I wore one of the outfits that Ethel had put together for me. It was a simple but elegant, fitted beige jumpsuit and a pair of black stilettos that brought a whole new level of pain to my feet. Sweety could walk in high heels as if it was second nature to her, and in that moment, I wished that she could transfer some of that talent to me.

Zeke offered me his arm when he noticed me wobbling a little. "You okay?" he asked.

"Yeah. I just don't wear heels this high usually, so it feels like I've got two torture devices attached to my feet."

Zeke let out a low laugh before suggesting that I take my shoes off until we got to The Official's floor. "Nah, it's cool," I told him. "I gotta get used to them anyway, right? Ethel said that high heels are like a part of all female Org members' uniform or whatever."

"Well, you can hold onto me if you need help with your balance."

"Thanks."

When we got into the elevator, Zeke gave me a brief recap. "Remember that when The Official speaks to you, you should answer. You can drop that part of your persona with him, okay?"

"Okay," I answered.

The doors opened up to the fifth floor of the hotel, and we walked down the hallway, stopping at room 510 which was right at the end. Zeke knocked on the door and, a moment later, a huge man in a black suit opened it. Zeke nodded at the man and said, "Knight."

"Gage," the man replied with a voice so deep that it was almost a growl. His green eyes fell on me briefly, but he didn't say anything. He stepped to the side, and we entered the suite. It was exactly the same as our room, except for the fact that it had one king size bed and not two singles.

There was a coffee table next to the balcony doors and sitting at it were two men, one young and one older. The older man was reading a local newspaper, the ankle of one leg placed on top of the knee of his other leg in that relaxed manner that men do. The younger man, however, looked anything but relaxed. He gripped the arms of his chair tightly, and his jaw was clenched.

The older man looked up from his paper, and I got a better look at his face. He had a white strip of hair at his hairline amidst his dark brown strands, and a neat salt and pepper beard. His eyes were dark and held an alertness that was a little disconcerting. The younger man had dark hair and dark eyes too, but he was clean shaven. He looked to be in his early thirties.

Zeke and I stood before the two men and they both got to their feet. "Thank you, Knight," the older man said.

Knight, who had been standing behind us, replied, "Sir," before he walked over to stand next to the younger man in front of us.

The older man then spread his arms wide as he exclaimed, "Zeke, my boy! It's so good to see you. And I see you've brought me a guest."

Zeke took a step forward and awkwardly received the hug that the older man offered him. "Yes, this is Ella-Cherie Silver," Zeke said. "Ella, this is The

Official."

This is him. The Official smiled and opened his arms wide again as he moved closer to me. "Ella-Cherie Silver," he repeated, giving me a hug too. "How are you, my dear?"

"I'm fine, thank you, sir. It's a pleasure to meet you," I replied politely.

"Indeed. I'm happy to finally meet you, too. You have been quite a topic of discussion amongst the members of The Org," he said. When I didn't respond to his statement, he continued. "You are stunning, Ella. Such an exotic face." He cupped my chin gently and studied me.

I held back the urge to roll my eyes and forced a smile to my lips as I said, "Thank you."

The Official abruptly dropped his hand and turned to Zeke. "So, my son, who decided to endorse Miss Silver, hmmm?"

"Both Smithson and me. He just managed to give her his pendant before I could give her mine," Zeke answered calmly.

"That is not the way things are supposed to be done. Smithson should have consulted with me first," The Official said with a furrowed brow.

I couldn't place The Official's accent. It was a smooth hybrid of intonations and, even though it wasn't too thick, I clearly heard that he rolled the "r" in his words.

"I agree that we both should have consulted with you first, yes. But, in this matter, all I ask is that you trust our judgment. Ella is special. She's a great asset to have. We didn't want to wait too long to get her on board."

I stood there in silence, listening to Zeke's explanation. He was a brilliant liar. So brilliant, in fact, that I almost believed him for a second. It wasn't what he was saying, but how he was saying it.

The Official raised one eyebrow. "What is her talent?"

"She has many," Zeke said, but didn't elaborate further.

"That's funny because, from the background check that Alissa did for me, it appears Ella here is just an ordinary, everyday citizen," The Official said as he reached for a folder that was on top of the little coffee table and opened it to reveal the contents. I glanced down briefly at the documents in the folder that appeared to contain detailed information about me. "A normal, innocent girl."

"She does seem that way, doesn't she?" Zeke said flatly.

The Official squinted his eyes at him. "You are being very secretive. I don't like secrets," he said. *That's ironic.* He inhaled deeply then shook his head slowly. "But you have never steered me wrong before, Zeke, so I would like to think that this instance is no different. If you say that she is truly useful to us, then I believe you." When The Official said that, the younger man standing next to Knight rolled his eyes.

"I appreciate your confidence in me, sir," Zeke said. "I assure you that Ella will be a great advantage to us. Her seeming innocence is her strength. The best kinds of Org members are the ones that no one suspects. She'll fit in with us just fine."

The Official came to stand in front of me. "I consider all of the members of The Org to be my children. I see them as my family. And in any family, loyalty comes first. Always. Do you promise to always be loyal to me, Ella? And to me alone?" he asked me.

I felt shivers go down my spine at the thought of committing myself to something like that. Shivers of fear. "Yes," I said hoarsely.

The Official smiled wide. "Then welcome to The Organization, my child." He kissed me on both cheeks and then took a step back. "I'll put out the word that I have accepted Ella's endorsement," he said to Zeke before asking him, "Is that all?"

"Almost. I would like to request that Ella come with me whenever I'm carrying out any of my duties, including my meetings with you. She's going to be my right hand, and I need to show her all the ropes before she can start handling duties on her own. Also, I would like her to enter as top-tier."

"Understandable. That's fine with me, my son."

Zeke looked at me and said, "Before we go, I should complete introductions. Ella, that's Jet, The Official's son. And you met Mr. Knight, Jet's bodyguard."

"Welcome to The Org, Ella," Jet said, completely monotone. There was no warmth in his words. His accent, unlike his father's, was distinctly American.

"Thank you," I replied.

Zeke put his hand on the small of my back lightly and said, "We should be leaving now, Ella." He turned to The Official. "Thank you for your acceptance, Official. If you need anything, sir, you know where to find us."

"Of course. Enjoy your stay here," The Official said with a warm smile.

As we made our way to the door to leave, accompanied by Knight, I played our short meeting back over and over in my head. The Official seemed friendly, and his demeanour was fatherly but, like I said, I'm good at detecting vibes. The Official, despite his jovial manner, was not a good man. I could feel it. His aura told the story of something more sinister. Even if I hadn't known that he ran a network of assassins and drug dealers, I still would have been able to sense the cruelty radiating off him. And he was the worst kind of bad guy because he was the deceptive kind. The kind of bad guy that made you question your own instincts, made you almost want to trust him. I only hoped that I got out of The Org before he could ever reveal to me just how bad he was.

****

Both Zeke and I got back to the suite much more relaxed than when we had left it. "That went well, right?" I asked enthusiastically.

"As well as it could have," Zeke answered.

"We were in there for, like, five minutes. It was actually kind of anticlimactic," I joked.

"It was, wasn't it?" he replied with a smile.

I sat down on my bed and thought about the three men that I had just met. "Hey, why is Knight assigned to only be Jet's bodyguard? Doesn't The Official need security, too?" I asked out of curiosity.

"Knight's father used to be Jet's bodyguard. He was assigned that duty by The Official as soon as Jet was born. His sole purpose was to protect *him*. Unfortunately, Knight's father died about nine years ago and, after that, Knight took over as Jet's security. Technically he protects both Jet and The Official but, because he specifically watches over Jet, everyone just refers to him as Jet's bodyguard. Also, they're close. Jet doesn't go anywhere without him. They practically grew up together, so they're like brothers. And I'm pretty sure Jet loved Knight's dad like he was his own father." Zeke paused, as if he were in thought, before continuing. "The Official has never used bodyguards. Maybe he thinks he doesn't need any because very few people know what he looks like anyway. Like I said, him staying hidden is his security. But, honestly, I think it's just because of his ego. I think he just doesn't want to feel like a coward."

"He sounds like a complicated guy, The Official. Just like Ethel told me," I mused.

"He is," Zeke replied.

"Is Knight's name really 'Knight'? Or is he a mystery as well? That name is way too coincidental in relation to his job, don't you think?" I asked him after a moment's pause.

Zeke chuckled. "No mystery, Ella. Just pure coincidence. That's really his last name. It's a family name. The Knights in The Org traditionally perform security duties. It's their skill, and they're born into it. We've never called them by their first names. They're all just referred to as 'Knight.' "

"So his dad was, what, Knight Senior?"

"Basically."

I snorted. "What is it with The Org and its members having no names?"

Zeke shrugged. "That's just the job." He changed the subject before I could get into my usual ten-thousand-questions interview mode. "We'll be here for another week. I'm thinking you could do with a little break after the time you've had. I'll book a couple of activities for us while we're here, just so we get back Stateside refreshed. What do you think?"

I smiled brightly at him. "Sounds like fun. I'm in."

****

I could tell that Zeke was feeling less tense, almost laid back, and it looked good on him. The Official's request to meet with me had obviously been weighing heavily on him, and I was glad to see that the burden had been lifted. It had been about an hour since our meeting, and Zeke had offered to take me on a tour of the resort and show me all the amenities that he had seen earlier.

As we walked down one of the resort's garden pathways, I was startled to see Smithson sitting on a wooden bench and casually people-watching. I had no idea that he was also in Zimbabwe and staying at the resort as well, but Zeke didn't seem at all surprised that he was there.

He stood from the bench when he spotted us approaching. The only indication that he hadn't been expecting to see us there was a slight tilt of his head and a brief narrowing of his eyes. "Gage," he said to Zeke in greeting.

"Smithson," Zeke replied.

Smithson looked over at me and said, "Ella. I'm glad to see you."

"Hey, Smithson," I greeted, still finding it difficult to believe that he was a killer. I reached behind me and took off the pendant that he had given to me, holding it out to him. "This belongs to you," I said quietly.

He took it from my hand slowly. "I guess this means that everything went well?" Smithson inquired

176

of Zeke.

"It did. We're all set," Zeke answered.

"Well then, welcome to The Org, Ella," he said with a smile, but there was sadness in his eyes. "I want you to know that we didn't mean for any of this to happen. But I'm glad that everything has gone as smoothly as it has, given the circumstances."

Smithson looked so sincere as he spoke that I struggled to maintain my disapproval of him. "Thanks," I replied quickly, and then forced myself to focus on the fact that he intentionally hurt people on a regular basis. "Hurt" being a very mild way of putting it. "I met your pal Al," I said before I could stop myself. I hated that I still found Smithson likeable. He obviously did terrible things, but I got the feeling that, deep down inside, he was a good man. Way, way deep down inside, of course.

"Al, huh?" Smithson raised one eyebrow inquisitively. "What makes you think we're pals?"

"You both kill people for a living," I stated flatly. Now that I had opened up that particular line of conversation, I wanted him to know that I was aware of his occupation.

"I see. And what do you think of…my pal Al?" he asked me, seeming completely unbothered by my statement.

"Well, she was sent to kill me so, needless to say, I'm not her biggest fan."

Smithson chuckled. "Al…Al is, uh, a different breed. And I know she can come across as a little overbearing, but she's not as bad as she seems, believe me."

I didn't understand how he could say that, given

the nature of her job, but I didn't argue. *Maybe they have some kind of killer-code that obligates them to protect each other's reputation,* I thought sarcastically.

"I heard you'd be here. Usual business?" Zeke asked him.

"Yup. Same old, same old. The Official asked me to handle something here. I obliged. And you two? What brings you here?" Smithson questioned.

"Random errands," Zeke answered cryptically.

Smithson gave Zeke a shrewd look before turning his gaze to the setting sun. The sky was a beautiful canvas of gold, orange, and purple. "He's here, isn't he?" he asked without looking away from the glorious Zimbabwean sunset. Zeke didn't answer, but Smithson nodded his head to himself anyway, as if he had received confirmation of the accuracy of his suspicions. "It's strange, you know? Speaking to a man I've never met. Staying at the same resort as him and not even knowing what he looks like. I could walk right past him." He glanced toward the massive resort building. "Everything is so secretive."

"That's the job," Zeke stated, just like he had when we were in our suite.

Smithson gave a small smile. "That's the job," he agreed. He checked his watch and abruptly announced, "I have a lot to do before I leave this place. I'd better get going. I'm sure I'll be seeing you both again soon."

He turned to walk away after we had said our courteous goodbyes, and I suddenly felt the need to thank him. The fact was that he had saved my life, and he deserved to know that I appreciated it. "Smithson," I called to him. He turned back around and I walked over to him, giving him a quick hug around the waist.

"Thank you," I whispered.

I let go of him and he was smiling, a real smile this time. There was understanding in his eyes. "Ella, it was my pleasure," he replied. Then he looked at Zeke and said, "Take care of this one. Something tells me she'll be good for us." He strolled away without any further explanation, whistling a random tune.

Zeke didn't respond to Smithson's statement but instead took my hand again and said, "Come on, let's head back up. We've got a busy itinerary this week, and we'll need to be rested."

****

Zeke wasn't kidding when he said that we had a lot of activities to get through. Our stay at Injabulo Ranch consisted of numerous indoor and outdoor pursuits including a cooking class which, of course, I excelled at. A couple of days into the week, we traveled to Victoria Falls for more water-based recreational fun before our stay in Zimbabwe came to an end.

We didn't see The Official again at all after our first meeting and, during our self-declared mini-vacation, Zeke and I started talking late at night just like we used to at The Lost Cantrell. It made me feel almost normal again, almost like my life was getting back on track. Almost.

****

We arrived back in the States jetlagged but relieved at how everything had turned out. Despite our long flight, Zeke got back into his usual work routine without missing a beat. It had barely been an hour since we had gotten settled back in his condo before he announced, "I have somewhere I need to be right now, but I should be back in a couple of hours. I'll be taking

CP along with me but if you need anything, just call."

"Oh, okay. That's cool," I replied, already missing the time that we had spent together in Zimbabwe as I watched him get up from the couch. "Um, can I ask you something?" I inquired tentatively.

"Sure," Zeke said as he put his jacket back on.

"Are you seeing someone?" I asked. He looked over at me with one eyebrow raised in question. "It's just that you go out a lot, and you've never brought anyone over or anything. I was just wondering if maybe you have a girlfriend somewhere whom you go to see? I know it's none of my business, but I just want to be sure that your partner is okay with you having a random woman in your apartment. And I don't want you to feel uncomfortable with bringing someone over just because I'm here."

Zeke smiled. "You don't have to worry about that, Ella. I'm not seeing anyone."

"Do you ever get lonely?"

"Not really, no. No time to feel lonely."

"So, you're okay with being alone? You've never thought about dating or finding someone to commit to?"

"I don't have enough time for dating, either. And I'm sure most women wouldn't approve of what I do for a living."

"What about the women in The Org? They would obviously understand your, uh, job." I faltered, unable to convincingly call being a part of a criminal network a "job." "None of them tickle your fancy?"

"No. But even if one of them did, I wouldn't be able to act on it. One of the rules in The Org is that members aren't allowed to become romantically involved. If any members enter into a relationship with each other and get found out, one of them has to go. One way or another."

"What? Why?"

Zeke shrugged. "It keeps emotions from getting in the way of work, I suppose."

"But Ethel and The Official dated, right?"

Zeke leaned against the front door, which he had slowly made his way to. "Yes, but that was before he made her a member. As soon as she became a part of The Org, he ended their relationship."

"That's crazy."

"That's the life we live."

"Is it worth it?"

He smiled sadly. "Not anymore. Maybe it never was. But it's what we deserve," he said. "A lot of members are in relationships with normal people whom they lie to about what they do and where they are. Doesn't seem fair."

"No, it doesn't," I said thoughtfully.

Zeke checked his watch. "I gotta go. I'll be back soon."

Just as he opened the door to leave, I stopped him. "Hey, Zeke," I called out. He turned back around to face me. "I know you said you don't get lonely, and that's great if that's the case. But, if you ever do, I want you to know that you have me now. For as long as I'm in The Org, you won't have to be lonely." I wanted us to be friends, and I didn't want him to only see me as some burden that he was stuck looking out for all the time.

He gave me a look that I couldn't read. "For as long as you're in The Org," he repeated slowly. "Best enjoy the time I have with you, then," he said with a soft smile.

"Best you do that," I replied light-heartedly, returning his smile. He studied me briefly and then finally turned to leave without any further prevention from me.

After he left, I let my thoughts drift to my official welcome as an Org member. On our flight back from Zimbabwe, just before we'd landed in the States, Zeke had told me that my welcome ceremony was planned for the next day. *Tomorrow. It's happening tomorrow.* I was going to become a member of a secret criminal organization, and there was nothing that I could do about it.

Chapter 12

The time for my official welcome ceremony came way too quickly for my liking. It had been just over twenty-four hours since Zeke had told me about the scheduled dinner, and I still didn't feel completely emotionally prepared for it as I psyched myself up to leave my bedroom. Ethel had helped me get ready for the evening's events, and I was feeling even less like myself in the figure-hugging, off the shoulder black dress that she had squeezed me into. I stared at myself in the mirror, trying to pull some relief from the fact that Ethel had told me she would also be attending my welcome ceremony, just before she had taken off to get a head start on us.

I eventually walked out of my room as I attempted, and failed, to control the incessant tremor in my hands. Zeke stood in the living room, wearing a fitted dark-blue suit and looking incredibly dapper. He smiled at me as I stepped into the room tentatively, donning another pair of torture-worthy heels. "You look stunning, Ella," he said.

"Thank you. You look really good, too."

"Thank you." He offered me his arm. "Ready?"

Nope. "Yup."

We headed downstairs where Chris waited for us at the car, looking rather dapper himself. I smiled at him and greeted, "Hey, Chris! Love the suit."

His cheeks flushed a little and he replied, "Thanks, Ella. You look great."

Zeke opened the car door for me, and I got inside, settling in the backseat. As he slid in next to me and closed the door, I turned toward him and asked, "This is a huge deal for The Org, isn't it? A new member being welcomed in."

"Yeah, it is. It doesn't happen very often anymore, and especially not in the way it's happening with you."

"So, should I be terrified or just anxious?" I asked with a nervous laugh.

Zeke's mouth curved up on one side. "Neither. Just be ready."

Fair enough. "I'm ready," I told him, trying to convince myself that it was true and getting acquainted with the feeling of resignation in my gut.

"Good," he answered. "Just one last thing." He took out a long strip of black fabric from his jacket pocket and held it up in front of me.

I stared at it blankly. "What's that for?" I inquired.

"This is for your safety. It's a good ol' fashioned blindfold."

I looked at him like he had just lost his mind, because he must have if he seriously expected me to willingly let him put a blindfold over my eyes. "You want *me* to put that on?"

"Yes."

"No."

"Ella…"

"No! Why on earth would I do that? I don't even know where you're taking me."

"That's the point. Plausible deniability, remember? I don't want you to see how to get to the meeting place so that if you're ever questioned, you won't need to worry about having to lie." He sighed when I looked at him skeptically. "I want to get you out of this, Ella. And as much as I need you to be prepared for anything that may come your way while you're a member, I also need to make sure that you don't see more than is necessary. For your safety. I want you to get back to your normal life soon.

"You won't be in The Org for long, so the route to the meeting place isn't something you need to know. As far as I'm concerned, this is the first and last time that you'll ever step foot in there, if I can help it."

I glanced at Chris, who had already taken his position comfortably in the driver's seat. He always managed to seem as if he wasn't listening to our conversations, but I knew that he was. I looked back at Zeke and studied his face intently.

I had seen with my own eyes just how brilliant a liar he was, so I had no idea why I still believed him. I guess it was because he always sounded so sincere. All brilliant liars do, I suppose. But, despite my reservations, I turned my back to him slowly, pointedly giving him an indignant glare as I did.

"Thank you," he whispered in my ear just before placing the fabric over my eyes. My view of the car's interior turned to pitch-black, and I shifted my body to face forward again.

"Let's go, CP," Zeke said.

****

After a drive that felt like it took hours, the car came to a smooth, quiet halt. Hands at the back of my head gently untied the blindfold, and then my eyes were once again free to behold the scenery around me. Truth

185

be told, the view wasn't anything to write home about. In fact, it was completely underwhelming.

I looked out of the tinted window of the car and squinted my eyes at what appeared to be an old, abandoned warehouse in the middle of nowhere. There was no lighting anywhere, save for the dim lights of the car that were still on. As my eyes adjusted to the poorly lit area, I could make out quite a large number of other vehicles in the dusty expanse surrounding the warehouse, but that was it. I turned my head and stared at Zeke, feeling mildly puzzled. "You said that a new member entering The Org was a big deal," I stated flatly.

"It is."

"Then why would you welcome them in a dusty, old warehouse?"

Zeke shrugged. "It's secluded. No one really comes out here. And it makes for good camouflage, don't you think?"

I snorted at his response. "So much for feeling special. Why did we even bother to dress up? I'm probably going to get sand in my shoes," I grumbled. My irritation was irrational, a mere symptom of my fear. I wouldn't admit that I was scared though. Instead, I muttered, "Secluded, my foot. Abandoned is more like it." I rolled my eyes and shook my head at the unimpressive venue, just for good measure.

"We're a criminal organization, Ella. We don't exactly tend to do things out in the open," Zeke told me matter-of-factly. I continued to stare at him in annoyance, and he added dryly, "I could always carry you in. Would that make you feel special?"

"Ha ha. Very funny, Zeke. Let's just get this over

with before I come to my senses and change my mind." I knew that I could only look for excuses to complain for so long before I had to suck it up and go through the process. Procrastination wouldn't help anything.

Chris switched off the lights and we all exited the car, making our way the short distance to the warehouse entrance in the eerie darkness. We stopped at the door, and I took a moment to exhale slowly and calm myself.

Zeke pressed his thumb against a small, inconspicuous black square on the side of the door, and a green light flashed over it briefly before a clicking noise sounded. He pushed on the door and held it open for me. I peeked inside and saw that there was no lighting within the warehouse either. It was completely dark. "After you," Zeke said. I gave him a hesitant glance and he reassured me, "Everything is going to be fine. This is the easy part, believe me. It's going to be smooth sailing from here on out."

I stepped into the warehouse cautiously. Zeke used the torch on his phone to light the way and, after Chris had closed the door quietly behind us, we made our way slowly across the empty room. "Where are we going?" I asked in a whisper that came out sounding way more panicked than I had wanted it to.

Zeke took a few more steps and then answered at a normal volume, "Upstairs." He pointed to a flight of metal steps leading to the next floor of the warehouse and added, "I'll go first so I can lead the way for you."

I followed him as he made his way up the stairs and, for a moment, I felt secure, thanks to Chris's presence behind me. But the closer we got to the next floor, the more I had to admit to myself that I was terrified. I had no idea what awaited me.

When we reached the landing, Zeke walked up to yet another door with yet another inconspicuous black square screen on it. He pressed his thumb to it as well but this time when he pushed the door open, the sight that greeted us was anything but empty and dark.

The brightly-lit room was full of people who were dressed just as fashionably as we were. There was soft jazz playing in the background, complementing the extravagant décor, and a plush red carpet leading from the door down the center of the room to a stage where a glass podium stood. Several round dinner tables were arranged neatly throughout the room, and the windows were all covered by heavy blinds. That explained why it was impossible to see any light from outside. The walls even looked to be soundproof. Just like Zeke had said, the place was camouflaged. The dull exterior of the warehouse was a clever illusion. *I guess this is a big deal after all.*

As we stepped farther inside, all the chatter that had been going on stopped, and the many faces in the room turned to stare at us. Zeke leaned in closer to me and whispered in my ear, "Our table is in the front."

Taking that as my cue to walk, I headed slowly toward the front of the room with Zeke beside me. We passed by several people who greeted him and Chris politely. Maybe they tried to greet me too, but I kept my eyes forward and my jaw tightly clenched. When we reached the front, Zeke guided me to the table nearest the stage. We sat down quietly, he and Chris looking quite comfortable and me looking quite the opposite, wondering what the heck was going to happen next.

I didn't have to wait long to find out. Zeke gave a

single nod to a chubby, balding, middle-aged man with a rounded paunch who was standing across from our table. The man walked up onto the stage, moving to stand behind the podium. As he did so, the rest of the guests took seats at the various tables in the room.

The pudgy man cleared his throat before speaking directly into the microphone. "Good evening, Members of The Org. Thank you for being present today for this very special event. An Official Welcome Ceremony." The man paused his speech as the guests all applauded in a controlled manner. When the room had quieted down, he continued, "I am your host, Judge Woods. As usual, I will be conducting the Ceremony proceedings." His eyes swept across the room quickly. "It appears that all the relevant parties are here, so there is no need for me to prolong this introduction. I know you're all anxious to meet the new addition. She has been endorsed by two top-tier members, after all." A few hushed whispers traveled throughout the room, and I had to make a conscious effort to not fidget in my seat. "Without further ado, I invite Ella-Cherie Silver and top-tier members, Zeke Gage and Colt Smithson, to the fore."

I followed Zeke's lead, rising from the table and walking up onto the stage. Smithson appeared from the other side of the room, where he had apparently been sitting at another table near the stage. Zeke stood closest to Judge Woods on my right side. Smithson stood to my left, and I glanced up at him briefly. The expression on his face was somber, nothing close to the usual joviality that I had come to know him for.

Judge Woods held out his hand toward the guests on our left, his eyes focusing on something in that general direction. It must have been some kind of signal because a young man stood up from a nearby table and walked onto the stage. He hurried toward the judge, carrying a medium-sized, square, black, velvet box. "Thank you, Colin," the judge said, taking the box out of the young man's hands. Colin quickly walked off the stage again, his head bowed. "Ella-Cherie, may you stand next to me, please," the judge requested politely.

Zeke stepped aside as I moved to stand next to Judge Woods, who turned to face me completely and said, "Ella-Cherie Silver, in order for us to accept you as a member of The Org, we need to know that we can trust you. The oath you shall take is the promise of your loyalty to The Org until your death. All you have to do is answer 'yes' to the questions that I ask you. Only if you agree with the terms, of course." From the way the judge glanced at his audience humorously and low chuckles flowed through the room, I figured not agreeing with the terms wasn't something they expected me to do, nor was it an option. "Do you accept the invitation to take this oath?"

I swallowed hard. "Yes," I whispered.

"Good. Let's begin. Give me your hand." I did as he said, and he took hold of my outstretched hand gently and placed it on top of the velvet box. "Ella-Cherie Silver, do you promise to serve The Org before yourself?"

"Yes."

"Do you promise to always put the other members, your brothers and sisters, first? To protect them when need be?"

"Yes."

"Do you promise to be loyal to The Official as

your leader? To be loyal to The Org as your family?"

"Yes."

"Will you honor your membership…" he began, and then paused to make sure that I was looking him in the eyes before continuing, "…until your death? Will you choose death before disloyalty?"

I forced myself not to blink as I answered. *Only liars blink when they're asked a question, right? Or do people blink when they're telling the truth?* In that moment, I honestly couldn't remember. But I kept my eyes focused on his anyway as I said, "Yes."

The judge smiled like a proud parent. "Gage, Smithson," he said, nodding at the two men who both slowly moved closer to him. Smithson took the black box from Judge Woods' hands, turned, opened it, and held it out toward Zeke, its contents clear to see. Zeke carefully pulled out the sparkling chain that the velvet case held and stepped behind me. "Ella-Cherie Silver, we welcome you," Judge Woods said as Zeke maneuvered the piece of jewelry over my head and let it rest around my neck like a decorated noose.

"We welcome you," everyone else in the room repeated in unison. It was the closest thing to a cult-like experience that I had ever witnessed in real life, and I had to swallow a couple of times to keep bile from rising up my throat. Judge Woods turned toward the other members who sat patiently at their various tables and addressed them. "As our new member, until death, we eagerly accept Ella-Cherie Silver. Top-tier."

The room erupted into applause and cheers, way more raucous than before. I looked around and took in all the smiles on the members' faces. *They're genuinely happy about this. About making me a professional criminal.* I forced a smile onto my face too, just to feign being grateful for their warm welcome. I had to. Plus, if I hadn't forced a smile, I probably would have cried. Or I would have hurled, and that would have been even worse than crying. "Now let the celebration begin!" Judge Woods exclaimed, his jowls quivering with his excitement.

I stared down blankly at my brand-new gold and black sapphire pendant. Top-tier, just like Zeke had requested. The room was still buzzing with uncontained energy when Zeke finally said quietly into my ear, "That's it, Ella. It's done."

I followed him off the stage, keeping my eyes downcast. We got seated back at our table and I glanced at Zeke, noting his completely calm expression and the way he rested his arm casually on the table surface. "It's time for you to meet some of the other members. Socialize a little," he stated, turning in his seat to face me.

"Socialize?" I asked. We were the only ones at our table, besides Chris, but we were still keeping our voices as low as possible.

"Yeah."

"But I don't socialize. I mean, I'm not supposed to talk."

"You don't have to talk. Just hang around and let them talk to you. And smile when you feel like it."

"I'll never feel like it around these people," I told him with a glare.

His eyes narrowed briefly, then he licked his lips before sighing and asking flatly, "How about a mild attempt at being courteous, then?"

I was on the verge of telling him exactly where the

members of The Org could shove that imaginary courtesy when a dark-haired man walked up to our table and introduced himself. I didn't pay attention to what he said his name was, but I did hear him mention that he was somehow involved with the FBI. He shook my hand firmly and told me that if I ever needed anything, he would be more than happy to help me with his "resources."

After him, more and more members came over to our table to congratulate me as if I had done something worth the praise. Sy, one of the men who had been in Zeke's suite the night I saw the whole gore-filled scene that had gotten me into this mess in the first place, was present as well. He greeted me with a bright smile and said, "We meet again, Ella. Better circumstances this time, yeah?" I smiled at him as convincingly as I could. "Welcome to The Org. Officially." He winked at me and strode away.

It went on like that for a while. Strangers welcoming me with joyous smiles. Lawyers, cops, businessmen. It was a melting pot of achievers. Criminal achievers, but still. "Ella," a smooth female voice said with an exaggerated affection that was undeniably fake. I looked up at the slim figure standing to the right of me, and my eyes eventually met Al's. Before I could register what was happening, she leaned over to give me a hug. "My, my, didn't you dodge a bullet?" she whispered in my ear, the tone of her voice overly warm in contrast to her cold words. She released me and walked away with a mischievous grin on her face. *Psycho*, I thought as I watched her sashay away.

Ethel came over and gave me a kiss on my cheek but didn't say a word. After that, I did my best to keep a polite smile on my face the rest of the night, and I moved around the room trying to mingle with the crowd silently as much as my anxiety would allow. Despite the location of the event, it was obvious that an Official Welcome was, indeed, a big deal. The food was delicious, served with a flourish by waiters who were apparently lower-level gang members, and the décor was classic. A whole lot of money had been spent to organize my welcome and by the end of the night I had to admit, even though I knew the kind of people that I was surrounded by, the mood in the room was pleasant. Regardless, I was still relieved when Zeke checked his phone and finally began to tell the other members that we needed to take off.

Everyone said their jovial goodbyes, and Zeke ushered me out of the warehouse, with Chris following closely behind. When we were back in the safety of the car, I let out a breath and asked, "How'd I do?"

Chris replied, "Great. You were a natural," at the same time that Zeke answered, "You did well, Ella."

I grinned at them. "An innocent girl like me fooling a room full of career criminals. Who would have thought?" I made it sound like a joke, but I was actually a little proud of myself for keeping my cool. "So, what now?" I asked Zeke.

"Now we go through the motions. Until I can get you out."

We were still parked outside the warehouse, and I glanced at it, my curiosity slowly rising as I thought about the people that I'd just met. "Were those all the New York members?"

"No. Not everyone is here tonight. It would be impossible to let every member in New York attend a welcome event here because of our numbers. And work still has to be done, so we need some members to stay on the ground. You just met the people who need to know you first. You'll meet everyone else on the job."

On the job. Through crime, you mean! Choosing not to voice my thoughts, I leaned my head against the headrest as I closed my eyes. "My feet are killing me. Can't wait to get back to the apartment and relax."

"We'll be back home soon, Ella. We just need to make a stop somewhere first."

I turned my head to face him without lifting it up from the comfortable position that it was in and looked at him through narrowed eyes. "Where are you taking me now, Zeke Gage?" I grumbled.

"We have to attend a meeting with a potential member. He might have some new business for us."

****

"Ethel's going to kill me if I ruin these shoes," I said with a groan as I lifted up one of my feet in an attempt to get a better look at the soles of my pricey stilettos. It turned out that the so-called meeting that Zeke had rushed us to attend was happening in a dingy alley behind a café that was frequented by college students. The ground was sticky, and there were even a couple of rats joining in our gathering.

"She'll understand," Zeke stated, completely unbothered.

"No, she won't," I muttered under my breath. Chris had dropped us off, as per Zeke's instruction, and he was apparently supposed to meet us back in the same spot after ten minutes. We'd been waiting in the alley for approximately four minutes already. I knew this because I kept checking the time on my phone, anxiously waiting to get the heck out of there. "Where is this guy? We've been here for four minutes." I looked down at my phone again. "Five minutes. We've been here for *five* minutes with no communication from this guy. I'm starting to get nervous."

"You're nervous? I hadn't noticed."

I rolled my eyes at Zeke's sarcasm. "I'm serious. Maybe he's not coming."

"Timing is everything, Ella," Zeke said calmly, just as a man wearing all black rounded the corner and came hurrying toward us. His messy blond hair was sticking out from under his beanie, and his brow was furrowed like he was worried.

"Am I late?" he asked when he reached us, concern lacing his voice.

"No," Zeke answered. "We're just early."

"Oh. Cool." The man looked around nervously before composing himself. "How you doin', Zeke?"

"I'm good, Ant," Zeke replied and then looked in my direction. "This is Ella. She's a new member. Ella, this is Antony Castle but everyone just calls him Ant."

Ant eyed me for a moment before saying, "It's nice to meet you, Ella. Congratulations on getting in."

I nodded once but didn't say a word. Ant gave me a questioning look. "She doesn't talk much," Zeke told him, leaving no room for Ant to become inquisitive. "Your message said you had some news for me."

"Oh, uh, yeah. So, I've got this cousin, right? Name's Benton but he goes by Benny. Bad Benny on the streets. Anyway, he runs the whole block where the Windton University campus is, just down the street over there." He pointed behind him and to his right. "He deals there full time through some of the students who're enrolled. He's making a killing off those college kids, so I was thinking that we could get him to join your crew. That would expand your dealer pool without you guys having to take his territory from him by force at some point. If we tell him that your syndicate is planning to run most of the city soon, but that you guys are willing to let him join and keep dealing around here as a member, then it's a win-win. As an incentive, maybe you can give him an extra territory to deal in later or something. You guys get a cut from his campus dealings since he'll be a part of your mob, and he gets to expand, too. Like I said, win-win."

Ant shrugged nervously before rambling on. "You said that if I can prove myself to you and show you that I can bring in new business then you'd let me join your secret group, right? I figure this is a good way to prove myself."

I had no doubt that this whole grand meeting was about drugs, and that made it all the more terrible to be in attendance. Zeke studied Ant in silence and the other man shrank back under his critical stare. Finally, Zeke spoke up. "All right, Ant. If you can pull this off, then you would have earned a spot. Entry-level, of course."

"That works for me. So I'll go ahead and set up a meeting."

"You do that," Zeke said just as Chris pulled into the alley slowly and came to a halt right in front of us. *Timing, indeed.* "Don't let me down, Ant." Zeke opened the back door of the car for me to get in and then swiftly followed after me.

"I won't, I promise," Ant replied quickly. His tone was determined as he spoke, and I found myself completely surprised, yet again that evening, at just how many people actually wanted to be professional criminals.

As we pulled off, I turned to face Zeke and asked, "How does Ant know about The Org? He's not a member yet, and I thought it was a secret."

"He overheard one of our guys slip up and mention Org business publicly somewhere. No names or details, but Ant's been obsessed with knowing more and being a part of it ever since," he answered.

"How much does he know?"

"Just enough for him to want in. Not enough to get him killed."

I looked out of the window, not needing any further details, but Zeke continued to speak next to me. "Now that we're done with all of the introductions, we can talk about your compensation."

"My compensation?"

"Yeah, as a member. For the work you'll be doing."

"You mean the criminal activity that I'm now a part of?"

Zeke shifted uncomfortably. "Yes, *that* work. Technically, you won't actually be doing anything. We just want the other members to think you are." He shrugged. "I'm assuming you'll want to make money somehow now that you won't be working at The Lost Cantrell for a while. Just something to make this whole ordeal worth the trouble."

Even though Zeke said, "*for a while*," I knew he meant, "*ever*." The Org didn't let members keep full-time jobs that weren't beneficial to its operations in some way, and we had already established that my being able to chef up 5-star meals wasn't exactly what they were looking for in a top-tier member. I swallowed down my anger at the situation and managed to say, "No, thanks. I'm good without it."

"Ella—"

"I don't want it," I cut him off sharply. "You honestly think that money will make *any* of this worth it?" I took a deep breath to calm myself down. "Please just let me preserve a small part of my soul. I don't want to get paid to be a bad person. I can't do that. I won't. I'll find another way to make money with my skills."

Zeke didn't push the matter, and we drove the rest of the way to his condo in uncomfortable silence.

Chapter 13

The best part about uncomfortable situations? They don't last.

Things got better after I told Zeke that I wouldn't accept any payment from The Org. In the weeks that followed my new membership, Zeke and I began to talk more. We spent time together because he took me along with him when he was going to meet other members, and he didn't have to hide me in the apartment anymore. We joked around, talked like friends and, because we spent all day with each other, we developed a familiarity that I enjoyed.

When we had free time, we would hang out in his apartment, just like Stace and I used to at our brownstone. I was gradually getting used to my new circumstances, mostly because the couple of weeks that I had been a member were highly uneventful. And uneventful suited me just fine. I had even started to relax, somewhat.

One particularly calm afternoon, when Zeke had a mostly free day, we were sitting in the living room together having one of our usual conversations, when a quiet knock sounded at the door. "I'll get it," I told Zeke, jumping up from the couch. This was another symptom of how comfortable I was in his condo. When I first moved in, I would have never answered the door myself because Zeke wouldn't have allowed it, fearing for my safety.

I looked through the peephole then pulled the door open with a smile. "Hey, Chris," I greeted. He was standing there alone, dressed in his usual shirt and formal pants combo.

"Hey, Ella," he said. I stepped to the side, giving him room to enter, but he stayed rooted to his spot. "I'm not coming in. I just came here to talk to you, actually."

"Yeah? What's up?"

He cleared his throat. "I was thinking that maybe I could go and check in on Stacey. You know, make sure she's okay. I had promised that I would, but I couldn't make the time because I needed to make sure you were secure, too. But, um, since you're a member now, you're safe. I figure I can check in on her?"

I smiled at him. "Are you asking my permission to go and see my best friend?"

Chris's face turned red. "Uh, yeah, I guess I am. I just want to know that you're okay with it."

My smile grew even bigger at his response. It was cute. But I didn't own Stace, and I definitely didn't have the right to speak for her. "I like you, CP. You're a good guy," I told him. "Honestly, it's up to her and not me. But if she said it's what she wants, then why not? I do recall her accepting your offer to check in, right? And I'd feel better knowing you're watching out for her anyway."

Chris exhaled softly and relaxed. "Great. Thank you."

"Sure."

He stood there awkwardly for a second then eventually said, "Well, uh, I'd better get going."

"Okay. Let me know how it goes," I replied with a grin.

Chris smiled back at me before walking purposefully down the hallway. I closed the door behind me and went back to the living room with a little bounce in my step.

"That was Chris," I told Zeke as I dropped my body heavily onto the couch again. "He wanted to know if I was okay with him checking in on Stace from now on. I am. I think she'll like that."

"CP is good people. I have no doubt that his intentions are sincere." There was something akin to affection in his voice when he spoke about Chris.

"Are you and Chris close?" I asked.

"We've known each other for a while now. I trust him with my life. He's never given me a reason not to."

"So he's like family to you," I stated.

"Yeah, I suppose he is," Zeke agreed.

I used the direction of our conversation as an opportunity to venture into territory that we had never been before. "Where's your real family?"

Zeke went still for a moment, his body tense, and then eventually he replied flatly, "My dad lives here in New York."

My eyes widened. "Wait, your real dad lives here? In New York?" I asked in surprise.

"Yeah."

"What does he do?"

Zeke scratched the back of his head and chuckled. "Uh, he's a pastor actually."

"Really?" I had to admit to myself that I wasn't expecting that answer.

"Yeah. Funny, huh? That he ended up with a son

like me."

"There's nothing wrong with you, Zeke. Nothing beyond redemption."

Zeke shrugged. "I guess."

"So, what's he like?" I asked, leaning in with interest.

Zeke smiled. "He's great. He's an amazing dad. How I turned out isn't any fault of his. He's kind and caring. Even now."

"You still see him?"

"Yeah, I go to see him often. He doesn't know what I do for a living, obviously. He's always trying to get me to attend church."

I perked up. "So we should go."

"I don't know."

"Why not?"

"I just don't think church is a place for someone like me."

"Trust me, church is exactly the place for you. People don't attend church because they're perfect, Zeke. They attend to be better. Everyone has their flaws."

He smiled, but it didn't reach his eyes. "I guess so."

I studied his sad face. "How exactly did you get involved with The Org, anyway?" I asked him, hoping he wouldn't close up on me.

Zeke leaned back, his eyes going a little distant. I held my breath, waiting patiently for him to speak. "When I was about fifteen years old, I started hanging out with a bad crowd. I gravitated toward them. The whole rebellious thing. Deep down, we were all decent kids. Just didn't know how to express ourselves, I guess. Anyway, one night, when we were about seventeen, the cops ran up on us while we were messing around where we shouldn't have been." He didn't bother going into detail about what exactly they were doing, and I didn't even attempt to get him to. Him opening up to me was enough.

"Everybody else got away, but I got caught. I hadn't even bothered running. So I was taken in and they called my dad to let him know that his son was a delinquent." He snickered. "They asked me a bunch of questions, like who I had been with at the time, what their names were. I didn't tell them, obviously. No one wants to be a snitch."

His mouth turned up in a self-deprecating smile. "Word got around about the preacher's kid who wouldn't talk. Turns out, one of the kids I was rolling with at the time had a dad who was in The Org. Lower-level gang member, but he made enough noise on the streets about me not snitching on his son that it piqued interests. It wasn't a big deal to me. I figured it was just the right thing to do. But everyone else thought it was heroic or something." Zeke shrugged and stared off at nothing. "A couple of days later, one of the cops who interrogated me shows up at my house while my dad's not home. He hands me a phone and says, 'Answer the next call.' It was crazy."

Zeke's life sounded like something straight out of a movie. "Anyway, I did. I answered the next call. And it was The Official. He said he wanted to meet me." Zeke's voice had been getting gradually quieter as he spoke and, at one point, he was momentarily silent, thinking back on his story, I assumed. "So that's how it happened. I met him, and he took a liking to me. It was obvious that The Official had a lot of connections in different places, so it felt like a good idea to join at the time. He made me his right hand eventually, and I've been that ever since."

Involuntarily, a laugh escaped me, and Zeke gave me a puzzled look. "You're laughing at me?"

"I'm sorry, Zeke. It's just…all this time I thought you were some crazy, bad kid from a terrible neighborhood and a messed up home. Turns out you're just a stereotypical preacher's kid. Rebellious."

He paused, pensive. "I guess I am, aren't I?" he said, his mouth twitching. And then he smiled. Not a small smile. Not a half smile. A big, wide, perfect smile. "My dad's a great man. Everyone expected me to be the same. I guess I couldn't deal with the pressure. Stupid, huh? I'm sure there are easier ways to deal with stress than joining a crime syndicate." He chuckled, shaking his head.

"It happens. Believe me, I know what it feels like." I remembered how despondent I felt before getting my job at The Lost Cantrell. "It's never too late to fix things. And if it means anything, I think you're a great man, Zeke. You lost your way, but you're not irredeemable. No one is."

"I've done a lot of bad things, Ella."

"I'm sure you have. But no one is unforgivable."

"You sound like my father."

"Clearly, your father is a smart man."

He smiled that wide smile again. "He is."

I grinned back at him. "You should smile like that more often. All the time, actually," I told him.

He almost looked shy as he said, "I don't think I've smiled like that in a while. But you make it easy."

"Yeah?"

"Yeah."

"Well, I'm glad I can do that for you."

"You've done more than that for me."

His eyes held that classic sincerity in them that I had come to know him for. I smiled at him through the awkward silence that lingered after his statement. His words had come out so involuntarily...so raw. I cleared my throat and changed the subject to lighten the mood again. "So, you're the next in command to The Official?"

"Yes."

"And where does Jet fit into all of this? What's his position?"

"I can't really say. He doesn't make any decisions, but he obviously has a top spot in The Org, just for being who he is. But The Official doesn't let him make any calls. He's more of a silent partner." Zeke shrugged. "Honestly, though, sometimes it's as if The Official resents Jet."

"Why would he resent his own son?"

"I don't know. Personally, I think he blames him. By his logic, his wife would still be alive if it weren't for Jet. She died giving birth to him. It's a crazy way of thinking, but I wouldn't put it past him." Zeke sighed and shook his head slowly. "The funny part is that he cares about Jet's safety too. It's like he wants to preserve that last piece of his wife that's in his son. One day, he has to choose one emotion. Familial ties are something." Zeke's eyes were distant, like he had drifted off into his own thoughts. I was convinced that if I had walked out, he may not have noticed.

"Do you love The Official? Like a father?" The

words were out of my mouth before I could stop.

He blinked at me. "What?"

I shifted, suddenly uncomfortable with where I had taken the conversation. "Well, it's just that he calls all of us his children. You've been in The Org since you were really young, and you two seem to understand each other. It's possible that you would have some…*familial ties* to *him*, right?"

Zeke looked even more uncomfortable than I was. "I'm loyal to him. But I don't consider him a father figure."

"Does he know that?"

Zeke was about to respond when his phone rang. "Gage," he answered. He listened for a moment then said, "Come on up."

After he hung up the call, I asked, "Who was that?"

"One of our contractors."

A few minutes later, a knock sounded at the door and Zeke moved toward it. He pulled it open and stepped aside as a man with a full head of white hair strutted in stiffly. "Gage," he said.

"Doc. How are ya?" Zeke replied as he closed the door behind the man.

"Keeping busy. That's what matters."

"We're always happy when you're working…I guess." The man gave Zeke what looked like an attempt at a smile, but it just ended up looking more like a sneer. Zeke turned to me. "Ella, this is The Doc. You can call him Doc. Doc, this is Ella, our newest top-tier member."

Doc nodded at me without a word. I nodded back.

"You can speak around Doc, Ella. He's The Org physician. Communication will be key in your relationship," Zeke stated.

"Oh, well, hi," I said hesitantly.

"Hello," The Doc replied. He was stoic, but he didn't make me feel uncomfortable.

"The Doc is here to get you acquainted with our practices. He helps if ever there's a medical emergency. We don't anticipate a lot of those, but it's important to have a plan if one does occur."

"Okay…" I dragged the word out and waited for a further explanation. It never came. The Doc simply strode toward the guest bathroom purposefully. Zeke and I followed, my curiosity piqued. The Doc placed the briefcase that he had been carrying down on the bathroom counter and opened it, revealing a strange looking machine that resembled a gun.

"What is that?" I asked nervously.

"That is what the good Doc here is going to use to insert a tracking chip just under your skin."

"Wait, what?" I stared at Zeke, wide-eyed. "You're kidding, right?"

"No."

"I'm not letting you put anything under my skin. No way."

"Ella, it's for your own protection."

"What does that even mean?"

"I need to be able to keep tabs on you when we're not together. To keep you safe. All members get one of these, so we can look out for each other. The Doc knows what he's doing. Don't worry; it's not his first rodeo."

I turned my gaze on The Doc, who was looking back at me with a bored expression. He certainly was calm, as a doctor should be. I sighed and closed my eyes briefly. I knew that Zeke wasn't going to let up. "Fine. It won't hurt too bad, right?"

"No, it just feels like a little pinch," Doc replied.

"Okay," I said on an exhale. "Let's do this."

Zeke took a step away from us to give Doc room to work. "Hold out your arm," Doc instructed. I did as he told me and shut my eyes. I smelled the alcohol as he disinfected a small area of my arm thoroughly. Then I felt the coolness of the small machine press up against the soft skin of my inner arm before the pain hit.

I learned that day that The Doc was a shameless liar. It wasn't a pinch. Not even close. It hurt. The chip was practically shot into my arm. I glared at The Doc as he started to pack away his kit, having placed a large bandage over the aching spot. "You know the drill. You can activate it in twenty-four hours," he told Zeke, ignoring the fact that my eyes were burning holes into his face.

"Thank you for your assistance, Doc," Zeke said.

"Of course. See you next time, Gage." He looked at my sulking face briefly and said, "Ella," with a nod.

"Doc," I grumbled back in lieu of goodbye and, for a second, I thought I saw a tiny smirk cross his face. He turned quickly, before I could be sure of his amusement, and left the apartment just as swiftly. I turned my narrowed eyes on Zeke. "My arm feels like it's been put through a grinder."

"I never took you for a drama queen, Ella," Zeke replied.

"I'm serious, Zeke. It hurts."

His eyes softened a little as he said, "I know. But it'll stop hurting soon, I promise. Give it an hour and you won't even feel it anymore, all right?"

"Okay," I said begrudgingly.

Zeke squeezed my shoulder before leaving the bathroom and when he came back a couple of minutes later, I could tell that he was all business again. "You can take a rest for a few hours if you want, but be ready to go by seven o'clock," he told me.

"Where are we going?" I asked.

"Ant got us that meeting with his cousin Benny. Seven-thirty tonight. We're going to be negotiating for his territory. You get to watch."

****

We walked into a small grocery store two blocks away from Windton University at about seven twenty-five p.m. I didn't even bother to check the name because I was so on edge. The store was empty, save for the young woman with short black hair and heavy eye makeup who was behind the counter, chewing gum. Ant, who had met us outside, addressed her. "Hey, Carey. We have a meeting with Benny."

"'Sup, Ant?" she responded, eyeing Zeke and me curiously. "Benny's upgraded his friends, huh?" She blew a bubble with her gum then finally said, "You can head through."

I rubbed self-consciously at the slight tugging feeling on my skin from the bandage on my inner arm. When I realised what I was doing, I dropped my hand quickly, not wanting to draw attention to it. It wasn't necessary for me to feel uncomfortable about it because my full-length coat obviously hid the evidence of my tracking chip fiasco, but I guess human nature isn't always sensible. Zeke hadn't lied though, because the pain had indeed almost totally faded.

We walked through the door leading to the back of

the store and went down a short corridor before entering a dimly lit room at the end of it. A guy with greasy blond hair sat behind a desk in the dingy room, with two big Latino men standing on each side of him. He clearly felt like he needed security. He also looked like the typical, lower-level criminal cliché.

As we walked in, the greasy-haired man looked up from behind his desk, where he was casually smoking a cigar. He gave us a wide smile, but there was nothing pleasant in his eyes. He put his cigar out in the ashtray next to him. "My guests have arrived!" he exclaimed, standing up and striding over to us. His two henchmen stayed in place, staring blankly at us. "Welcome, gentlemen," he said before turning to me and adding, "And lady."

Ant stepped forward and introduced us. "Benny, this is Zeke Gage. I told you about his business proposition. And this is Ella. She works with Zeke."

Benny took in our appearance and smirked. "Apologies for not dressing the part," he said, gesturing toward his worn gray T-shirt and jeans. "I didn't realize it would be this formal a meeting." Zeke didn't respond. I could tell that he was studying Benny and, if my Zeke-radar was correct, he didn't like what he saw. A painfully awkward silence ensued before Benny finally said, "I would offer you all a seat but, as you can see, we're a little short of those."

The room was actually bare, save for the desk and the chair that Benny had been sitting on. *So much for a warm welcome.*

"That's all right, Benny. We don't plan on staying long," Zeke replied.

Benny smiled again. "Straight to business. I like

that. So, what can I do for you, Mr. Gage?"

"This is more about how we can have a mutually beneficial business relationship. Ant tells me that you run this block, moving product through the university."

"That's right."

"We want in. Our organization is looking to take over the city. We want to work with other crews where possible, not fight them. So the proposition is that you join us as a member of our organization and we get a cut from your business on this block. We'll give you an additional territory to operate in, of course. You expand, we expand. You make money, we make money."

"So I would basically be working for you?"

"*With* us. You'd be working with us, Benny."

"And these territories would belong to you?"

"They would belong to the organisation under your sole management. You would still technically be in charge."

"And I give you a cut?"

"Yes. A fairly minimal one. In exchange for your expansion, among other perks."

Benny looked pensive before saying, "That's all well and good, but why would I willingly give away ownership of my territory and part of my money when I can just have all of it, like I do now? I would still be doing all the work and not even receiving my full due. Sounds like a loss. What's in this for me?"

"You get to be part of a powerful brotherhood. You'd be untouchable, Benny."

"What makes you think I'm not untouchable right now?" Benny asked.

Zeke's mouth turned up in a smile as he studied the

two henchmen behind Benny before turning back to the defiant man in front of us. "You in or you out?" he asked, ignoring Benny's question.

"Out. I'm not interested. It sounds like you want to control my business then make me pay you for it. That's a loss all round for me."

"Actually, working with us would get you way more money than you make now."

"Under your control. Why would I give up all my power?"

"Money is money, Benny. Don't get caught up with power."

Benny snorted. "Says the guy who would have all the power." He shook his head slowly. "I'm not interested in joining your little club. This is my territory. I run these parts. So you can take your offer and shove it up your—"

I didn't see Zeke's arm snap out. It happened so fast but, before I knew it, his hand was wrapped firmly around Benny's throat.

"Whoa, Zeke. Chill, man," Ant said shakily.

Zeke ignored him. "Here's the thing, Benny, I'm here simply out of courtesy. We have manners in my organization, believe it or not. Your cousin, Ant, was respectful to me, and so I thought I'd extend that to you." Zeke spoke low and calm even as his hand tightened around Benny's throat. He tilted his head at him as he watched the other man's face turn a deeper shade of red than I thought was possible, his hands clawing away at Zeke's grip. "But don't ever mistake my courtesy for weakness. That wouldn't end well for you."

Benny looked on the brink of passing out just as

Zeke released his grip. Benny coughed and spewed, gulping in air with wheezing noises. "So, here's what's going to happen, Benny," Zeke continued, all business-like as he said, "You *will* join The Org. You *will* work for me. You *will* do as you're told. And you *will* give up your territory to us. You're lucky I'm still willing to give you a chance."

I had been clenching my fists and grinding my teeth together, and I hadn't even noticed. I tried to calm myself, but the fear that something might kick off kept me unsettled. That, and how cold Zeke appeared in that moment. It was like the hotel suite at The Lost Cantrell all over again. It hit me then that this wasn't a negotiation at all. It was a takeover.

Once Benny had gotten the air back in his lungs, he yelled at his two henchmen, "What are you two just standing there for?" They didn't move. Just stood as still as they had been.

Zeke raised one brow, his amusement obvious. "Guess I forgot to mention that they work for me. They accepted my generous offer last week. Your right hands are smarter than you, Benny. They know what a good deal looks like. Did you really think I'd come here unprepared? I've known all your plans for longer than you've known I was coming."

Benny's face fell in shock, and I almost felt sorry for him. He had thought he was in control. His eyes met mine briefly, as if he needed an explanation of what had just happened.

"Don't look at her," Zeke told him harshly. Benny quickly averted his gaze, choosing to stare at the floor instead. I glanced at Ant, who looked even more uncomfortable than I was.

Zeke exhaled slowly, his restraint restored. "You know, Benny, the measure of a man is how he conducts himself when he thinks he has the upper hand in any situation. Needless to say, you've been found wanting." He shook his head at Benny before saying, "You have forty-eight hours to accept my offer. You don't, then we have no use for you. I don't have to elaborate." He looked at the henchmen, who were apparently future members now, and said, "Gentlemen." He took my hand and turned to leave, taking me along with him. Ant followed closely behind us.

Like loyal pets, the two henchmen, who I had previously thought were Benny's, followed us out, too. I risked looking back at Benny as we left. His face held a look of pure hatred and rage. It was unsettling, and the thought of being around him in The Org knowing that he held that much anger made it even worse.

We breezed past the gum-chewing girl without saying a word and walked out into the street, the cool air hitting our faces. Zeke made sure I was settled in the backseat of the car before closing the door and having a very hushed conversation with his new sidekicks and Ant. Chris stood with them, observing quietly as usual. I tried to listen to the conversation.

"What was that, Zeke? Benny's gonna kill me. There's no way he'll believe that I didn't know you would embarrass him like that," Ant said.

"You have nothing to worry about, Ant. You're one of us now. You kept your end of the bargain, and I'm keeping mine. We protect our members, even when they're still prospects. I'll be in touch soon with more details. For now, just lay low, all right?"

Ant nodded at Zeke's words, relaxing somewhat,

then left with the other two men, who almost seemed to be *his* security now. Chris got behind the wheel while Zeke settled in next to me. "I'm sorry you had to see something like that. Again," Zeke said quietly, searching my face with concern.

"It's okay. I was ready for anything to happen. I knew what I was walking into this time. Well, for the most part." I smiled at him, wanting to reassure him that I was fine.

"I don't want you to get used to this, Ella. You don't belong in this mess." He was clearly aggravated and becoming more so by the second.

"I know. But I'm in it for now. I have to accept it. We both do." I reached out and squeezed his hand. "I'm okay, Zeke."

He shifted to face forward. "Let's go home, CP."

Chapter 14

It had been a couple of weeks since the whole Benny incident, and Zeke had eventually stopped feeling guilty about putting me in another volatile situation. I didn't mind. I knew what I was dealing with now. In all honesty, "the Benny thing" (as we had come to call it) was nowhere near as traumatic as "the Hotel room thing." Plus, Benny had agreed to join The Org well within the forty-eight-hour ultimatum period that he had been given. He had no choice but to cooperate, and the situation didn't feel so volatile anymore.

So, I got over it and gave Zeke the time he needed to do the same. I was pleased when his mood finally started to become chipper again. Well, chipper by Zeke's standards. I was even more pleased when he randomly walked up to me in the kitchen and said, "I was thinking that it's just about time that things went back to normal for you. Well, as normal as possible," he said with a shrug.

"Yeah?"

"Yeah. You should go to see Stacey."

I stood up from my stool. "I can see Stace again?"

"Yeah, you can. It's been close to two months, and you're officially a member now so your safety is no longer an issue. CP tells me that she always mentions how much she misses you. It's about time you guys reunited."

I smiled widely and jumped up and down on the spot. Zeke laughed at my antics. "I take it you're happy?"

"I am. So happy. When can I see her?"

"Whenever you want to. Even today, if you're ready."

I was more than ready.

****

"Basically, you're telling everyone that you and I will be opening a restaurant together and so you won't be returning to The Lost Cantrell. We bumped into each other in Paris and decided that we would make good business partners. You as the chef and me as the investor. Monsieur Cantrell has told all your former workmates the same thing, as per our discussion." Zeke had been briefing me the whole time on our way to see Stace. I still had no idea how on earth we would pull off such a tremendous lie.

A thought occurred to me as he spoke. "Monsieur Cantrell is obviously an Org member, right?"

"Yes, Ella, he is."

"Top-tier, too?"

"No. But close. He's pretty high up."

My former boss was a part of a secret criminal organisation. I should have figured, given how comfortable Zeke was with him, but I hadn't had much time to process much of anything. My brow furrowed at the thought. I felt Zeke's hand touch my shoulder gently. "He's a good man, Ella. He's a member of The Org solely to provide his accommodation to us when we need it. The Lost Cantrell is a safe place for us to conduct our business. And, believe me, he doesn't like it any more than you do. He was practically threatened to join because certain members wanted his hotel as their business arena. The Org gives ultimatums sometimes when they want to coerce someone to join in order to benefit from that individual's position without any unnecessary removals. That's what happened in Monsieur Cantrell's case. He joined to protect his daughter."

All I could feel in that moment was sympathy for Monsieur Cantrell. He had been bullied into joining. "Like what you did to Benny? That type of ultimatum?" I asked Zeke.

"Yes. Like that."

"So you threatened Monsieur Cantrell to join, too?"

"No. That wasn't me. That was the guy before me."

"Who was the guy before you?"

"I don't know. It was way before my time. I hadn't joined yet. The Official told me about him. Didn't give me a name though. Didn't mention what happened to him, either. He just let me know that I would be taking over from the previous guy. No one ever talks about him." Zeke shrugged. "Anyway, Cantrell has been a member for a long time. Longer than most."

I looked away. "Thanks for letting me know that," I said quietly.

The car came to a halt. I hadn't noticed that we were already at my old place. The place where Stace and I had made our home. I stared out the window, taking deep breaths. "Are you ready?" I heard Zeke ask next to me.

"Yes," I replied on an exhale.

I got out of the car on shaky legs, taking small

steps slowly toward the door. I already had my story in place, and Zeke had given me a detailed description of Paris and The Lost Cantrell restaurant there, but I still felt like I had no control of the situation. I turned back to look at Zeke and Chris, who were still seated in the car. They weren't staying because they wanted Stace and me to have time alone, and I watched as the car quietly pulled off into the street.

I knocked on the door three times and waited. After a couple of seconds, the door swung open. "Hey, stranger," I said awkwardly.

Stacey's face lit up like fireworks on the 4th of July, and she screamed loudly as she jumped up and down excitedly. Before I could say more, she grabbed me in an unrestrained hug. I laughed and hugged her back tightly, fighting all my emotions in order to keep the moment light. "Ellzy! Oh my gosh, Ellzy! You're here! You're back! You're back! You're back!" Her excitement was contagious. Always had been. She pulled away and grabbed my hands, giving them a firm squeeze. I hadn't gotten a word in since I had greeted her. I didn't need to. I just wanted to bask in that moment for hours, being with my best friend again.

Once she had pulled me just inside the apartment and closed the door behind us, she hugged me again. Even tighter this time, which I didn't think was possible. When she let go, her eyes were so full of happiness. "Hands down, the best welcome home reception ever," I told her, grinning widely.

"When did you get in?" she asked.

"Today," I lied.

"Why didn't you tell me or call? I would have met you at the airport." She almost looked hurt.

"I wanted to surprise you. And, anyway, Monsieur Cantrell offered to have the hotel driver pick me up on arrival, which was really nice of him, given the circumstances."

Stace frowned. "What circumstances?" Then she looked around my feet in confusion. "And where's your luggage?" She looked up at me, and her brow creased with worry. "Ellzy, is everything okay?"

A small smile slid to my lips when the realization hit me that I had missed Stace's overprotective nature. I cleared my throat. "Stace, I'm not going back to work at The Lost Cantrell," I said slowly.

Her eyes widened. "What? Why? Did something happen?"

"Yeah," I said simply, then when Stace's face grew even more worried, I quickly added, "Something amazing. While I was in Paris working at the branch there, I bumped into Zeke Gage. You remember him, right? Well, he travels a lot on business, and he just happened to be there when I was."

Stace narrowed her eyes at me. "Okay," she said, dragging the word out.

"Well, he ate a couple of the dishes that I prepared at the restaurant, and he's decided to invest in our own restaurant. Together."

Stace gave me an incredulous look. "Seriously?"

"Yeah. He's a businessman, after all. He's always looking for new opportunities, and he believes we would make a good team." It was a bold-faced lie.

"Are you sure you want to do this, Ellzy? I mean, it is an amazing opportunity, but do you trust the guy? And, I mean, The Lost Cantrell was your dream."

"Having my own restaurant is my dream, Stace," I

told her truthfully.

"So are you and Zeke...?"

She left the question hanging in the air, but I caught her meaning. "No, no. It's nothing like that. Strictly business." I took a deep breath before I told her the next big lie. "But here's the thing, Zeke wants to get things moving on this whole project, and our time management is super important at this point. We figured that in order for us to reach our deadlines, we're going to need a lot of sleepless nights and a lot of hours to be put in. So, we'll be staying together for a little bit to stay within our time limits."

Stace's face fell, and it nearly broke my heart. "You'll be living together?"

"Yeah. Just for a few weeks."

"And you're sure you two are not...?" She let it hang in the air again.

"I promise you that we're not. It's just business."

"And you're sure that his intentions are pure?"

"One hundred percent, Stace."

She sighed. "So you won't even be staying home with me tonight?"

Home. And then my heart broke for real. "Not tonight. But soon. Give me a few weeks to get settled into this new business arrangement. I'll be home in no time."

They were all weak lies, but Stace trusted me. So I felt like even more of a heathen when she simply smiled and said, "Ella, look at you. You're already becoming the top chef that I always knew you'd be. Traveling and owning your own restaurant. I'm so proud of you."

"Thanks, Stace. And I promise I'll be back home as

soon as possible."

She perked up. "I'm going to hold you to that. Now, tell me everything." We sat down on the couch in the living room together, just like before. "What are your plans for the restaurant? What was Paris like?"

I smiled mischievously. "If I tell you all about Paris and my future restaurant, will you tell me all about Chris?" I asked, wanting to change the subject for as long as possible.

Stace blushed, and we both burst out laughing. And that's how the rest of the day went. We laughed and caught up and laughed some more. When night came and it was time for me to leave, I held onto her like she was a lifeline in deep waters and I couldn't swim.

Zeke and Chris had come to pick me up, and Stace made it a point to give each of them an earful. "I want her back in a couple of weeks. She promised me that she'll only stay with you for that long," she told Zeke.

He held his hands up in a mock gesture of surrender. "Just a couple of weeks," he promised her.

I hoped he wasn't just telling her what she wanted to hear because Stace took promises seriously. She turned on Chris. "And you, why didn't you give me a heads up and let me know that my best friend was starting her own restaurant?" she asked him. Her voice had taken on its usual joking tone.

Chris laughed at her dramatics. Even though it was a light moment, I still felt bad for the guy because he probably had no idea about the cover story either. "Uh, sorry, Stace. I figured Ella would want to surprise you."

That appeased Stacey and she backed off, turning back to me. "Will I see you some days, still?"

"I'll try to come over every day until I move back

in, if you'll let me," I replied.

"I'll allow it," Stace said, and I smiled at her humor.

Zeke's voice piped up then. "Oh, before I forget," he said pulling out an elaborately wrapped box from the back seat of the car. "Ella was in such a rush to get to you after she left her luggage at my condo that she forgot to bring the gift that she bought for you with her," he told Stace.

I had no idea what he was talking about, but I played along. "Oh, yeah. Thanks for remembering," I said, trying not to sound like a programmed robot.

Stace squealed. "Oh, my gosh! A prezzy! What is it? What is it?" She took the box and opened it up using the car hood like a table. Inside was a beautiful gold necklace, with a diamond pendant in the shape of a heart. It was a classic piece of jewelry. She gasped, and I saw tears spring to her eyes. She reached for me and pulled me into a tight hug. "Oh, thank you, Ellzy. I love it. Thank you, thank you," she said happily, giving me a kiss on the cheek.

"You're welcome, Stace," I replied, still trying to sound human. I was a mix of emotions in that moment. I felt like a terrible friend for not even thinking of bringing Stace something back from my fake Paris trip. I felt happy to see her happy. And mostly, I felt grateful to Zeke for being so thoughtful all the time.

"Ella has excellent taste," I heard Zeke say.

"She does, doesn't she?" Stace said, staring at her new necklace. I gave Zeke an appreciative look while Stace admired her gift.

"Well, we'd better be going. Ella. CP. Ready?"

Chris and I gave confirmation that we were good to

go and, after hugging Stace for what felt like ages, we got into the car and headed for the condo.

"Thank you for today, Zeke. It was…I needed this," I told him quietly on the ride home. "And that pendant was perfect!" I added with gratitude.

Zeke smiled. "Well, Ella, you do have fantastic taste."

I rolled my eyes at him, but I know he didn't miss the smile on my face before I turned away to watch the bright city lights through the window.

****

The next day, Zeke took me to see everyone at The Lost Cantrell to say my goodbyes and tell them all about my restaurant plans in person. Even though it was all make-believe, I had gotten fairly good at convincing people of my stories. Monsieur Cantrell was obviously in on it too, which made it easier to sell the lie.

Bernie had shrieked and come to give me a hug when she saw me enter the lobby. Then she had promptly begun to call everyone else from the kitchen. They all welcomed me with hugs, and even Melany wasn't as rude as she used to be. And then Monsieur Cantrell came over. I almost got emotional when I saw him, all the images of that terrifying night coming back to me. I hadn't seen him since then.

"Congratulations on your new business venture, Ella. Or, should I say, Chef Silver," he said with a smile. "You deserve this opportunity." His smile grew even wider when he said, "It's so good to see you. Truly."

Hearing him say that, and knowing the reason why he was saying it, was enough to make me do something that I never thought I would. I hugged him. It was brief but…it was a hug. And the best part about it was that he hugged me back. And it was stiff but…it was a hug. From Monsieur Cantrell. That's what mattered. I took a step back awkwardly and said, "Thank you, Monsieur."

I chatted a little more with my former workmates, who were now my friends, while Zeke spoke to Monsieur Cantrell off to the side. I didn't have to guess what they were discussing. I pushed the thought aside and focused on the fact that I was able to socialize with The Lost Cantrell staff again.

Then it was finally time to say my farewells. I left The Lost Cantrell feeling lighter and happier than I'd been in a while. And even though it was a lie, it made me happy to know that everyone else believed in me.

****

"Thank you for letting me see everyone," I told Zeke once we were back at the condo.

"You're welcome, Ella. It was about time, anyway." He shrugged. "Now all we have to do is come up with a name. But I'll leave that up to you."

I frowned. "A name?"

"Yeah, for our restaurant."

"That's real?" I asked him.

"Of course. You're an amazing chef, Ella. And I need to invest in more…legal ventures. I think we'd make a good team."

I couldn't believe it. "You really think I could run my own restaurant?"

"There's no doubt in my mind. I know you may think that it's money from criminal activity but, at the end of the day, the profit will be from your hard, honest work. And, if it'll make you feel better, you can give me all the capital back after we're up and running. No handouts and no blood money."

I hadn't noticed that I was smiling until my cheeks started hurting. "Zeke, I..." I didn't have the words to express how grateful I was to him. But in that moment, I knew that I cared about him. We had grown close, whether we wanted to admit it or not. And I cared about him. I really, really cared about him. But it felt awkward trying to say that. So instead, I rushed over to him and hugged him. I hugged him like I wanted us to merge into one person. He stood stiff while I squeezed the heck out of him, clearly taken by surprise. "No matter whatever happens, Zeke. I'm so glad I met you. You...you're awesome," I whispered.

Zeke's arms came up slowly and wrapped around me as he returned my hug with his own warm one. "I'm glad I met you too, Ella."

I stepped away and studied his reaction as I asked, "Can we stay friends? Always. Even after I get out, can we stay close? We'll talk all the time, like we do now?"

He grinned at me. That perfect smile again. "Of course we will. We'll be in business together, remember? Either way, I'm so used to having you around now, I'd probably feel a little empty without you." His eyes held a tenderness that I hadn't seen in them before, and I believed that he meant what he had said.

Chapter 15

The days turned quickly into weeks, and my new normal had become comfortable, maybe even a little enjoyable. Especially on the days when I managed to forget about The Org and its activities.

One morning, Zeke and I had breakfast together like we always did, the mood even lighter than usual. I jumped up onto the kitchen counter, just like I used to do at my and Stace's brownstone. "I'm seeing Stace again today. We're meeting at The Hot Shot Cafe later on in the evening, after she knocks off."

"Yeah? You two like that place, don't you? Haven't you been there three times this week already?"

The Hot Shot Cafe was relatively close to the brownstone we used to share, and Stace went past it on her way to and from work. Plus, the food was great. It just made sense. "Yeah. The coffee is amazing. And it's great being able to actually catch up in person."

"I wish you never had to be separated from her in the first place."

I shrugged. "That's the job, right?"

Zeke smirked at my joke and replied, "Right."

We finished our breakfast, and then he left to run his still mostly secret errands, for the sake of "plausible deniability" on my behalf. When he went out without me, he was usually gone the whole day until about eight o'clock. It gave me time to think up recipes that I wanted to try at our future restaurant, so the moments alone were useful, but I had accepted the fact that I enjoyed having Zeke around and I was okay with that.

One thing about meticulous recipe planning though? It made the clock move quicker. Before I knew it, it was time for me to start preparations to see Stace. I always timed myself so that I arrived at the cafe about a half hour before she and I would be meeting. I enjoyed watching people walk by. Probably because I had developed a new appreciation of other human beings ever since I had been locked up in the condo, before becoming a confirmed member. I just wanted to be outside, experiencing human contact.

I was sitting at our usual table, staring out of the window next to it, with about twenty-five minutes to spare before Stace arrived, when someone sat down heavily in the seat across of me with a sigh. I turned to look at the person, perplexed. My perplexity changed to surprise and, soon after that, caution when I looked into Benny's face. He grinned at me. I frowned at him. I wanted to ask him what he was doing there but caught myself when I realised that I needed to be in character.

"Hey, darlin'," he drawled. "Mind if I sit down?"

You probably should have asked that before you sat down.

"You alone?" he asked, looking around.

He knew I was alone. I stared at him, hoping my annoyance at his presence would show through my expression.

"Look, I'm not here to cause any trouble, okay? I can't get hold of your boy, Gage. He's not answering my calls, and it's important that I talk to him because I've run into some issues with my subordinates. You two are a team or something, right?"

I blinked slowly but still said nothing.

"Well, you're a lot easier to find. So, here I am."

I didn't like that he said that. He must have seen the look on my face because he began to explain. "It's not a secret you've been coming here. Plus, I come by this street sometimes for certain business, and I've seen you here. Decided to try my luck today. I was hoping you'd show up again since Gage is so hard to reach. I figured either one of you will do. I don't normally deal with women but, hey, you're basically my superior anyway."

When I remained silent, he leaned back in his seat. "Whatcha doing here, anyway? Waiting for that cute friend of yours that lives around here?"

I clenched my fists. Hearing him mention Stace sent a chill through me.

He grinned again. "Relax. The streets talk. And like I said, you haven't exactly been hiding your whereabouts. But I'm just here for you."

I put my hands in my lap and waited patiently for him to get to the point or leave.

"I need this situation handled. If I could get in contact with Gage, I wouldn't even be here, all right? Just hear me out so you can tell him my problem when you see him."

I considered his words and then gave him a single nod.

"Okay, now we're getting somewhere." He looked around briefly. "Not here, though. We have to talk where there ain't this many ears."

And my guard was up again. I wasn't going anywhere with him. I folded my arms and settled comfortably in my seat, letting him know I wasn't going to budge.

"I just need a moment of your time in private. My car is right over there in the middle of a busy street." He pushed a coaster around the table. "I mean, you don't want your pretty little friend to get here while I'm explaining my woes to you, do you?"

I scowled at him. He really was annoying.

"All you have to do is watch a quick video of my so-called loyal squad ripping me off. I need help giving them some discipline before they run my business into the ground. And my business is now officially Org business, remember?"

He was looking at me as if I was being unreasonable by not going with his idea. I didn't like the thought of getting into his car, but I didn't like the thought of him being around Stacey either. I also couldn't let anyone figure out that I wasn't built for the crime life because that would reveal that Zeke had lied to save me. It wasn't a risk I wanted to take. So I stood, checking approximately how much time I had left before Stace arrived at the cafe from work, and walked out with Benny toward his car.

It was certainly parked in the middle of a busy street, just like he said. It was a royal blue Camaro, and I noticed with relief that it didn't have tinted windows. There was no way I would have gotten into it if it had tinted windows.

He opened the passenger door for me. "Milady," he said with mock chivalry.

I got in and sat rod-straight, waiting for him to round the car and get into the driver's side. He closed his door after he was comfortably seated then turned to me. "Was that so hard?" he asked.

I thrust my hand out irritably for whatever he wanted to give me, a sign to let him know that I wanted to get it over and done with.

"No small talk? Okay," he said as he leaned closer to me, tapping away on his phone and opening his video player. I flinched away from him, and he smirked. "Do I scare you?" he asked.

I gave him my best blank stare, composing myself. He handed me his phone as a video played. A video of me and Stace sitting inside The Hot Shot Cafe the previous day. I turned to look back at him angrily just as he tapped my arm quickly but lightly, and a pin prick pain hit the spot that he had touched. I looked down at my arm and saw a small, blue square device pressed into it. Before I could even think about what to do next, the first wave of dizziness hit me. Even if I had wanted to speak, there's no way I could have because my tongue felt heavy and my head started to feel light.

Benny put a finger under my chin and pushed my head back slowly. "See, your boyfriend Gage didn't know that I've got some tricks too, did he?"

His face became blurred just before keeping my eyes open was no longer an option. My body slumped against the door, and I let the darkness take over. To the outside world, I probably just looked like a girl who had been picked up by a friend and was now casually resting her head against the window. But I knew the truth. I knew what had really happened. And just before I lost consciousness, I thought, *How could you be stupid enough to let yourself get drugged?*

****

My head felt groggy, like it was stuffed full with

something. Not something nice, though. No, not something nice. It felt like it was stuffed with lead…and barbed wire. A combo along those lines. My hands were tied behind my back, and I was sitting in a cold, hard chair that already had my back aching. I lifted my head slowly and looked around the room I was in. It was dingy and gray, with a single table in the middle of it. *What the…?* I closed my eyes briefly, my mind trying to make sense of what was happening.

Then I remembered. *Benny.*

The events from before came rushing back to me. I inhaled, and the smell of the musty, damp walls engulfed me. *What is it with these criminals and abandoned warehouses?* I thought as I tested the tightness of the restraints around my wrists. As I expected, they were pretty darn tight, digging mercilessly into my skin. I hung my head forward again, my energy levels too low for too much exertion, then groaned when my temples throbbed from the movement.

"Finally, you're awake. I thought I'd have to pull you out of a coma or somethin'," a voice said enthusiastically.

I snapped my head back up quickly, too quickly, and the room spun a little, accompanied by even more throbbing. When my vision became normal, I clearly saw Benny standing in front of me, next to the lone table. I had no idea where he had walked in from. His eyes held a maniacal look that made goose bumps form on my arms.

"Look at you, Ella," he said, shaking his head at me. "Look at the position Gage has put you in. I know you must be wondering why it's you here right now, and not him. The answer to that is simple. You're easier to get to, and I have no doubt that you being here would hurt Gage more than any torture I could ever attempt to put him through. See, he slipped up, Ella. He slipped up and tried to cover it up, but I caught it. I saw it, Ella," Benny said poking at his temple, before continuing his monologue. "He cares about you. Rumor has it, Gage doesn't care about anything or anyone. But you"—he wiggled his index finger in my direction like a teacher scolding a child—"he feels something for you. I saw it in his eyes. You're the key. It's a classic strategy, am I right?"

He turned away from me to face the table and began fiddling with whatever was on it, but he kept talking. "I know you technically didn't have anything to do with that humiliating hostile takeover I went through. I get how this may seem unfair." He looked over his shoulder at me and added, "But I'd be lying if I said I didn't get any pleasure from this." He smiled his cruel smile again.

Even though I felt like I'd been run over by a bus and was truly terrified, I stayed in character. I didn't speak. Not only because I didn't have the energy for it, but because I didn't see the point of encouraging Benny to continue talking. I didn't want to engage him in any way. It wasn't worth it. I saw in his eyes then that he was an unreasonable man. I just wished I had seen it more before.

Benny noticed my resolute silence. "It's going to be fun trying to get you to talk. Maybe you'll even give me a little scream, if I'm lucky." He walked up to me with his hands behind his back. I watched him through heavy eyelids. "Now, I would hate for you to somehow get away from me when the drugs fully wear off, so I've come up with a little contingency plan, just in case." He pulled his hands out from behind his back, revealing a small knife in each one. Then he plunged them into each of my thighs in one swift motion, leaving them sticking out grotesquely.

I didn't scream. I couldn't. My breath caught in my throat, and my mouth gaped open as I stared at Benny's work, but no sound came out. The pain was so intense that it took the air out of my lungs. When my brain finally reminded me that I needed to breathe, all I could do was try to gulp in air, making choking, wheezing noises. I was sweating profusely and felt close to passing out from the plain shock of having been stabbed. Instead, I gritted my teeth and glared at Benny, refusing to let him win.

He stretched his hand out, placing it at my throat and squeezing hard. "You're tough, aren't you?" he said, tightening his grip and cutting off my air supply in the process. He was doing to me what Zeke had done to him. I was close to passing out again when he finally let go with a gleeful laugh. He bent in front of me and stated, "By the end of tonight, I'm going to hear that voice of yours, begging for mercy and screaming."

Challenge accepted, I thought. As I steeled myself for whatever Benny had in store, my eyes drifted to a spot behind him, and I blinked a couple of times to make sure that I was seeing correctly. And that's the moment I knew Benny would hear my voice after all. I gave him a weak smile as I said, "Oh, Benny, I guess I forgot to mention the tracker in my arm."

My words didn't register to Benny until it was too late for him. Zeke had tackled him to the floor before he got any words out. As they tussled, I slumped to the side, too weak to keep my body upright anymore. My chair fell over from my weight, having been leaning precariously as my body went limp, and I hit the ground hard on my side, still tied to it awkwardly. My head started to hurt in a whole new way, and I knew I had just added a nasty gash on my temple to the other injuries I had collected that day.

I watched from the floor as Zeke, who was with Chris and Al, took out a whole lot of anger that I'd never seen in him before on Benny, before pulling out an object that gleamed under the dim light. He pointed it at Benny.

"Gage, wait," Al said, as Zeke's shoulders rose and fell with his heavy breaths. She had both her hands up. "Gage, it's not your job to do this. This isn't what you do. Give me the gun." Zeke was still pointing the gun at Benny, his hand steady. I heard a small clicking noise.

"Dammit, Gage! This isn't you! You don't want to do this. Trust me. Don't do it." I had never heard Al yell before. She was always so cool and calm. She lowered her voice again and said, "Zeke, please. Just give me the gun. It's not who you are." Her voice was actually gentle as she pleaded with him.

I must be dreaming. My vision was getting blurry again, and the voices around me started to sound distant. My eyelids began to close against my will but before they did, I saw Zeke's face as he kneeled beside me. "Hey. Stay with me, Ella. Stay with me." His hand felt warm against my cheek.

"I'm with you," I managed to breath out. And then I wasn't with him anymore.

Chapter 16

Beep. Beep. Beep.

My body was stiff and aching. I heard distant voices again, less aggressive ones this time. Familiar, calming ones.

"I'm hungry."

"You're always hungry, Sweety."

"Okay, well I'm hungrier than usual then."

"I don't know if that's possible with you."

"Trust me, Mom, it's possible."

"You are your father's daughter," Dad quipped.

"Where are Angel and Stace?" Mom asked.

"Angel had to take a call or something. Said she'd be right back. Stace is out in the hall," Sweety replied while sending a text from her phone, barely looking up as she spoke.

I watched my family talking through my slightly opened eyes. I had missed them so much, more than I knew before that moment. "Could you guys keep it down? I'm trying to rest here," I joked. My voice was scratchy and weak, but it sounded worse than I really felt.

They all turned to stare at me, surprised. Then they were all right by my side, hugging me and teary eyed. Angel and Stace walked in right then. Everyone was talking at the same time, but I got the general idea. They were all thrilled that I was awake...and alive.

"Do you remember what happened?" Angel asked me.

I remembered everything. "Uh, it's all a little blurry right now. Maybe you guys can jog my memory."

"Someone attempted to mug you on your way to meet up with Stace. Apparently, you fought back and wouldn't let him take anything. Eventually, some witnesses noticed, and the guy ran away but he hurt you pretty bad. You were conscious enough to tell the witnesses to call your, uh, roommate, Zeke, from your phone before you passed out. The cops seem to think the guy had been watching your routine, since you and Stace have been meeting at the same cafe at about the same time. He targeted you. They're still looking for the suspect."

What a story. I had no doubt that The Org had covered its tracks thoroughly, too. "Who knows what would have happened to you if those two witnesses hadn't come around," Mom said, shaking her head. "Your father and I never wanted you to move to New York, you know?"

Witnesses, huh?

"You know you could write a rap song now, right? Like, on a whole gangster tip," Sweety piped up. Mom gave her a withering look, and I laughed. Sweety winked at me and rubbed my hand just as Zeke walked into the room.

Everyone greeted him cheerfully and with a familiarity that took me aback. They clearly liked him, even though they obviously hadn't known him for long. "We'll give you two some privacy," Mom said with a twinkle in her eyes. Did they have their own ideas about the nature of the relationship that Zeke and I had? Probably. But I didn't have the energy to worry about it.

"We'll be right outside, Ellzy," Stace said, squeezing my hand before they all left the room.

Zeke came to stand at my bedside. He looked full of grief. "Ella...I'm so, so sorry." His voice was quiet.

"I'm really happy you're here right now," I said, ignoring his apology. I didn't want him to feel bad anymore. It wasn't his fault that Benny was a cruel, vile man. "And thank you for saving me."

"It should have never happened."

"But it did. And you saved me. So, thank you." He had that same agitated look, like he wanted to hit something, so I grabbed his hand and squeezed it gently. "I'm safe now. That's what matters."

"Yes, you are. Benny can't hurt you ever again."

I cleared my throat. "Is he...?"

Zeke nodded.

"Did you...?"

"No. Al took care of it. That's her job." He said it as if he regretted not being the one to have done it.

"I'm glad you didn't," I told him.

He studied me and said, "You're the only reason I didn't. I knew you'd expect better from me. I didn't want to let you down."

I smiled at his words. "You didn't do it because you're a decent human being. That's why."

He shook his head. "A decent human being wouldn't have put you in this situation, Ella. I hate to see you like this. In this gloomy hospital room."

I took in my surroundings as he spoke, noting that it was anything but gloomy. There were loads of

239

colorful flowers, balloons, and gifts that filled the room. "Gloomy? It looks like a party in here. Who sent all of this?" I asked him.

"Staff from The Lost Cantrell," Zeke said, then hesitated before adding, "And some Org members."

"Oh. That was nice of them," I replied. "I guess." I yawned, an overwhelming flood of exhaustion suddenly washing over me.

"Get some rest, okay? We can talk more later," Zeke said, rubbing his thumb across the back of my hand gently.

"Okay," I answered, but I didn't let go of his hand even as I fell back to sleep.

Chapter 17

My family stayed in New York with me for a couple of weeks. Monsieur Cantrell had generously put them up at his hotel for their visit. Seeing them every day was bliss. It made my whole healing process easy. When they finally left to return to their lives, I was just about back to normal, besides a slight limp. Okay, it was more than slight, but I chose to be an optimist about my new, temporary walk.

After I had left the hospital, I settled back into our condo quickly. Even though I was healing well, the doctor at the hospital had still instructed that I take it easy, and so had Doc. So take it easy I did.

Zeke walked into the living room while I was lounging comfortably on the couch, reading a magazine. "I've booked us the penthouse suite at The Lost Cantrell. Just a quick in and out, for tomorrow. We'll spend the night," he stated. I gave him a quizzical look, and he chuckled. "It's nothing sinister. The Official has requested to meet with us, and I figured that's as good a place as any to do it. He had wanted to meet soon after your accident, but I told him that you needed to rest before making any trips. That's why we're staying in New York for the meeting."

I sat up straighter on the couch. "He's going to be out in the open like that?"

"He'll use the back entrance to come up."

Of course. The back entrance. "What's this meeting about?"

"He didn't divulge much, but he did mention that he wants to see you and make sure you're okay. Apologize for your ordeal."

"Oh. Can't he do that over the phone?" The last thing I wanted was to see The Official again.

"He wants to see you…physically. I know you don't want to go, but it won't be for long. And you'll still be able to rest your legs in the suite."

"Okay. I'll come." Not that I had a choice in the matter anyway.

****

Walking into The Lost Cantrell again, but this time as a guest, was strange. It felt like I was watching someone else's life, not living my own. We had entered hurriedly, leaving no time for me to see anyone I knew except for Bernie.

Zeke and I had taken the elevator up in silence. I had been a ball of nerves the whole day, not just because I would be seeing The Official again, but also because of the few bad memories The Lost Cantrell now held. The day before, when Zeke had told me about the meeting with The Official, I had been fine. I had basically been resigned and not bothered. But that morning, I had woken up a rattled mess. Trauma was a trip. It could show its lingering effects when you least expected it.

The elevator doors opened up to the penthouse suite floor, and I hesitated briefly before stepping out. Zeke opened the suite door and, again, I hesitated. "Ella, it's okay." His hand trailed down my arm gently before he took my hand in his. "Everything is okay now." I let him lead me into the room, just as I had that night.

The suite looked the same. It was pristine. Perfect. I knew better now, though. I knew what secrets it held. Zeke put our luggage down and straightened. "The Official will be here at eight. We should be settled in by then."

"Okay."

Zeke studied me before saying, "Don't worry. He won't be here long."

He kept saying that, but a minute with The Official was too much, as far as I was concerned. "I just want to get this over and done with. Whatever it is."

"I hear you." Oddly enough, Zeke sounded as if he just wanted to get it over and done with, too.

****

I hadn't stopped checking the time on my phone since we had settled into our suite. *Seven fifty-eight p.m.* My hands shook a little. The Official would be arriving soon. I was still holding onto the unrealistic hope that he might not make it for the meeting.

Zeke had ordered himself a drink and was sipping on it casually, no stress reflecting in his demeanor. I was surprised that he had allowed room service up. That was a change from his rules during his initial stays.

I looked down at my phone again. *Seven fifty-nine p.m.* "Is there any chance of him not...?" A knock sounded at the door, cutting my question short.

Zeke put down his drink and stood. "No, there's no chance of him not showing up," he said in a low voice as he brushed past me.

He pulled the door open and, much to our surprise,

Ethel walked in with The Official, looking sheepish and uncomfortable. I glanced at Zeke and caught his micro reaction. Someone else may not have noticed, but I knew he was on high alert, however, in the way that his jaw muscle ticked and his eyes narrowed very briefly. He closed the door behind them slowly and stood next to me. No one sat.

"How are you, my children?" The Official asked.

"We're fine, sir," Zeke answered for the both of us.

The Official stepped closer to me, taking my hands in his. "I'm glad to see you are well, my dear. When I heard the news, I was mortified. Needless to say, that villain was dealt with accordingly."

I smiled stiffly. "Yes, so I heard."

He released my hands and turned away. "I know you still need rest, and I don't want to burden you with work, so I won't take up much of your and Zeke's time. I'm sure you want to know what this meeting is all for." He turned to face us again. "Seeing Ethel and I together may be a surprise to you, my children. I didn't tell her the reason for this gathering. I wanted you to all hear my plans together. The decision to reconcile came after a long battle with myself, but I've decided it's time to focus on the important things. I'm here because I have come to the realization that family is all that matters. Loyal family." The Official gently touched the silver ring on his wedding finger before taking it off and putting it in his inner jacket pocket. "That being said, I don't think my son, Jet, is loyal to me anymore. I don't think I can trust him."

Zeke frowned. "Why? Did something happen?"

"No. But it's the way he looks at me. I can see it in his eyes. He is not loyal. Anytime now, he will turn on me. Maybe he is even planning his attack already. I can feel it."

"But he hasn't explicitly given you a reason to not trust him?"

"Snakes are never explicit, Zeke. They move undercover, quietly through the grass before they strike and kill. And that's why I must strike and kill first." The Official nodded his head to himself a couple of times, clearly in agreement with his own twisted logic. "I would like you to get rid of Jet. He can no longer be trusted."

As much as I tried to hold in my shock, I felt my eyes widening. Ethel gasped and said, "You...you can't. He's your son. Your only son. You're his father!"

The Official took her hands in his comfortingly. "Please don't get upset, my love. It's not as bad as you think, believe me. Jet is not my only son. All of the members are my children. *Our* children. And we are going to have even more children together. Born into our family. A family, like you always wanted. Loyal from the beginning to the end. And that's what this meeting is really about."

Zeke was as stiff as I'd ever seen him, but his eyes narrowed marginally as he studied The Official, who continued speaking. "We are going to allow relations within The Org. Beneficial relations. Pairings to bring Org children into this world. And you, Zeke and Ella, will be the first to start this family." He exhaled before continuing. "You know, my father was a bigot of extreme proportions. The idea of races mixing so commonly would have sent him straight to the grave, were he not already dead. But I know better than him. You said Ella was special. I see that now, my son. She will be the beginning of The Org truly becoming a family. She will create the first to be born into The Org."

I glanced at Ethel, wanting to be sure that we all heard the same insane thing, and saw the absolute horror on her face. I cleared my throat and croaked out, "You want us to have children for The Org?"

"Yes. And you and Zeke will make the first one. You already care for each other, and you are my most beloved children. I want you to have this honor." He took Ethel's hand again. "Ethel and I will be their parents. You will raise them. We are going to create true Org members. A true Org family."

I noticed, then, how manic The Official looked. He had mastered the art of speaking gently all the time, and it hid his obviously psychotic nature. But it was clearly on display now. He was insane. Paranoid beyond reason.

Zeke's face remained blank, like he was unmoved by what he heard. "I understand. We'll get the job done," he said suddenly. I looked at him in complete disbelief. "Ella and I appreciate you giving us this responsibility, sir."

The Official flashed Zeke a bright smile. "I knew you would never let me down, my son. You have always been loyal and seen the bigger picture."

"I do see the bigger picture, sir. And you're right, we need to strike first." Ethel looked just as disgusted as I was as Zeke continued. "We need to set up another meeting in about a week to hash everything out. I hope you'll still be available in New York then. In regards to Jet, we need to keep you safe from him until we have a solid plan. I don't trust any phone communication. You need to stay off the grid completely. No calls or messages." Zeke tapped a finger against the back of the couch, pensive. "Have you ever left your phone lying around in Jet's presence?"

"Maybe once or twice," The Official replied. "You think…?"

"We can't risk it. It's a good thing you don't have a tracking chip like the rest of us, but it wouldn't take him long to bug your phone so he can track your whereabouts that way." Zeke paced, looking anxious. "Where is it? Do you have your phone with you?"

"Yes."

"Give it to me," Zeke said, holding out his hand. "If Jet plans on following you and harming you somewhere where no one will see, it's best that the phone is with me. He won't be expecting that."

The Official handed Zeke his phone, panic on his face. "So you've seen it in his eyes as well, then?"

"Yes, sir, I have. But I didn't mention it because I didn't want to overstep. Now I see that there's a real threat and we need to take care of it."

"Zeke, no," Ethel said incredulously.

Zeke ignored her plea. "You can't stay with Ethel. Jet knows about your relationship. He may be counting on you being with her. You have to find somewhere to hide out alone for the week. All cash payment, of course."

"Of course."

"Let's meet back here in exactly a week, same time."

The Official nodded, pulling Ethel toward the door.

Zeke's brow was still creased with concern when he opened the door for them to leave. "I promise to take care of this for you, Official."

"Thank you, my son."

As the door closed on them, Zeke's face became a blank canvas again. No emotion at all anymore. It was strange watching his expression go from worried to…nothing. That was it. His face held nothing in it. He looked cold.

"What was that?" I asked him when enough time had passed for me to be sure that The Official and Ethel had left our floor.

"That was us giving The Official what he wants, Ella," Zeke replied flatly, still staring at the door. Then he turned to face me. "And now, we have time to formulate a plan."

Chapter 18

We waited patiently in the suite for The Official to show up again. He wouldn't be with Ethel this time. At least, that's how Zeke had arranged it to play out. I was pacing up and down the room while Zeke sat calmly on the sofa. He watched me, but remained silent. "What if he doesn't show up?" I asked.

"He will."

"But what if he doesn't?"

"He will. Now please stop pacing? You're making me nervous," he said, sounding completely *not* nervous. In fact, Zeke had been the perfect picture of composure the entire week since our last meeting with The Official.

I checked the time on my phone. It was almost eight o'clock. One more minute. "Zeke, this is—" A sharp knock at the door cut me off, just like the last time. The Official clearly didn't believe in being fashionably late.

"Don't be scared," Zeke said gently. He opened the door, and The Official hurried in.

"Hello, my children," he greeted, sounding breathless.

"How are you, sir? We're glad to see you made it," Zeke replied.

"Yes. I stayed well-hidden, just like you said."

"Good. I think it's safe to say we have avoided any

unnecessary complications, thanks to your cooperation, sir. Just so you know, I've restructured our plan to make it more convenient."

"Convenient," The Official repeated. "I like the sound of that."

"Yes, convenient. Well, convenient for Ella and me. For you, it's dependent on how you choose to proceed."

The Official frowned. "What do you mean?"

"I'm tired, sir. I'm tired of being what I am. I want to be better. And I can't be better while I'm still in The Org. Ella made me realize what I really want. And it's not this."

"I don't understand, my son." The Official looked genuinely confused.

"Ella and I want out. We don't want to be a part of The Org anymore. I don't suppose you might grant us that wish and let us leave peacefully?"

The Official snorted as if he had heard some kind of bad joke, shaking his head. "You know the rules, Zeke. No one leaves. Not in this life."

"Hmmm. I thought you might say that." The air was thick with tension, and I jumped a little when another knock came from the door. Zeke opened it, and Jet and Knight strode in. The Official's eyes were wide, darting between us and the new guests. "I hope you don't mind that I invited some company to our discussion. You see, Jet here has come up with some new Org rules. Rules that suit most of the members better than what's been in place all these years. All members now have the option to leave The Org and live normal lives, as long as it's amicable. They can now buy their way out, settle their debts to The Org. The amount and type of payment will be determined by Jet, of course. And the best part is that everyone who leaves holds a peace treaty with The Org. No member can hurt them in any way, or they will be dealt with accordingly. We had to put something in place in case any one member holds a grudge against another, you know?" Zeke paused, checking his watch. "A lot of the members are getting up there in age and want to retire from their jobs. The very jobs that made them relevant to The Org. They want an option to leave. *We* are giving them one."

"Jet doesn't make any rules or decisions. And he has no right to come up with any ideas. He has no authority," The Official scoffed.

"Yes, he does. Because he is in charge of The Org now."

"Excuse me?"

"He said I'm in charge now," Jet answered.

"Your son didn't take kindly to you wanting to get rid of him permanently, Official. He decided to strike first," Zeke stated calmly.

The Official's eyes were dark, his rage evident. "You think you can kill me? Disloyal filth!" The Official bellowed. "I own The Org, you fools! You can never kill The Official!"

"That's where you're right," Zeke said coolly, staring him in the face. "The Official isn't going to die, sir." He took a few steps forward. "You see, no one knows what you look like, except for us here in this room and Ethel. And to our knowledge, The Official looks like that." Zeke pointed a finger at Jet.

Realization crept onto The Official's face before a psychotic, murderous fury entered his eyes and had me stepping closer to Zeke. "You could never be me!" he screamed at his son.

"Don't worry about your reputation, Father. I promise to always do what needs to be done for the betterment of The Org. Starting today," Jet stated.

"Ethel knew I was in danger. She will find out that you betrayed me and tell the other members!" The Official was frantic.

Zeke shook his head slowly and said, "No, she won't tell the other members anything." He looked down before adding, "Ethel said to tell you she's sorry."

For a moment, The Official looked hurt as the reality that his last hope, his Ethel, had turned against him, too. The moment didn't last long enough for him to seem humane to me, though. And just as he lunged toward Jet, Knight pulled a large syringe from behind his back and plunged the needle into The Official's arm, forcing him down onto the sofa. The Official seemed to wither and age in an instant, losing all cognizance.

I swallowed hard, waiting for the drug to fully settle in. "That's it?" I asked no one in particular after a minute had gone by.

"Yes," Zeke answered.

"But he will live, right? Like we agreed?"

"Yes, Ella. I gave you my word. The drug just incapacitates him. This will be his life now, confined to one place. But he will live."

"Like a vegetable," I said, sad that things had reached that point.

"He'll be cared for in one of the best old age homes in the world. It's better than what he deserves," Jet threw in.

Zeke turned to him. "We've settled our debt. Ella and I are free now. Chris, Hector Cantrell, and Ethel, too."

"Yes, you are. Thank you."

"You've put the word out?"

"I sent Al a text yesterday as The Official from his usual number stating what the new rules are from now on and that she must communicate with our members through our usual channels. I also told her to include that the five of you have taken the option of settling your debts and leaving The Org. She didn't seem surprised. And she didn't suspect a thing, either."

"So, we're safe to move freely?"

"All formal announcements will still be made at the next Welcome meeting of new Org members, as is protocol, but Al has been doing the preliminary communication. So, yes, you're safe. No Org member can touch you. Not any of you." Jet held his hand out to Zeke, and he took it, shaking it firmly. Then Jet held his hand out to me. I shook it, feeling awkward. What had been done was hardly pleasant. Hand shaking was too casual an act for it. "We'll be on our way," Jet said cheerfully.

Knight effortlessly lifted The Official into the wheelchair that would be his permanent seat. It had been placed inconspicuously to the side of the sofa before the meeting, in aid of the plan to fake The Official's major stroke. Jet whistled a tune as he and Knight wheeled the former Official out into the hallway and into the elevator. And as the doors closed on them, Jet finally let a smile touch his lips. It wasn't overtly menacing, I suppose. Just one of relief, maybe even of feeling victorious. But it did cross my mind how strange it was that he was smiling after what he had done to his own father. I knew it probably meant that The Org had a long lifespan ahead in his hands. He wanted the power. *That's not good.*

"Hey," Zeke said next to me. "You okay?"

"Yeah, I'm good. But I could use…"

Zeke closed the gap between us, engulfing me in a warm hug that felt like home. "Let's get out of here, Ella."

We waited for the elevator to come back up and walked in wordlessly. The trip down was just as silent. But once the doors opened to the hotel lobby, the atmosphere shifted. I felt the stress seep out of me and when I glanced at Zeke, he was smiling. He took my hand as we headed for the exit.

Monsieur Cantrell was behind the reception with Bernie, and he looked up from whatever he was doing as we went by. Zeke gave him a single nod and he nodded back, his shoulders relaxing and sagging forward as if a burden had been lifted from them. He knew he was out, too.

Chris was waiting for us outside, leaning against the car with his hands in his pockets. When he saw us, he rushed forward, embracing Zeke quickly. "Man, am I glad to see you guys," he said with an embarrassed grin.

"It's good to see you too, brother," Zeke replied.

"So, it's done?"

"Yeah, CP, it's done."

Chris stared down at the pavement. "So, where do we go now?"

Zeke inhaled deeply and exhaled. "I don't know.

Can we just enjoy having nowhere to go right now? Just enjoy being a little…lost?"

"You're not lost, Mr. Gage," I told him with a grin. "Not anymore."

"I still can't believe you guys turned the tables the way you did. It's something that no one would have expected. It's so covert," Chris said.

"That's the job, right?" I joked.

Zeke laughed and shook his head lightly. "That *was* the job, Ella. That *was* the job."

A word about the author...

Shamiso Mlilo Lezard was born and raised in the city of Bulawayo, Zimbabwe. Faith in God and family are the most important things to her. She lives in the City of Kings with her husband, and you will always find her spending time with the people she loves most, or participating in one entertaining activity or another. She is a passionate writer and hones her craft as a Social Media Journalist.

She also has a really keen interest in the culinary arts…because food is happiness.

The Lost Cantrell is Shamiso's debut novel.

Shamiso loves to hear from readers and other writers via her online platforms:

Website: https://www.shamisolezard.co.zw

Twitter: https://www.twitter.com/shamiso_lezard

Instagram: https://www.instagram.com/shamiso_lezard

Thank you for purchasing
this publication of The Wild Rose Press, Inc.

For questions or more information
contact us at
info@thewildrosepress.com.

The Wild Rose Press, Inc.
www.thewildrosepress.com